"I have come to make you a proposition, Mr Wilder."

Laura Middlebrook's gaze settled directly into his, stealing the breath he had been about to take. "As you may or may not know, I have an inheritance from my grandmother, a lump sum amount as well as a healthy trust."

"How fortunate for you," Sean said. "There is a point to you offering me this financial information, I presume?"

"Indeed," she said. "Every farthing will be yours unconditionally if you agree to take on the task I'm about to propose."

How serious she looked about it. She probably wanted him to investigate someone who had offered for her. Wanted to see whether the rascal had a mistress tucked away or if he might be prone to reckless gambling.

Sean only hoped the man in question deserved her. "Must be very important to you, this proposal."

"Quite," she answered. "I wish to be married."

"I figured as much," he said. "Very well, then. Who is this lucky fellow you have set your sights upon?"

"You, sir," she replied with a dimpled smile. "I want to marry you."

A painter of historical events, Lyn Stone decided to write about them. A canvas, however detailed, limits characters to only one moment in time. 'If a picture's worth a thousand words, the other ninety thousand have to show up somewhere!' An avid reader, she admits, 'At thirteen, I fell in love with Emily Brontë's Heathcliff and became Catherine. Next year I fell for Rhett and became Scarlett. Then I fell for the hero I'd known most of my life and finally became myself.'

After living for four years in Europe, Lyn and her husband, Allen, settled into a log house in north Alabama that is crammed to the rafters with antiques, artefacts and the stuff of future tales.

Recent novels by the same author:

To my sisters Kaye and Rhonda and their heroes,
Tom and Doug.
Thanks for your love and support,
for losing sleep to finish my books,
for Sunday morning coffee in Atlanta,
and most of all, just for being who you are.

her forehead against the flocked wallpaper and squeezed her eyes shut. She had not misheard. They were definitely speaking of her.

Dr. Cadwallader had attended her not two hours ago to ascertain what had caused last night's fainting spell. He'd advised her to leave off lacing her corset so tight. The wretch should have told her the truth. But maybe he was right not to, considering her present reaction. She wished to heaven she hadn't heard anything at all.

Maclin's words jerked Laura's attention back to their conversation. "Granted, she's not much to look at, but I swear I've never seen another with such heart, you know? A real goer, admired by everyone, too. Must be quite a blow to face losing her like this. Shall I pour us another brandy, Lamb? You look pretty fashed."

Lambdin grunted his assent and Laura heard the clink of crystal. So, that was all? They were going to dismiss her impending death as a "damned shame" and have another drink? For a moment she feared she would cast up her accounts right there on the foyer floor. Was the sudden nausea she experienced now a symptom of whatever sickness she had? Laura swallowed hard and sniffed. Tears dripped onto her bodice and she hadn't even realized she was weeping.

"Shouldn't she be isolated to keep this from spreading?" Maclin asked. "I shudder to think of all you have at risk here."

"Doc swore it isn't contagious. Quite a rare condition," Lambdin replied. "Caused by an insect bite, he believes. Said it's not terribly uncommon in some parts of the world. Certainly is hereabouts, however. The disease lies dormant, he says, for years in some instances. And then—"

Laura heard the snap of his fingers, followed by a few seconds of silence before he continued. "She'll weaken toward the last, as I said. I really hope Laura won't guess how

Chapter One

Midbrook Manor, Bedfordshire, England
October 1889—

"Will you tell Laura she's going to die, Lamb?"

The words halted Laura Middlebrook just outside the study door. She automatically sought purchase against the wall to keep from crumpling to the floor. Breath stuck in her throat. Surely to God, she had misunderstood!

James Maclin's words to her brother reverberated in her head almost blocking out her brother's answer. "No, no, of course not. The poor girl would be terribly upset. Little point worrying her about something she can't possibly help. Wish I didn't know myself since there's nothing to be done for it."

"Doc Cadwallader assured you of that?" James asked.

"Yes. Damned shame, isn't it? Doc says the end should come quickly without any prolonged suffering. There'll be progressive weakness. Then she'll simply lie down one day and that's that. All I can do now is make her last days comfortable as I can."

Maclin's grievous sigh echoed Laura's own. She leaned

serious it is until it's over and done. Easier on her that way. Perhaps not knowing will prevent her dashing about unnecessarily trying to find a cure. There simply isn't one to be had. Poor Laura, I dread it for her. You won't let on to her, either, will you, James?"

Laura covered her mouth with a fist to stifle a wail of despair. She squeezed her eyes shut and shook her head in denial.

"You know I won't. How long does Doc think before this runs its course?" James asked.

"A few months at most, maybe less," Lambdin said sadly. "Damn it, James, I shall miss her, y'know."

Laura pushed away from the wall and staggered back toward the stairs. She couldn't think what to do next. Her first inclination had been to rush in and demand that Lambdin tell her everything Dr. Cadwallader had said about her condition. But she figured she had already heard as much as she could deal with for the moment.

Maybe the doctor was wrong. He *must* be mistaken. She'd never been ill in her life. That attack of vapors last night resulted from wearing tight stays, as he had said, and she had imbibed more wine than usual at dinner. Surely, the combination had caused her faint. But the doctor would never lie to Lambdin about such a matter. Why on earth would he?

When the door knocker sounded, Laura looked down and saw that she was gripping the newel post as though it were a lifeline. Her fingers wouldn't obey her command to turn loose. Dumbly she watched Lambdin exit the study and answer the front door.

"Ah, Mr. Wilder! Father wrote to us about you," her brother said. "Isn't every day one gets a visit from a Scotland Yarder out this way. I'm Lambdin Middlebrook."

"I am no longer with the Yard," the man corrected quietly.

"No, no, of course you aren't. Should have paid more heed.

I thought Father said…well, you were to uncover something havey-cavey about the shipping, weren't you?" Lambdin probed.

Lord, Laura wished Lambdin would stop nattering, pay the man and send him away. She needed desperately to learn more about Dr. Cadwallader's predictions for her.

The visitor shifted his leather case to his left hand. "Yes. My business, Wilder Investigations, is an individual concern. Your father's aware of that, if you are not."

"Ah, yes, that's it!" Lambdin gushed. "A private enquiry agent! Of course, I remember now. Well, come in, come in!"

The guest entered and shook Lambdin's outstretched hand. Even as he did so, the man's piercing green gaze fell on her. Dimly Laura registered the impression of emeralds set in gold. Golden skin, sun kissed, as though he dwelt in warm, southern climes. Soft, dark and wind tossed waves framed his strong features.

The stranger projected a gilded warmth that drew her, as though somehow he might banish this frightful coldness if she let him. Then, suddenly, he deliberately did something to shutter all that, and the intensity of his regard made her uncomfortable.

Laura sucked in a deep breath and tried to muster what composure she could. He made her feel like a bug pinned to a collection board. Pinned by those eyes. Eyes that seemed to ferret out everything. Once again, something flickered briefly in their jeweled depths. Compassion?

Could he see at a glance that she was doomed? Dying, even as he watched? She couldn't bear it.

With a sob she couldn't contain, Laura took to her heels and clattered up the stairs.

The upper hallway had never seemed so long. When she finally reached her room, Laura slammed the door behind her, turned the key and threw herself across her bed.

She was not going to die. She wasn't! There was some

ghastly mistake here. The doctor was old, confused. Or Lamb and Charles were playing some horrible joke on her. They knew she was eavesdropping and were teaching her a lesson. Perhaps she had imagined it all. Or her ears had deceived her.

Oh God, she couldn't be dying. She flatly *refused* to die!

Sean Wilder looked a question at his host, though he didn't bother to ask who the scurrying little rabbit might be. He didn't usually affect women quite *that* profoundly. And—modesty aside—when he did so they usually ran to him, not away. True, his size intimidated some. That must be the case. She was a wee mite of a thing.

Pretty, too, he had noticed. Petite and curved in all the right places. He would bet the hefty fee from his last case that her shape was natural, and not the result of fashionable underpinnings. That umber hair of hers gleamed like flawless satin against her well-shaped head. Made a man wonder what it would look like loosened from that untidy chignon and swinging free about her shoulders. He recalled then that those wide gray eyes had already been wet when he first saw her. She hadn't run from *him,* then. Perhaps she had just received a dressing-down from Middlebrook for shirking her duties.

"My sister," the fellow explained, summarily dashing Sean's theory about a rebuked servant. "Been off her feed here lately. Sorry if she seemed rude."

"She seemed upset," Sean said bluntly.

Middlebrook shrugged. "Oh, you know, women suffer these megrims time to time. Had the doctor to her just this morning."

"Nothing serious, I hope?" To his surprise, Sean found himself wishing very hard that the man's answer would alleviate his worry. Why the hell should he care one way or the other? The girl meant nothing to him. God only knows he had seen scores of women in straits far more dire than this pampered pigeon's worst nightmares. But for some reason, he needed to know what was wrong.

Middlebrook obviously took Sean's question as a polite response and ignored it as he led the way into a well-appointed study. The young man introduced his friend who was busy pouring drinks. "This is Mr. Sean Wilder, James. Sir, my neighbor, James Maclin."

Sean noted Maclin's hands tremble on the decanter and glass and the fellow's dawning expression of awe. So, this one was no stranger to London's gossip mill. Affecting his most enigmatic smile, Sean slowly inclined his head in greeting. He rather enjoyed Maclin's discomposure. Fostering his black reputation remained one of the small pleasures Sean allowed himself.

"Don't mind James," Middlebrook said. "He's only hanging about to see my new foal when it arrives. Interested in breeding, sir?"

"Not at all," Sean declared abruptly. He had little use for horses other than their getting him from one place to another. They were fractious beasts at best, and he had never had the slightest desire to own one. Besides, distractions from business at hand always bothered him and he did not intend to encourage this one. The lovely watering pot dashing up the stairs had proved distraction enough already. He could ignore fury, petulance, even outright seduction, but a woman's tears stopped him in his tracks every time. What in the world could have set her off like that?

Middlebrook looked miffed at Sean's disinterest in his stables. "Very well, then. Have a seat if you will. You have the information my father requested before he left? I recall I'm to forward it to him as soon as he sends word where to post it."

Sean shook off thoughts of Middlebrook's sister and drew the documents out of his case. He hadn't the time or the inclination to get involved in anyone else's problems.

Still the young woman had looked so confoundingly tragic, clutching that stair rail. He could still envision the white of her knuckles and the trembling of her full lower lip. Damn! He shook his head to clear it of the troubling image.

He knew better than this. Once a man let a woman get close enough to make him worry about her, he might as well go ahead and lift his chin for the throat-cutting.

No, a real attachment didn't bear thinking about. He had already traveled that scenic route twice with young ladies of good name. The first time proved devastating. The second had only pinched his pride, of course. One learned.

If he had any driving ambition at all, it was to avoid any emotional entanglement with another female. Now, a physical entanglement would be welcome as hell, he thought, repressing a smile. But Miss Middlebrook was not that sort.

Best get his business completed and remove himself from the vicinity before the idea of seducing her took root.

"You should pass these reports along as soon as possible so your father can take action on them. He is losing a fortune even as we speak," Sean advised the lad.

A pair of old Middlebrook's shipping managers were skimming funds on both sides of the water. Middlebrook had specifically asked him not to kill anyone involved. Some wag or another must have added "paid assassin" to Sean's list of dubious talents. The thought prompted a grin. Fear certainly had its uses.

"I assume he left instructions as to my remuneration?" Sean asked politely.

Sean had sensed the fear underlying the elder Middle-brook's disdain the day he had hired him. But only once in this business had someone tried to cheat him. One of his clients—a banker, ironically—had refused to pay once Sean had completed a job for him. A neighbor discovered the man dead of knife wounds the very next day. Never mind that Sean had spent the entire evening with the chief inspector of Scotland Yard. Never mind that the real culprit had been caught and punished by hanging. The gossips would have it that Wilder "had his ways." Sean didn't mind. Reputation was everything in this business.

"Oh yes, of course. I'm to see to it." Middlebrook stashed the folder of facts in the desk drawer and handed over an envelope containing a presigned cheque. Sean verified the amount and they shook hands. "Tea's in one hour. You'll stay, of course?"

The boy's offer of refreshment was solely due to ingrained manners, Sean knew. He meant to refuse, but on second thought, accepted. He would see the girl one more time. Just once, to find out whether she was recovering from whatever had caused her tears.

Not that he cared all that much. It was that cursed curiosity of his. Besides, a four-hour trip loomed ahead and he felt sharp-set even now. He only hoped he wasn't delaying his departure for a mere handful of cucumber sandwiches.

"James and I are just off to the stables. You're welcome to join us," the lad said.

Sean smiled at the halfhearted offer. He had put the lad off with his bluntness. Of course, that had been his intention, but it served no purpose now. He had the balance of his fee in his pocket and an hour to kill before a free meal. "Yes, I could use a brisk walk after that carriage ride. I'll admit knowing nothing about the business, Middlebrook. What sort of horses do you breed?"

That did the trick. Middlebrook and Maclin carried the conversation, with Maclin darting anxious looks as though he expected Sean to make off with all the cattle. Suppressing satisfied laughter, Sean only needed to add polite grunts and hums of feigned interest.

Normally he would not have bothered with this little pup and his horse-mad prattle. He would have taken his leave the moment the boy forked over the blunt. Sean assured himself that only hunger had prompted his acceptance of the invitation. The young man's weeping sister had little to do with his tarrying at Midbrook Manor.

Getting involved with a woman like this one, however intriguing she might be, would prove foolish at best. Camilla Norton had intrigued him recently, too, he reminded himself with a barely restrained grimace. And for all his experience with women, that relationship had proved fiasco enough for the year. Give him a good, honest whore any day of the week.

He had his life sorted out just the way he wanted it now and he wasn't about to muck it up again. Control, that was the thing. He had worked damned hard to attain that and, by God, he meant to keep it, too. No more women messing about with his finer feelings, what little there was left of them.

This curiosity about Laura Middlebrook was only that, Sean decided firmly. Simple curiosity. The girl would be well over whatever was wrong with her by teatime. He would fortify himself with whatever culinary delights were offered at tea, see that she was fine, and then he would be on his way.

When the time came, tea proved interesting. Not the tea itself, Sean mused, but the serving of it. Miss Middlebrook poured. All over the table, as a matter of fact. He had to shove back sharply to keep from getting a lapful. She reacted strangely, as though the accident rated a distant second to whatever really concerned her. Even her brother's sharp curse didn't seem to register.

She summoned a maid and had the mess cleared away. Then she retired to her own chair with a cup and gave rein to her preoccupation. Sean wanted desperately to ask what that was.

Instead, he consumed every morsel set before him, absently

answering Middlebrook's questions between bites of delicious little spiced beef pies and cakes iced with lemon sugar. Very deliberately, he concentrated on the food, ignoring the girl.

"So, your mother lives in Cornwall? Lovely place, I've heard. Never been there myself. My betrothed has an aunt and uncle who reside in Trevlynton, though, on the coast," Middlebrook chattered on. "Just got myself spoken for, y'see. Nineteen's rather young to get myself yoked, but I was lucky to find a pearl like Jillian. Can't let her get away. Are you wed, sir?"

"No," Sean snapped. He had shot the boy a threatening look before he realized the question wasn't meant as a taunt.

Suddenly Sean could not wait to get away. This empty-headed chatterbox and his gape-mouthed friend annoyed him. As did his own inclination to sort out the little Middlebrook beauty's dilemma. "I am poor company this afternoon, and I do have things pending in town," he said curtly. "I will excuse myself now and head back."

"Of course," Middlebrook agreed rather heartily. "Good of you to come all this way to deliver the results of your enquiries."

Sean inclined his head. "Your father compensated me well for it. Part of the job."

"Laura, fetch Mr. Wilder his hat and cane, would you? There's a dear," Middlebrook said. Maclin exhaled with what appeared to be profound relief.

The girl set down her cup with a clatter, rose hurriedly and immediately tripped on the edge of the rug. Sean caught her before she hit the floor. She shuddered in his arms like a wounded bird. He battled the urge to embrace her fully, to calm her trembling, to try to make her smile. A dangerous impulse, and a stronger one than he wanted to admit.

But what had her so flustered she couldn't even take tea properly? Devil the little chit, she couldn't even walk straight.

"There now," he soothed. "Are you steady?" He lowered her to the settee, knelt and took her hands in his. "Did you injure yourself?"

Her head shook frantically. When she finally did speak, the words issued on a gasp. "Fine. I'm fine." She snatched her hands away from his and buried them in her lap. "I'm all right."

Middlebrook had gone around the back of the settee to rest his hands on her slender shoulders. There was nothing else Sean could think to do but rise and take his leave. Certainly the wisest course. "If you're certain?" he said, still unwilling to leave her in such a state. He was definitely not behaving like himself at all. "I'll see myself out."

She nodded, seeming only a bit less muddled. Her shoulders squared like a little soldier's, and a strained smile stretched her lovely bow-shaped lips. "Goodbye, Mr. Wilder." She drew in an audibly shaky breath. "Do...do come again."

Come again? Not bloody likely he'd do that. Sean located his hat beside an Oriental urn in the foyer. The cane was missing. His favorite sword cane, too. But after a few moments of looking about for it, he abandoned the search. The loss of it seemed a small price to pay for getting himself out of Midbrook Manor in a hurry. The need to hang about until he had satisfied his concern for Laura Middlebrook bothered him far more than the cost of a new cane.

He had concluded his business here and that was all there was to it. No need to think about Miss Middlebrook any longer. He would put her right out of his mind, where she belonged.

"Don't you *know* who he is?" Maclin demanded of Lamb the moment they heard the front door close. "You haven't any idea, have you?"

Laura leaned against the rolled arm of the settee, unable to shake the weakness in her limbs enough to rise. She only hoped Lambdin and James would leave her in peace and continue their visit elsewhere. With her eyes trained on the two, she tried to will them away. The effort to speak seemed too great.

"You heard him," Lamb said idly as he nibbled on the last ladyfinger. "Enquiry agent. Dreadful old bore, wasn't he?"

"Bore, my Aunt Fanny! That man is the talk of the town, he is! You wouldn't know, stuck out here in the wilds as you are, but they say he's directly out of the stews. Whitechapel, in fact!" He paused to shudder. "Born a bastard in a whor— uh…house of ill repute."

Maclin narrowed his eyes and leaned forward to shake a finger under Lambdin's nose. "And you'll never in a thousand years guess who they say his father is!"

"Who?" Lamb asked, polishing off the last of the cakes. He licked a sticky finger and smiled at the prospect of James's tattle.

"The prince. Yes, Old Bertie himself!"

Lamb laughed and waved off the idea as he stood up and stretched. "Nah, Bertie was straight as an arrow! A right prig of a fellow, else the queen would've sent him packing."

"Little you know, you old rustic! They say Wilder's mother suffered a comedown of one sort or another. Very wellborn, so I heard, but her family booted her right out, just disowned her, and then she…"

"Here now!" Lambdin interrupted, stepping around the end of the settee and laying a hand on James's shoulder. "We'd best leave off with this. Laura's not up to snuff at the moment and this is no topic to trouble her with. Not proper anyway."

He leaned down and took her elbow. "Come on, old girl, why don't you go upstairs and have a lie down, eh? Looks a bit peaked, don't she, James?"

She allowed him to lead her to the stairway. With a murmur of thanks, she did as he suggested. Lord knows she felt good for little else at the moment. And James's tale of Mr. Wilder's ancestry made her slightly more ill than she already was.

Laura welcomed Lambdin's belated concern. She knew he soft-peddled it so as not to alarm her further and she appreciated that. But she couldn't stand that he had told James Maclin of her illness, even though his doing so did make perfect sense. He had wanted someone to talk to about it. She wished for the same, but Laura knew instinctively that anyone's pity would undo her completely.

Had Lamb also told the man who stayed for tea? *Did you know my poor old sister's dying, sir? That's why she tore off in such a snit. Can't control herself. So sorry.*

No, Lamb would never do such a thing. Even so, Mr. Wilder had seemed a trifle too curious with all that staring he had done. A handsome man of the world such as he shouldn't have glanced twice at a clumsy country girl who was "not much to look at." James Maclin had described her that way to Lambdin, and in exactly those words.

Wounded vanity ought not to mean much at this point, but it certainly did. Here she was, old, ugly, and…dying. She shrugged off her self-pity with no little effort, busied herself undressing, and then donned her best nightgown. No use to go on and on about it, she told herself sternly. She would just forget she had ever heard it. It wasn't true in any case. She was fine. Just *fine*.

The bed felt too soft when she lay down. Would they cushion her coffin, she wondered? God, she had to stop these morbid thoughts. What use was it to dwell constantly on what would happen? She should concentrate on the time she had left, such as it was. If it was true. Could it be?

Laura yanked the covers over her head and curled into a ball. So many things she had yet to do. Her entire twenty-five years had been spent here in the country looking after Lamb and the estate while their parents either traveled or lived abroad.

She knew more about farm matters than most men. With her gone, the haughty Mr. Williams might have to live up to his post as manager, she thought with a smirk. Thus far, all the man had seemed capable of was warding off her suitors, few as they were, and bailing Lamb out of trouble now and again. He had certainly proved proficient at both. Perhaps with his task as watchdog cut in half by her demise, he would have time to see to the business of running Midbrook's farms. God knows she was sick of paperwork. Perhaps He did know, and that was why...

She would be gone. No more. *Dead.*

For a long time—perhaps hours—Laura lay there contemplating. Slowly she came to terms with what she had heard. At least for the moment. Strange, how she could almost tolerate the horror of thinking about it.

Not that she looked forward to dying, but reluctant acceptance was better than outright hysteria. She could not allow herself to fall apart.

Her brother had borne the news with surprising strength. And she knew now that she would not ask him to discuss the matter with her. Somehow his determination to spare her the dread of death seemed conscientious, something Lambdin almost never was.

Dr. Cadwallader had obviously advised him, and both believed they were doing the right thing to pretend to her that nothing was wrong. The least she could do was humor them and appreciate their misguided thoughtfulness. She would not speak of it to them. Ever.

Laura decided the thing that bothered her most about dying was that she had never really lived. Life had slid right by her, day after boring day, year after boring year. She had not even had a happy family life to compensate.

Gifts had arrived, expensive things which hardly made up

for the lack of parental involvement in her life or Lambdin's. But some treats had been thoughtfully chosen—Lamb's prized Arabian, Caesar, and her own beloved little mare, Cleopatra. Her parents had shipped them all the way from Egypt. Ostensibly, the horses were for breeding purposes, but Laura just knew her parents had their children's pleasure in mind when selecting those two.

How had they known her one great joy was riding? And that she would adore the mare with all her heart? Perhaps Mother and Father did care in their own distracted way. Would they miss her when she was gone? Would they even know the difference?

Father was not really her father, of course. Not as he was Lambdin's. Still, he had adopted her when he married her widowed mother, giving Laura his name. She had never dared ask for more than that for fear Father would change his mind and she would be an outsider. As it was, she received the same infrequent attention as he gave the son he had sired.

At times she believed Father originally purchased the remote manor and its accompanying acreage just to keep her and Lambdin isolated and out of trouble.

That had certainly been his motive for hiring Mr. Williams as manager. As for her situation, the number of available suitors had kept her opportunity for misdeeds to a minimum. Thanks to Mr. Williams's vigilance regarding those few fellows, she had just celebrated her twenty-fifth birthday without any hope of a proposal, proper or otherwise.

Now she would die an old maid. *Laura Ames Middlebrook, Proper Spinster.* Unwed, untraveled, unremarkable. What a truly rotten epitaph.

Exhaustion finally took over and the next she knew, morning had dawned. The bright sunlight streaming through the tall casement windows seemed out of keeping. She wanted rain, lots of it. And cold, mourning winds soughing through the eaves.

Suddenly Laura leapt out of bed in an unexpected fit of rage. She threw open the windows and stalked out onto the balcony, beating her fists against the railing. Damn it all, this was unfair! When was she supposed to live? Really *live,* instead of existing in this bucolic little burg, counting sheep and cows, and worrying over crops that were not even hers? Why did she have to do all the work while her parents made merry abroad and her brother played with his horses?

Well, no more!

She slammed back into the bedroom. Lead crystal perfume bottles crashed against the wall leaving gouges in the plaster. *No more!* The piecrust table cracked beneath the weight of her heavy water pitcher, scattering knickknacks everywhere. *No more!* Her breath heaved out in furious pants. One swipe of her arm cleared the mantel.

She looked around desperately, hands fisted and lips tight. Panic overwhelmed her. She slid into a crouch by the bed, her nightgown bunched at her knees, glass from the photograph frames biting into her feet. And she wept.

Chapter Two

Ten days later, Laura had gotten herself in hand. She had taken control. Her course was set now. No more useless grieving, she had decided firmly. No more self-pity. Time was running out and she must make the most of what was left to her.

Lambdin had seemed agreeable when she announced her decision to go to London. He had said it was a famous idea to strike out on her own, and had even promised to create a diversion so that Mr. Williams would not notice her leaving until it was too late to stop her. Obviously, poor Lamb didn't want to endure what was coming any more than she did. He never could face a crisis with any grace. Laura determined that she would.

Better to distance her mind from everything at home. She might long for Lambdin and her wonderful little mare, Cleopatra. Perhaps she would even miss silly old James and the villagers, but she would not return. Mere existence would no longer serve.

Once she had arrived in London, Laura had prepared herself immediately, with every intention of experiencing life to the fullest extent. Beginning without delay.

First she had confirmed Dr. Cadwallader's diagnosis. The

young doctor she had visited agreed with the findings the very moment after she had listed her symptoms. He specialized in treating young women and their ills, he had assured her. Though the man proposed a lengthy and rather expensive treatment, Laura had declined when he offered no promise of a cure. Obviously, there remained little anyone could do for her condition. That only strengthened her determination to carry out her plans. Voracious shopping had occupied the time she might have spent in further useless moaning about her fate. She found that if she stayed constantly on course, never stopping to think too deeply, she absorbed the pain of acceptance gradually.

Why, by this time she could even look forward to the bit of time she had coming to her. What adventures she intended. And not for tomorrow. Today was the thing. Right this very moment.

Laura straightened her skirts and strengthened her grip on her new parasol. Her hair lay expertly coifed under an elegantly feathered chapeau. An undetectable touch of cosmetics brightened her complexion and lips. Her frightfully expensive gown fitted superbly over delectable silk underthings. She wore the confident air of a woman who knew she appeared at the height of fashion.

The only accessory that did not coordinate perfectly was the expensive malacca cane, the one with the hidden catch, a sword cane. Just carrying the thing made her feel totally invincible for the moment.

Heads turned as she entered the Everton Building of Public Offices and crossed to the ironwork lift. They recognized a woman with a purpose when they saw one, Laura thought with a lift of her chin and a secret smile. Death be damned. Today she would begin living every single moment to the hilt. And given a bit of luck and a little more time, she would hire Mr. Sean Wilder to help her do it.

Once she reached the third floor, Wilder Investigations proved easy enough to find. The opaque, half-glass door stenciled gold and black with the company name stood open.

Laura allowed herself a moment to observe the man she had come to see. She watched the broad back and shoulders stretch against a dark brown gabardine coat. He was even larger than she remembered.

Conservative dresser, she mused. The earthen hues he seemed to prefer accentuated his coloring. Like the suit he had worn on his visit to the country, this one seemed designed to avoid ostentation. Not pricey, yet hardly cheap, and cut extremely well. No jaunty plaids or racy houndstooth for this fellow. His clothes were ordinary to a fault. Considering his extraordinary physique, however, Laura knew very well he could not have bought this suit ready-made.

She almost laughed at his studied attempt to avoid drawing attention to himself. Maybe he thought such was necessary in his line of work. He might as well wear glitter-paste stones and purple satin for all the good it did him. Sean Wilder couldn't go unremarked in a crowd of thousands.

His size and good looks only accounted for a portion of that remarkability, however. Something within the man exuded absolute self-reliance, maybe even danger. Attractive trait, that. Adding intelligence, a sinfully handsome face, and compassion to his list of attributes, Laura knew she had selected the nearly perfect man.

There was his reputation, of course. There were truly wicked rumors about his sordid past, as well as his present endeavors. But those only added to his appeal as far as she was concerned.

When Laura saw him straighten and begin thumbing through the papers he had drawn out of his files, she took a deep breath and rapped on the door frame with the head of his cane. Time was wasting.

"Just leave the coffee on the desk," Sean muttered. "There's tuppence for you on the blotter there." He flicked through the folders in the oak drawer and cursed when he found the one he wanted, misfiled. He pulled it out and riffled through it.

Good thing he had kept his own personal notes while he worked for the Yard. He needed access to the official records, but these jottings he had saved were better than nothing for the moment. Whoever had sent him the threatening letter this week must be one of the miscreants he had given evidence against at one time or another. There were certainly enough candidates for a lengthy list.

He favored George Luckhurst, a well-educated fellow he had nabbed for a murder down near Buck's Row. The note's penmanship indicated it had not been written by one of the usual inhabitants of his former beat. The folder in one hand, he reached atop the filing drawers and scanned the open missive again.

You bastard, I will destroy you.

Luckhurst had escaped later during a transfer from Fleet to another facility. Could be him, Sean mused as he laid the note aside. He would ask Inspector MacLinden about the fellow.

"Mr. Wilder?" a soft, musical voice enquired.

Sean turned swiftly. Papers from the folder in his left hand slid to the floor and scattered. He hardly noticed. The vision in lavender georgette smiled and inclined her head. "My apologies for interrupting your afternoon, sir, but I've come on a matter of business. Also to return your cane." She glided forward and gently laid the object across his desk.

Recognition brought with it a fierce ripple of pleasure. He could hardly credit the change in her, but there was no mistaking who she was. Those huge, gray, dark-lashed eyes. That tender, expressive mouth, today unhampered by its former tremble. "Well now, if it isn't Miss Middlebrook."

"You remember me!" she exclaimed, dimpling. "I should have expected you would, given my behavior when you visited. I do apologize. You must have thought me the worst sort of ninny."

"Not at all," he replied to the flirtation. Then more to the point, he added, "Where is your brother?" Sean, more than most, understood the dangers of a woman going about without protection. "Surely you haven't come here alone?"

She nodded slightly and sent the long, delicate feather in her hat swaying. "I'm afraid I have. Not at all the thing, is it? But my business has nothing to do with Lambdin, or my father's dealings with you, for that matter. May I sit?"

"Yes, of course." Sean pulled one of the captain's chairs around to a more convenient position and held it for her to be seated. Then he took the other facing her and leaned forward. A subtle hint of jasmine surrounded her like an aura and drew him closer to the source. Warnings of danger clanged like bells on a fire wagon inside his head. He ignored the sound and smiled.

What an amazing metamorphosis. Gone were the out-of-date clothes and haphazard hairstyle. The gorgeous gray eyes looked clear and direct, so unlike the teary, heart-clutching sight they had appeared when he first saw her. That sunny smile of hers, which he hadn't been subjected to until now, could melt stone. Sean felt entranced in spite of himself. His better judgment didn't seem to count for a damned thing.

He deliberately shook off the abhorrent thought. Entranced, indeed. The girl had come to discuss business, not to be ogled. Sean straightened in his chair and forced himself to relax. "So then, what may I do for you, Miss Middlebrook?"

She wound her hands together around the silken cords of her reticule, betraying a subtle attack of nerves. "I have come to make you a proposition, Mr. Wilder." Her gaze settled directly into his, stealing the breath he had been about to take. "As you may or may not know, I am moderately wealthy in my own right. I have an inheritance from my maternal grandmother, a lump sum amount and a healthy trust, plus stock in several companies. I reached my majority six months ago and control it, independent of my stepfather or brother."

"How fortunate for you," Sean said, amazed that her family let her wander out of the house alone. The woman needed a constant keeper if she bandied about facts such as this. "There is a point to your offering me this financial information, I presume?"

"Indeed," she said. "Every farthing I own will be yours unconditionally if you agree to take on the task I'm about to propose." Her perfect brows drew together. "And, sir, I *do* pray you will."

How serious she looked about it. Sean smiled and nodded to himself. She probably wanted him to investigate someone who had offered for her. Wanted to see whether the rascal had a mistress tucked away or if he might be prone to reckless gambling. Simple matters, easily unearthed. One should also discover beforehand any dangerous or peculiar sexual habits, as well, for her safety's sake, but she would never think to ask for that.

At any rate, Sean admitted she showed a modicum of good sense in checking a suitor's background. He only wondered why the men of her family left it to her to determine the fellow's worth.

Sean hoped the man in question deserved her. The gossamer cloak of innocence she wore could too easily be ripped away, leaving her victim to some scoundrel bent on ill use of that lovely body and the little legacy she mentioned.

As for the offer of her whole inheritance, he knew that a few hundred pounds would seem a fortune to this little country rustic. That hardheaded stepfather of hers would never allow her control over more than that, Sean felt certain.

She regarded him steadily, as though she were taking in every nuance of his expression. A bit unnerving, that regard of hers. And women never unnerved him. He knew them too well.

He shifted, leaned back in his chair and crossed his arms over his chest. "Must be very important to you, this proposal."

"Quite," she answered. "I wish to be married."

"I figured as much," he said, fully intending to send her down the hall to an acquaintance of his who handled such personal investigations. He usually limited his own tasks to matters of commerce. Nevertheless, he was curious enough to wonder whether his own intervention might not be more helpful if warding off a rake became necessary. Why not give the lady a hand with this? He had only one small case pending, and that figured more in the nature of a short holiday.

"Very well, then. Who is this lucky fellow you have set your sights upon?" he asked politely.

"You, sir," she replied with a dimpled smile. "I want to marry you."

Him? She wanted to marry him? Sean choked back a laugh. He sucked in a deep breath and bit his lips together. He must try not to sound condescending or he would hurt her feelings. She obviously considered this a legitimate proposal. Damned serious business, too, judging by the look of her.

"Well now, I am truly flattered, but I'm afraid I must decline, Miss Middlebrook. I have no desire to enter into the wedded state. I've been there, you see, and I can't say that I liked it in the least. Nothing personal, you understand."

For the first time, she appeared somewhat flustered. Sean watched as she recovered her decorum and lifted that sweetly rounded chin. Her words held a slight ring of desperation. "You are a man of much experience, are you not, Mr. Wilder?"

"Yes, you could say that, however—"

"You have traveled? Faced dangerous situations? Known a great number of...of women?"

Sean felt uncomfortable with her frankness, but only because of her obvious innocence. He couldn't think of a soul he knew well who possessed that quality. His wife surely hadn't, and Camilla wouldn't know the meaning of the word.

How much did this Laura Middlebrook really know about him? he wondered. Rumors abounded, of course. He had even created some of them himself. But the truth about him was even worse. He might have to give her that truth to dissuade her from this madness.

For now, he simply answered, "Yes."

"I have been in town for a week, sir. I have made it a point to ask about you." She looked neither apologetic nor embarrassed by the admission, he noted. "Please don't be upset about it. I'm certain you make enquiries about people every day as a matter of course, given your line of work."

Sean straightened and leaned forward again, his face not an arm's length from hers. "Does your brother know you have come to me with this ridiculous proposition?"

She shook her head and brushed her feather aside with one gloved hand. "Of course not. He would never have allowed it." Annoying how quickly she had recovered that composure of hers, he thought.

"I shall be direct with you, sir," she said, lowering her head and peering up at him through those long, dark lashes. "I need a husband immediately, one who knows the ways of the world and how to take me about in it. I mean to travel as far and as fast as I can, see everything possible, do everything possible."

"Indeed." He cocked one brow, encouraging her to continue.

"Yes. And that doing everything must include marriage.

Therefore, I want someone appealing, someone with expertise in that area. So I chose you."

"May I ask why? We are practically strangers."

She answered immediately, as though she had her answers catalogued. "As I said before, you are a man who knows his way about, Mr. Wilder. Also, I sensed your sincere concern for me when I was so distraught. That speaks well for your character, I believe, since you didn't even know me at the time." Her head ducked shyly again and he lost sight of those luminous gray eyes as she added, "And I do find you enormously attractive."

Sean crossed his legs to hide his sudden reaction to that bold statement. He swept away images of long, liquid satin hair drifting across his bare chest, of sweet young breasts pressing against him, of smooth, slender limbs entwined with his. His avid response, along with her presumption that he was for sale angered him. She *must* know of his childhood—a time when he had been bought and paid for—to suggest such a thing. "A stud for your stable, eh?" he asked with a harsh, forced laugh.

She raised her head and arched one beautifully shaped brow. "Certainly not! I wish to hire you. To exchange six hundred thousand pounds for a few months—perhaps only weeks—of your time."

"Six hundred thou…?" Sean swallowed hard to prevent choking visibly. "I do believe you are mad."

"No," she declared reasonably, "I am merely trying to arrange all that has been left to me, and help someone in the process." The gray eyes increased their earnest regard. "I would like for that someone to be you."

Sean had a sudden desire to shock her out of her pantalets. "Just how much do you know about me, Miss Middlebrook? Let us set your facts straight, shall we?" he dared.

She nodded amicably. "My solicitor has it that you were indigent as a lad."

"A real beggar from birth. Brought up in a whorehouse," Sean affirmed. "That is no secret. All of London knows it."

Her lips pursed and the eyebrows raised a fraction as she continued, "He says that a wealthy benefactor rescued you and saw you properly educated."

"Ah, the *royal benefactor* story again," Sean said, pulling a wry face. "Triggered by my uncanny resemblance to the old Prince Consort."

She inclined her head smiled doubtfully. "True?"

"Would you like it to be?" he countered. The last woman he asked that certainly had.

"No, of course not. Yet I can see how the idea might be helpful to you. Gain you entrance into certain circles for in-vestigative purposes and all that." Her small gloved hand executed a wave of dismissal. "Judging by his pictures, you look nothing like Prince Albert did, by the way. And he probably died before you were ever born!"

"Just after," Sean supplied. "I am twenty-eight."

"Well, much as she adored the prince, Her Majesty would hardly dote on you if it were true. Ridiculous notion. I cannot imagine how the gossip started unless you initiated it yourself for the very reason I mentioned." She ran her pink tongue over her bottom lip. He followed the motion of it with salacious interest. "Well, did you?" she asked.

Sean laughed sincerely this time, in spite of himself. The little minx was as charmingly direct as she was beautiful. All of a sudden, this interview was highly entertaining. "As a matter of fact, I did. You've caught me out," he admitted. "Although the command for a private audience with the queen to ascertain the truth of the rumor certainly did nothing to quell it. Quite the opposite. And she quite liked me afterward, by the way. I confess, it was my saintly grandmother who finally rescued us for my mother's sake, not Her Majesty for the prince's."

Miss Middlebrook nodded, a smile tugging at her beautifully shaped lips.

"Surely you shan't stop here? Please, do go on!" Sean invited.

"Very well. You have a manor in Cornwall," she stated.

"Compliments of my unsaintly grandfather," he supplied, amused by her aplomb and surprised by his own willingness to abet her rather thorough background enquiry.

"Once you finished at Oxford, you enlisted in the army, spent two years in Africa, then resigned and took a position with Scotland Yard."

He smirked, narrowed his eyes and leaned back in his chair. "And soon took my leave of *that*. Tedious livelihood."

"Since you have entered into your private enquiry business, you accept dangerous assignments for exorbitant fees. Therefore, I conclude that you have constant need of large sums. I can make those risks unnecessary, sir. All you have to do is marry me."

"So you want me to squire you about and take you to bed?" he added with blunt sarcasm. "In exchange for your money."

"Exactly." Her nod was succinct.

He held on to his fury with both hands. It was that or wring her presumptuous little neck. "As I divine it, you aren't looking for a permanent attachment. So what, may I ask, do you intend to do after you have experienced these 'months—perhaps only weeks' of nomadic, marital bliss and unloaded your considerable fortune?"

She lowered those gorgeous eyes again for a mere second and then refastened that determined gaze on his. "I am going to die."

Sean felt his lungs collapse and his stomach lurch. For a long moment he couldn't speak. Then, as dispassionately as he could manage, he looked directly into her eyes. "There are far worse things than death, Miss Middlebrook."

She didn't even blink at his insensitivity. "Yes, I expect so," she said in a small voice, "however, I haven't needed to face any of those as yet."

Intently Sean searched her face, took in the slight movements of her hands, her body, for signs of a lie. "Illness?"

"Yes," she affirmed, and hurried on, saying things that barely registered through his hidden shock, "but my malady will be nothing dangerous to you. It is noncommunicable and hardly even noticeable. Just a jot of dizziness here and there, leading to a quick and painless end, so I understand." She smiled. She actually smiled. "I've already seen to the…final arrangements. So you needn't have that bother."

Appalled by her words, Sean struggled to utter some denial, anything to refute them. But the certainty in the depth of her eyes, augmented by her courage, convinced him she spoke the truth as she knew it. He reached out and grasped her hands in his before he thought what he was doing. Her steady grip affected him more than a copious flood of tears would have done.

"You should see another doctor. Get another opinion," he suggested evenly, burying his pity. She would not want that. "I will find a good one for you. Go with you, if you won't go alone."

She squeezed his hands again as though to comfort *him*. "Dr. Cadwallader has served as the county's only medical resource for man and beast since long before I was born, Mr. Wilder. I have implicit faith in the man. However, I will confess this last diagnosis of his did shake it a bit. I saw one of his younger colleagues the day before yesterday. I explained Dr. Cadwallader's findings and my symptoms. He concurred immediately."

"Perhaps there is some treatment—"

She rolled her eyes and smirked. "Oh, Dr. Smithers had some idea of confining me to bed, dosing me daily with a concoction he admittedly brewed up on his own. But he flatly refused to state just what that medication would alleviate. Certainly not my demise. And thus far, anticipation of that is all that really troubles me. His vague answers and nervous disposition told me all I needed to know. Other than making himself rich at my expense, there is nothing he could do. And I don't plan to waste my last days lolling about in a sickbed, ingesting heaven knows what, when I feel just fine as I am. For now, anyway."

Sean sighed, feeling a regret such as he had never known. His own problems seemed trifling in view of Laura Middlebrook's dilemma. Then it occurred to him. "You had only just found out about this that day I came to your home, hadn't you?"

"Yes, and you were very kind to me then. As I said before, that is one reason I chose you to help me."

"I cannot do this, Miss Middlebrook, even if I wanted to. There are obligations, you see. I'm preparing to travel to Paris before the end of the week. Tomorrow, in fact. I am already committed to a case."

"How marvelous!" she said, grinning. "I've always wanted to go there!"

Sean quickly shook his head. "This jaunt will be no pleasure trip," he lied. "It could very well prove dangerous. So you see—"

"I promise not to distract you from your work. And, as for the danger, I have very little to fear, now have I? Perhaps I could even assist you."

"Don't be absurd! That's impossible."

"Come now, you won't be discommoded by this. I promise. All you need do is tolerate my presence for a bit. You needn't nurse me if I sicken, or feel you have to mourn when…well, when everything's over and done. Please marry me, won't you? Just for a little while?"

Her desperate look of entreaty made him blink against a burning in his eyes. He never wept. Never let himself care enough to weep. Tears never solved a damned thing, he knew that. But his inability to reassure her, this damned helplessness to alter what she faced, wreaked havoc with his senses. He swallowed hard and shook his head, struggling one last time to deny her. But the wall Sean had hastily constructed eighteen years before to encase his innermost self simply collapsed. He felt it crumble to dust.

"I intend to go with no regrets, Mr. Wilder. And I promise to leave you with none," she declared softly. "Please, sir, do we have a deal?"

"Yes," he whispered hoarsely. He heard the word come out of his mouth and scrambled to form another that would retract it. Hell, he hadn't meant to agree. "Look, I don't…oh hell, I wish…"

She released his hands and stood abruptly. "Wishing is for fools and dreamers, Mr. Wilder. Now, step lively! We can make the magistrate's office before closing if we hurry."

What was he doing? Sean wondered frantically as he pulled his office door shut and rushed to catch up to her. What in the holy name of God was he doing?

"'Under the power vested in me by the Commonwealth of Great Britain, I pronounce that you are husband and wife,'" Sir Buford Mallory intoned as though he did it every day. Sean couldn't imagine weddings all that commonplace around here, Mallory being a senior justice and all. She had said the old curmudgeon was a friend of her grandmother's solicitor. Sean had met him officially while employed by the Yard. The blighter had more than a few screws loose. That condition must be highly contagious. At the moment, everyone in the room seemed afflicted, himself most especially. The *Book of Offices* snapped shut.

Sean blinked sharply at the sound and looked down at the girl whose fingernails were cutting into his palm. She immediately rose on tiptoe and planted a quick, noisy kiss on his open lips. Good God, he was married. Again. An involuntary shudder of foreboding racked his spine.

"There now!" she said brightly, turning to the magistrate. "Where do we sign, sir?"

She had handled everything, Sean thought with disbelief—the special license, the official to do the deed, the rings, even the kiss. He was amazed there was no choir and banks of flowers crowding the chamber.

The old judge shoved two papers across his desk and pointed to a blank spot on the first. Sean watched her write her name on both in bold, flowing script. She did it without a tremble, without a speck of hesitation. *Laura Malinda Ames Middlebrook.* His own fingers felt numb as he took the pen she offered and scratched his own signature.

"Cavendish?" she asked with a grin. Her shoulders shook with what he supposed to be a quiver of mirth. "How terribly awesome!"

"My mother's maiden name," he justified his middle one defensively. He was damned if he would explain the other two, both products of a whore's whimsy. His glare fastened on her wide gold ring as it disappeared beneath the lavender glove. The band she had slipped on his finger felt abominably tight at the moment.

She pulled a face as he looked up again. The corners of her mouth turned down even as her eyes sparkled with merriment. "I'm only teasing. Cavendish a wonderful name. Sounds as if it needs a *Lord* in front of it, at the very least."

He quirked a brow at her impertinence. "Don't you wish."

She ought to have looked properly chastened, but Sean heard the barely squelched giggle.

Her persistent good humor made him want to shake her till her teeth clicked. Was she bordering on hysteria? How could she smile? How could she jest?

All the way over to the law courts here in the Strand she had chattered incessantly, interrupting herself to clasp his arm excitedly as they walked. Sean had no idea what she'd talked about. He had been too preoccupied thinking of the horrendous step he was taking. Correction: *they* were taking. And never, not once during that whole time, had he uttered a single word to halt this travesty. Where the devil was his mind? What had happened to all that control he'd thought he had?

Why hadn't he sent her and her nonsense packing, he asked himself with a sharp shake of his head. He was afraid he knew. He was terrified that he couldn't deny this woman anything she asked of him. Because she was going to die, he told himself, forcing the dreaded thought to the forefront of his mind. Compassion was the only reason he had agreed to this. He thought surely he had killed that feeling along with the others, but what else could it be?

He could not bear for her to face what was left of her short life alone. Yes, that must be it. Compassion. Well, surely he could afford to exercise that full measure in this instance. Where was the harm? It was not as though he must devote the rest of his life to it. Only the remainder of hers.

The brother, that young scamp who was about as deep as a dish of tea, would be no consolation whatsoever in her final days. He would likely spend most of them mucking around the damned stables with his bloody stupid horses. Those parents of hers were still racketing around the globe just as they had been doing most of her life, from what he knew of them. Sean hated the thought of Laura left in the care of a hired servant or some such.

"Tell me truly," she said, as they made their way out of the building and into the approaching twilight, "doesn't it feel wonderful to be wealthy, Mr. Wilder? Aren't you glad I had this idea? Think of the freedom this will offer you!"

Freedom? Sean glanced down at her, hoping the horror in his eyes was concealed, for he knew it was there right enough. He had totally forgotten the original transaction, the money. Had not really thought of it once she had told him she would soon die. *Bought.*

He changed the subject abruptly, unwilling to dwell on that one, lest he resort to cruelty. No point to it now. He might not relish the idea of being purchased again, but Laura certainly had no evil intent. The other had happened so long ago he seldom thought of it anymore. He wouldn't now.

"Shouldn't we dispense with formality?" he asked, striving for civility. "Shall I call you Laura?"

She beamed. "Of course you may! And I shall call you Sean. Unless you prefer *Cavendish,* of course. How should you like that?"

"I should *hate* that," he remarked as he turned her in the direction of his rooming house.

"Are you hungry?" He didn't think he could force down a bite if his life depended on it. His stomach felt like a melt pot full of lead. Perhaps some kind of illness had struck him, as well. Would that explain a total change in character?

She shook her head, setting the jaunty ostrich feather waving. "Not hungry really, but coffee would be nice. Yes, we shall have that and a sweet in lieu of a wedding feast. Perhaps then we should go home." She clutched his arm with both hands. "You are taking me home with you, aren't you? We can discuss our trip to Paris. Have you wine? We could buy some champagne along the way if we pass a wineshop. Oh, I do love walking this time of day, don't you? The sunset would probably be glorious if we could just see past the fog."

Before he could tell her it wasn't fog at all, just the usual dirty air of London, she had skipped to the topic of their crossing the channel.

When she pulled him into a tea shop, where she ordered coffee and lemon cakes to celebrate, Sean allowed her to chatter on, changing subjects by the sentence. He supposed that might be how she coped, never dwelling on any one thing long enough to form a profound thought. Thinking, living, only for the instant.

If only he could make her forget completely, make her smiles real and heartfelt. Did he even remember how to do that for a woman? Had he *ever* done it at all?

Chapter Three

∾∾∾

Laura swept into his apartment and did a quick pirouette around his drawing room. She sailed her wide-brimmed hat at the window and began tugging off her gloves. "Oh, Sean, this is wonderful! All browns, greens and brass. So masculine, just perfect for you.

"Oh look!" She scooped up the open sketch pad he had left on the divan. "You draw, too! I love to draw. I knew we had things in common. You're very good," she said, examining the picture he had done of an old man who ran a paper stall down the street.

He took the book from her and snapped it shut. "Sometimes I use it for work. Sketches help to locate people on occasion. Things such as that. Just picked it up, no formal training or anything. It's nothing much."

She laid a hand on his arm. "False modesty doesn't become you at all. Tell the truth, you enjoy it. It shows in the work, Sean."

He nodded and smiled shyly at her praise. "I suppose I do. Do you always say exactly what you feel, Laura?"

She considered that for a moment. "Yes, why shouldn't I? Honesty's very important to me."

"The most important thing," he agreed. "Though I encouraged those ridiculous rumors about my parentage, doing so was more of a private joke than any deliberate falsehood. Tweaking London's nose, so to speak." He framed her face with his hands. "I vow never to lie to you, Laura. About anything. I value truth above everything. It is so very hard to come by."

His seriousness was not lost on her. "Then you shall always have it from me, Sean. Always."

He suddenly looked so sad she couldn't bear it. Laura wondered whose dishonesty had affected him so profoundly. And how quickly could she erase the memory? With one hand, she brushed a windblown lock off his brow and smiled up at him.

"Have you a kitchen? I can cook!"

"No." He took her by the shoulders and stared deeply into her eyes as though looking for something hidden. "No kitchen."

Laura sighed, totally entranced by the power of his gaze. "You have eyes like spring leaves, Sean. I do love the spring."

He laughed softly, his head moving back and forth. "Laura, Laura, I don't quite know what to make of you."

"Make me a wife, then. No point in delaying. Show me what to do." The thought of lying in his arms sent heat streaking through her body. She felt slightly dizzy from it and prayed she wouldn't swoon. That would frighten him off for certain.

With a soft curse, he firmly set her away from him and covered his face with one hand. "Damn! Give me a moment here, will you?"

She gave him a moment. The silence grew so loud she couldn't bear it. "Does it put you off, then? My illness, I mean. You really don't have to do anything if you don't want. Just being married is quite—"

He whirled abruptly and kissed her. Laura felt her thoughts dissolve and sizzle like butter in a saucepan. She opened her mouth when he urged it, and took him in with a greediness that shocked her. He tasted faintly of sweet coffee and something uniquely male. Overwhelmingly male. God, how delicious! His tongue demanded a response and she gave it, meeting his determined forays with eager inexperience and delight. Her breasts swelled against their binding silks, begging more pressure from the stiff brocade of his waistcoat.

When he finally released her mouth, Laura realized her knees had given way completely. She hung in his embrace like a puppet cut loose of its strings.

His harsh breath rushed out against her ear. One large hand gripped the base of her neck and the other cupped her just below her ruched-up bustle.

She could feel a taut ridge of muscle pressed firmly to her front. Well, at least he wasn't too put off, she thought with purely female satisfaction.

"What comes next?" she gasped.

With a groan of exasperation, he swept her up in his arms and sat down on the divan. "We have to talk," he said, settling her on his lap.

Those wonderful hands of his stroked up and down her arms. She supposed that was meant to calm her. *Ha!* "No, we don't need talking," she argued, seeking his mouth again. She felt starved for him, and so very much alive it hurt.

He turned his head to avoid the kiss. "Yes, we *do!* Wait a moment!" His breathing slowed to nearly normal as she waited. "Now then," he said, and cleared his throat. "About your luggage—"

"Bother the luggage. It's not going anywhere." She tugged on his tie, watching the bow unravel.

"Laura, I'm warning you. Behave yourself!" Sean admonished sharply, and pushed her far enough away to see her face. "Look, everything's happening too damned fast. I need time to think. There are things we need to consider...to plan."

Laura reached up, cradling his face with both hands. "No," she said gruffly. "Plans require a future, Sean. Do you understand that? There is only here and now. This moment. If you can't bring yourself to do this, just say so and I shall get up. If you can, then for heaven's sake, please do it!"

Sean leaned his forehead to hers and sighed. "This seems wrong, Laura. We've only known each other less than a day."

"A lifetime," she whispered as she turned her head to meet his lips. He surrendered with a tortured groan.

She tried to record his every touch, every nuance of his heated kisses, every word fragment that passed his busy lips. No use, she decided, and abandoned herself to the sweeping fire he ignited.

How had they gotten from the divan to his bed? She gasped at the feel of silk sliding off her hips. The rustle of his clothing sounded like the sweetest music in the world.

Suddenly the muscled, hair-roughened texture of his bare chest brushed over her own soft curves. Lips blazed a path down her neck, across her chest, and settled on a tightened peak of need. Her breath hissed in through her teeth. His palm glided over her knee and trailed up her inner thigh. Anticipation immediately lost its appeal. She wanted him *now*.

"Open, sweetheart," he whispered, tasting her ear. "There now," he crooned as his fingers worked magic. "Hot, you are so incredibly hot! Feel that. Do you like?"

"Mmm. I like," she agreed, arching into his hand. "Yes!" When she thought she could stand no more, he stopped. Laura would have pleaded if she'd had a voice left.

"I know, I know," he soothed as he rose above her. "You might not like this part," he warned softly. "Try to relax. Let go."

She felt his male part nudge her gently and automatically lifted herself toward it.

"Steady now," he said, thrusting gently, seating himself more firmly against her tight resistance. Then he plunged.

Laura struggled to get even closer, but he held her immobile with the weight of his body and his hands on her shoulders. "Don't rush me. You'll regret it," he murmured, and claimed her mouth again.

Tenderly at first, then growing insistent, his tongue invaded, moving in and out rhythmically, until her entire being focused solely on that act. Before she knew it, his lower body echoed the motion. How wonderfully pleasant, she thought, feeling herself join the intimate dance he created.

Pleasant quickly escalated to sublime with the marvelous friction inside her. Laura groaned into his mouth, wishing he would hurry. She didn't understand her urgency, didn't care at this point, but he seemed to sense her need and increased the pace to a fever pitch.

"Ah, now!" he rasped as the first shudder of ecstasy shook her. The rippling force of pure pleasure sent her flying into a void of star-studded nothingness. *Everythingness,* she corrected with a shaky last thought.

When feeling returned, she opened one eye. Sean lay plastered to her side, muscles glistening with sweat, his chest heaving with exertion. Spent. Laura smiled. "Better than talking, hmm?"

He grunted a soft laugh and nuzzled his face into the curve of her neck. "Better than anything."

She couldn't say when she drifted off to sleep, but when she woke it was to the smell of food. He had anticipated her hunger. Known what she needed before she even realized it, just as he had last evening. And he didn't waste a moment. The idea that Sean would go to such lengths to please her warmed her heart. What a husband! No one could ever say Laura Middlebrook Wilder hadn't made at least one truly excellent decision in her lifetime.

"Thank you, God." She closed her eyes and whispered with a grin. "I don't think I'm quite so angry with You anymore."

Sean hefted the tray onto his left palm and entered the bedroom. The newly arrived letter in his pocket rustled as he turned to close the door. This one, delivered right to his rooming house, bothered him more than the one sent to his office. *Prepare to die,* it said. Someone—very probably Luckhurst—was toying with him. But he couldn't concern himself with that right now. The writer of the dratted things would surely give up the game by the time Sean had finished his business in Paris.

If the fool meant to frighten him, Sean could almost laugh at the pitiful effort. For the past ten years, he had lived daily with danger that bore no forewarning at all. His first ten years of life had been much the same. Worse, really, due to lack of training to deal with the perils he encountered. Watching his back became second nature, a way of life. These little scare tactics didn't unnerve him in the least. But they did present a bothersome puzzle, and puzzles distracted him from more important matters.

He would have to dismiss the letters. Just forget them. Today he had a greater puzzle, a distraction and an important matter all rolled into one. A wife.

Sean smiled at the sight greeting him as he entered the bedroom. Laura nestled amid the pillows with the sheet tucked just beneath her arms. Her smile shamed sunshine and was, thank God, not so rare.

"Food!" he announced as he carefully set the tray on the bed beside her. "Don't fidget, sweetheart. You'll spill the tea."

"Mmm," she agreed, snatching up a fat sugared biscuit. Her cheeks puffed out like a chipmunk as she chewed. The blue gray eyes rolled with pleasure.

He had to laugh. "Such a greedy child!" Had he ever seen anyone so gluttonous for every moment's worth of joy?

Recalling the reason for her hedonism sobered him immediately. She never knew just how many moments she had left. Laura could only be certain of this particular one.

"Such a gloomy face!" she admonished, drawing her brows together. "Don't frown so. It puts lines between your eyes."

"Don't talk with your mouth full," he said, tapping her nose with his finger.

She choked down the food and took a swallow of her tea. "When do we leave?"

"Two hours," he told her. "We must be at Dover by this evening. I sent to the hotel for your things. They should arrive directly. Will you need a maid?"

"Never had one. Will you need a valet?" she teased.

Sean grinned at the thought of having someone dress him. Now someone—this particular someone—*undressing* him was a different matter altogether. No time for that now, unfortunately. He handed her a sausage. "Silly widgeon. Finish your breakfast while I draw your bath."

He left her tucking into the substantial plate of bangers and eggs he had requested from the kitchen downstairs. The announcement of his sudden marriage had prompted instant motherly attention from his landlady and her staff. Until this morning, he had only been the object of curiosity and gossip who hardly rated a wary word of greeting now and then. Now he was "the young bridegroom."

Falling fully into the role certainly tempted him. There was nothing he'd have liked better than to crawl back into that bed and spend the day with "the young bride." He couldn't recall

ever having held a more responsive woman in his arms. She
made love the way she did everything else, full steam ahead
and damn the consequences. The mere thought of her enthusiasm had his body thrumming even now.

He turned on the tap in the huge, claw-foot tub and tested
the temperature of the water with the back of his hand.

The timing of this unexpected honeymoon could be worse,
he supposed. What if he were embarking on a case involving
a life-threatening situation? There had certainly been a wealth
of those, not that he minded. Danger proved addictive. He
thrived on that sort of job and it was what he did best. For the
past few years, Sean admitted, the adventures held far more
appeal than the rewards. This coming endeavor, however,
only relied on his keen eye for deception and his solid reputation as a reliable courier.

Working for Burton was child's play, a holiday in fact. This
time he only had to verify the authenticity of a painting. If
genuine, he would complete the deal for Mr. Burton, director
of the National Gallery, bring the picture home, and that
would be that. No rush, no danger, large fee. Not that he
needed the money particularly, but one never had too much
of that commodity.

Laura would be disappointed when he told her about the
tame task, he thought with a smile. After his warning of
possible danger, she would be geared up for murder and
mayhem. Her thirst for adventure would be amusing under
different circumstances.

His heart contracted painfully every time he thought of
Laura dying. How could he bear to watch that bright little light
blink out? The world would seem a dismal place without it
now that he knew her. She touched him, threw his senses
awry in some way he couldn't quite fathom; had done so
from the moment he had first seen her. Innocence, he

supposed. Something he'd had so little experience with in his twenty-eight years. Surprising he even recognized it at all.

This whole affair seemed unreal. The hasty wedding, the lovemaking, and letting her accompany him to Paris were all so uncharacteristically impulsive of him. He could scarcely believe he had allowed any of it. For a man who planned every move he made with the precision of a well-oiled machine, Sean knew he had slipped an important gear somewhere along the line.

In his early life, quick decisions had equaled survival. But later, he had learned to consider the long-term effect—weigh all his options, however briefly—before he acted. For the first time since the wedding, he forced himself to stop and think exactly where all this might lead.

Laura had given him no time to plan or consider or project. Because she had so little time to give. So little time.

Steam from the bath made him sniff. Surely that was what caused his eyes to water this way. He shut off the faucet and brushed a hand over his face. Laura Middlebrook had blown into his life like a whirlwind. She stirred up feelings he thought he had eliminated, and some he hadn't known existed at all. How did he think he could direct events toward a satisfactory future? Laura would not have one. God, how that thought hurt. It shouldn't bother him this much. He, of all people, knew there were things worse than death. He'd even told Laura as much. Cruel truth.

But he had never met anyone as alive as Laura. He must be out of his mind to admit such a thing, even to himself, but he could love this woman, was probably half in love with her already. After letting down his guard and risking it that once with Ondine, love only equaled disaster as far as Sean was concerned. It ripped away all the hard-earned control over his life as though it were wet tissue paper. He needed control the way he needed air to breathe. How could he possibly surrender that again?

Despite their recent betrothal, Camilla Norton's subsequent desertion had not affected him much. Not in the least, except for the small dent to his pride. He would suffer a great deal more than that with Laura's leaving, unless he took immediate charge of things.

If he continued down this road with her, the outcome could only be total devastation. After Ondine's untimely death, he'd had fury at her betrayal to sustain him. Even then, the pain of loving her and losing her had almost destroyed him. He had rebuilt the wall inside himself once. He didn't think he could do it again. This time he would be left with nothing but soul-deep grief. There would be no saving anger to draw on. Nothing.

The only prudent course was evident. He had to back away from her now, to distance himself from what would continue to grow between them if he allowed it. Given his upbringing, Sean knew he was as well versed in sex as any male on the planet. But with Laura, sex was not just sex. It was a mutual giving, a bonding of spirits he had never encountered before in his life, even with Ondine. And Sean realized that the physical union would only strengthen his love for Laura into a veritable necessity he could not live without.

He could never abandon Laura, however. She was his wife now and needed protection and support, certainly more than most wives did. But he must discontinue their intimacy before his need for her grew to unmanageable proportions.

How to do that would take some planning in itself. Denying her anything would be damned difficult, next to impossible, but he knew the alternative would prove worse. Loving her fully, without reservation, and then watching her die would tear the heart right out of his chest. A living death.

"I'm ready," she said from the doorway.

Sean pushed up from the edge of the tub, hardly daring to look at her, unable not to. She stood gloriously naked but for the sheet loosely draped over one shoulder, the dark satin of her hair wound in a precarious loop on top of her head. The invitation in her smoky eyes set him afire. Acceptance almost fought its way out of him despite his recent and very firm resolution. Stuffing his hands into his pockets, he skirted around her, muttering something inane about seeing to his packing.

It was a narrow escape. The first of many, he predicted.

"No one in the world needs this many clothes," Sean growled as he hefted a leather-bound trunk off the dock. A huffing porter struggled with the other.

Laura laughed and stepped aside and out of his way. "Of course they don't. Where's the fun in buying only what one needs? I'm afraid I did reduce your future inheritance considerably this past week, however."

Sean shot her a dark look.

She wondered why he resented it so whenever she mentioned her legacy. Pride, perhaps. His mood would lighten once he had loaded the baggage and they settled in for the crossing.

Laura left him to it and went to grasp the forward rail. France was out there. She even imagined she could see it, a faint gray line, probably the point near Calais. Perhaps what she saw were only swells of waves. Excitement skipped through her veins like little fairies. By late tomorrow they would be in Paris, City of Light. How she had dreamed of such places.

"Should be a fair enough crossing," Sean remarked as he joined her, that hoped-for smile in place. "Are you a good sailor, Laura?"

"Yes!" she answered immediately, thinking of the little sail boat she and Lambdin kept on the pond. "Oh, I can't wait, Sean! My insides are fluttering like the seabirds." She pointed up at the dizzying flock of gulls that circled the wharf.

He chuckled. "Be still, widgeon. You're rocking the boat."

"Don't be silly. This thing's a ship. 'Twould take a gale to rock it." She drew in a huge draft of the damp, salty sea breeze and sighed it out. Huge arms surrounded her and she leaned back against his solid chest, covering his hands with hers. "I feel so happy, Sean. So very happy, just at this moment."

Again he laughed, the rumble vibrating through her back and settling around her heart. "We haven't even done anything yet," he reminded her.

She tugged loose and turned to face him. "But we have, Sean. Think of it! In the space of twenty-four hours, I've become your wife," she said, feeling the blush color her cheeks, "and embarked on yet another exciting adventure! Will you show me Paris? Will we have the time?"

"I will make the time," he declared, brushing his hand down her face to cup her chin. "You shall see everything there is to see. The Tuileries, Bonaparte's Tomb, the Arch, the Louvre. All of it."

"What else? What else? Tell me more!" she demanded with an impatient bounce.

He shook his head. "Isn't that enough? Oh, all right, then, how's this? The tallest structure in the known world, three hundred meters. Will that do? There is this tower in the middle of the city, built for the Exposition."

"Oh, I read of that," she said excitedly. "It's costing them millions!"

"In francs, yes," he agreed. "But I'm afraid it's too ugly to thrill you much."

"No, no, I shall love it," she said, shaking her head. The mist-dampened feather on her hat drooped across one eye.

"Let's get you inside before you're completely soaked. I think the wind is picking up."

In her excitement, Laura hadn't even noticed they had

gotten under way. Obediently she accompanied him to the cabin where they could pass the short trip in comfort.

Half an hour later, she dashed out and back to the rail. Sean held her fast as she leaned over and lost her breakfast and luncheon. When her stomach had collapsed in on itself, she drooped in his arms and rested against him.

"It's too soon," she gasped, squeezing her eyes shut against her disappointment. "I thought it would be all right…but I don't want to…go yet."

His arms tightened around her, one hand pressing her now-hatless head against his chest and the other holding her whole body snug against his. "You're not going anywhere!" he snapped furiously. "You hear me? Not anywhere but to France. To see Paris. To dance away the night. To laugh and eat beignets, drink café au lait, the best champagne…."

"Oh, God, don't speak of food!" She pushed him away and retched again.

He enfolded her more softly this time. "This is only sea-sickness, Laura. You won't die of it, I promise, no matter how you feel at the moment."

Somehow she didn't quite believe him. From the desperate way he held her and the tone of his voice, he must not quite believe it, either.

For the remainder of the crossing, Laura lay cocooned in a blanket Sean had secured from one of the stewards, expecting to breathe her last at any moment. By the time they reached Calais, she found herself embracing the thought. Anything would be better than the misery she endured.

"I'll send for a doctor, darling," Sean whispered against her ear as they disembarked. He carried her in his arms toward one of the waiting carriages for hire.

"First we'll go to a hotel and get you to bed."

Laura allowed herself to doze in the carriage. She felt the

sick dizziness subside a bit when he deposited her on a cushioned armchair near the innkeeper's desk. "Sean?" she called when he started to step away from her to register.

"Yes?" he answered immediately, hurrying back to kneel beside her and take her hands in his. "What is it?" The sharp concern on his face made her smile.

"I feel much better. The sickness seems to be fading." In fact, she felt a bit hungry. "Do you think we could order up some tea? Maybe a few salted biscuits?" Laura watched his wide shoulders droop with what she suspected was relief.

"Anything," he answered on a protracted sigh. "Whatever you want. Will you be all right here for a moment?"

She nodded and smiled again, putting more energy into it than she really felt. Perhaps she would have a reprieve after all, another day to enjoy. During the few moments it took Sean to arrange for a room, she recovered completely. Nothing of her illness remained save a bit of weakness in her knees when she first stood alone. She insisted, over Sean's objection, that she could manage the stairs to their rooms on her own two feet.

When the doctor arrived, he caught Laura with her mouth full of savory chicken stew. "Good day to you, Madame Wilder," he greeted her. The newness of the address thrilled her into a happy grin.

"The *mal de mer* abates, *oui?*" He continued, "I am Dr. Louis Grillet, at your service."

Laura swallowed again and held out her hand. The handsome rascal kissed it! Lingeringly. She shot a glance at Sean. He was frowning ominously at the physician's gesture. Lord, he looked jealous.

"*Enchanté*," she announced sweetly just to further gauge her husband's reaction. He stepped nearer. If the doctor had not been leaning against her bedside already, Laura thought Sean might have pushed between them.

Something inside her did cartwheels, and it had nothing to do with her formerly unsettled stomach. "You were kind to come so quickly," she said to Dr. Grillet, "but it looks as though I don't need you after all. As you can see, I am fine. Appetite restored," she said pointing toward her half-empty tray of food, "and no lingering effects. I suspect my husband and I may have overreacted."

"Perhaps a more thorough examination is in order, none-theless," Grillet suggested with a sly smile. "If you would wait outside, Monsieur Wilder?"

"I think not," Sean growled menacingly. "If she says she is fine, then she is fine." He handed the doctor several bills, neatly folded. "For your trouble. Good night."

The curt dismissal prompted a Gallic shrug from Grillet and an inner squeal of delight from Laura. She hugged her arms over her chest to calm her heart. Her husband acted like a smitten lover. She didn't even mind if he was pretending. The very fact that he troubled himself to assume such a role told her that he cared.

"You were wonderful!" she said once the doctor had gone.

"More like ridiculous," he declared, sinking onto the bed and pinching the bridge of his nose with his fingers.

Laura started to reassure him, but when she leaned forward away from the pillows, her head spun dangerously. He noticed when she swayed to one side and righted her with his hands on her shoulders. "Lie back. And don't worry, it's just the effect of the laudanum. I promise that's all it is."

"Laudanum!" She bolted upright and nearly screeched the word.

"I had the cook add a bit to your tea. It will calm your stomach and allow you to rest well tonight."

"I will not be drugged! Not *ever!*" Laura fumed. "How dare you lace my tea without so much as a by-your-leave? Don't you understand? I want awareness, Sean. Every single moment, I want to know exactly—"

"Oh, Laura," he said, shifting nearer and sliding his arms around her loosely. "Never again, I promise you. Damn it all, I should have known better. I didn't think."

"Will you hold me?" she asked, burying her nose in the soft wool of his jacket and pulling him closer. "I was afraid today," she whispered the words, barely hearing them herself. "I *hate* being afraid!"

"I know," he answered. She thought she heard a slight catch in his voice. "Everything will be all right," he added. "You'll see."

"You won't leave when I sleep, will you?" Laura hated herself for clinging, but the night ahead frightened her witless. What if she simply drifted off into nothingness and stayed there forever?

"I won't leave you," he promised fervently. His lips pressed against her temple and hovered there as he spoke. "I vow I won't leave you, Laura. Not even for a minute."

With a sigh of relief, she let the reality of his strong embrace bear her into a world of dreams where nothing else dared touch her.

Chapter Four

Sean knew he could have left Laura last night and she would never have known the difference. He could have seen to their bags, which were no doubt stacked in some corner belowstairs awaiting his instructions. He could have ordered a late meal for himself so that his stomach wouldn't be growling now like a bear just out of hibernation. But a promise was a promise.

"Where is it?" she mumbled, squinting up at him.

"What?"

"The cat."

"What cat?"

"The one that slept in my mouth," she muttered. "I know I have fur on my tongue."

Sean laughed softly and pulled his arm from beneath her neck. He propped on his elbow and raked the length of her body with his gaze. "If there is a cat, it's probably lost in the wrinkles of your skirts. We're both a mess. I should have undressed us."

He wouldn't discuss with her why he hadn't done that. He could not have borne holding her with nothing between them. The pain of their closeness, even fully dressed as they were, had nearly killed him. The powerful urge to give comfort with, as well as to, his body would have wrecked his resolve if he hadn't left the fabric barriers exactly as they were.

Laura shifted and rubbed her eyes with her fists as a child might do on waking. He brushed the loosened strands of her hair back from her forehead and kissed her brow. "How do you feel?"

She laughed softly and shook her head. "Fuzzy. Could we have some breakfast?"

"Certainly!" he said, rolling off the bed and trying to straighten his clothes. "Right away." Then he stopped what he was doing and braced one hand on her shoulder. "Will you be all right while I go and order?"

"Of course. Go ahead. I'm quite recovered." She marched to the washstand and began splashing her face in the water. He watched her for a time to see how steady she was. Then, satisfied she told the truth, Sean left her to her ablutions while he arranged their passage on the train bound for Paris.

A little while later, they sat in the dining room of the hotel drinking the café au lait he had promised her.

Sean thought she looked a bit washed-out. He hoped that was only the result of the medicine he had ordered last night and her earlier bout with the nausea on the ship.

"So, tell me about our business in Paris," she demanded with a bright smile.

"*Our* business?" he asked with a quirk of his brow.

"You don't think for a moment I'm going to let you prevent me playing investigator! Now, tell." She threw him a saucy wink over the edge of her cup.

Sean fought the urge to embellish his current case, to offer her some trumped-up derring-do to take her mind off her other problem. No, he wouldn't lie. After all his insistence on honesty, she deserved better than that. Still he found himself tempted.

"My—our—employer is Mr. Frederick Burton, director of

the National Gallery. He has set me the task of examining a painting offered for sale by a Monsieur Charles Beaumont. If the provenance proves legitimate and it is what he says it is, I—we—are to purchase it with the funds provided and take it safely home."

"And?"

"That's it," he declared, noting her frown of disappointment.

"I thought it would be something more—"

"Dangerous? Yes, I knew you expected that. But it needn't be so dull. If you like drawing, then you must be interested in art. This Monsieur Beaumont may have a fine collection as yet unseen by the public. He's claiming a Rembrandt, at any rate. Won't you find that interesting?"

She looked distracted. "How will you know if this picture is the real thing and not fake?"

Sean allowed his pride to show. He didn't often do that, but he wanted her approval. Enough to boast a bit. "I *know* Rembrandt. I'll wager I could tell you how many hairs in each brush he used in every known painting he produced. No one knows him as I do. I've already discovered two forgeries formerly attributed to him. That's how I landed this case." He grinned at her astonishment.

"You said you never studied painting."

"Art history," he admitted wryly. "Rembrandt was always my favorite. I've read everything ever written about him and his work. Later, as I traveled, examining his paintings and his technique in museums became something of a hobby. More like an obsession, really. I've seen them all. At least those not in private, inaccessible collections such as Beaumont's."

"So you will simply look at this painting, decide if it's real, and buy accordingly?" she asked.

"Of course not. I'll check the provenance and establish how it changed hands through the years, as well as examining the brush strokes, colors, composition and so forth. Burton and I did that together with a fourteenth-century Duccio a few years past in Florence, though I'm not really well versed on Italian painters. I've acquired lesser pieces for him since then. This is the most important thing he has trusted me with alone."

Her eyes looked a trifle glazed as she said, "I'm fascinated!"

Sean laughed aloud and shook his head. "You are not, you little liar! You're bored to tears. Come on, you wanted sordid disguises, flying bullets, mad dashes through the back streets. Admit it."

"Childish, aren't I?" She laughed, too, and blushed. Sean was delighted to see color in her cheeks, whatever the cause.

"Wonderfully so," he said, standing and offering his arm. "Now let's go to Paris, shall we, Mrs. Wilder? On my word, I promise you won't be bored there."

They arrived at the Hotel Lenoir very late that evening. Both were travel weary, but Sean noticed nothing faint about Laura. She seemed to have bounced back readily enough from her ills of the day before. While that relieved his mind somewhat, he couldn't feel completely at ease.

There would come a time—probably quite soon—when she would not rally. Something vital shrank inside him every time he let himself think of that.

He tried to picture it, though, so that he could accept it when the worst happened. Laura still and white, beautiful in her final repose. Himself, stoic without and crushed within. It was no use. He could not make himself imagine. There was no preparing for such a thing anyway. Almost as heartbreaking as facing the actuality would be the pretending beforehand, the smiling and making of ordinary conversation, living as though there would always be a tomorrow for Laura. That much he must do for her, no matter how difficult or painful.

Facing the most deadly, knife-wielding bully in White-chapel had not prompted such dread as he felt now.

Sean knew now that he hadn't fully understood what he faced until Laura had fallen sick on the ferry. Death was no stranger to him, of all people. Sean could not begin to count the bodies he had viewed over the years, in the bowels of London, on battlefields, during days with the Yard and afterward. But thinking of Laura lifeless? His mind rebelled.

How could he go on this way, wondering if every breath Laura drew might be her last? And if it was this miserable for him, what the devil must it be like for Laura? Surely she marked the apprehension in his eyes every time he looked at her.

If only they could forget she was to die. Like being ordered not to think of elephants, he thought with an inner scoff. He could at least make *her* forget for a time. That would be something, anyway.

Sean glanced around the modest bedroom of Hotel Lenoir and thought perhaps he should have taken Laura somewhere fancier. Somewhere grand with a suite of rooms. Instead, he had selfishly chosen this place with its antique patina and its shared necessaries down the hall because the memories of his times here gave his soul comfort.

Right now he could use all the comfort to be had. For three school vacations during his adolescence, he had come here with his new friend, Eugene Campion. He and Camp had been the odd men out at Eton their first years there. Camp was the bastard of Baron Nesbitt Lorne, who had the good grace to see his natural son educated. And Sean, a product of the London stews, had a noble grandmother who had finally seen fit to rescue him.

Both benefactors believed they were doing the right thing by their respective charges. But neither Camp nor himself had had the background or a good enough grip on the king's proper English to make themselves accepted. In the interest of self-defense, they had befriended and protected each other.

Accompanying Camp to his mother's family in France for a few weeks of summer holiday had given Sean the only semblance of normal family life he had ever experienced. If life in a Parisian hotel could be considered anywhere near the norm, he thought with a wry smile. It ranked far above a brothel or the halls of Eton, Sean knew for certain.

When the boys had gone on to university, Annette Lenoir Campion had married and moved to Florence. Later, he and Camp had enlisted together and served two years in Africa. On returning, Sean had sought employment with Scotland Yard and Camp had gone on to medical school in Italy. Madame and Monsieur Campion, Camp's aging grandparents, had sold the hotel to a cousin whom Sean had never met.

Now, whenever he or Camp traveled to Paris, whether their visits coincided or not, they always came here. With its fond memories, the old Lenoir had become a sanctuary of sorts. He had never even noticed its genteel shabbiness before today.

Laura returned from the bathing room down the hall looking refreshed and rosy in her prim white robe. He noticed bare, pink toes peeking from beneath the hem.

"Into bed with you," he ordered with a forced smile. When he had tucked her in like the child she looked, he kissed her brow and turned to leave.

"Where are you going?" she asked before he could escape.

"To scrape off some travel dirt," he replied, knocking dust off his trousers. "Go to sleep, Laura. We have a big day tomorrow."

She squirmed impatiently and smoothed the covers over her knees. "I thought you might want to...well, you know."

"No!" he said, rather too quickly. In view of her confused look, he felt compelled to offer some sort of explanation. "It's too soon, you see."

Her eyes widened as though to take in this new bit of information. "Too soon? You mean you can't...manage?" The gears of her mind were nearly visible as she considered that. "How often can you, then?"

Oh Lord, he had spun a web now. And tangled himself up in it. He thought she would assume he meant it was too soon for *her*. He could not make love with her again. He would be totally, completely lost in her if he did. She already had half his heart. How was he supposed to guard the rest? He'd have nothing left to go on with.

"Well," he said, looking everywhere but at her, raking his mind for something, anything, to extricate himself. "Once a month," he declared, warming to the prevarication. "You understand your woman's cycle, don't you? Men have cycles of a sort, as well, you see. It's not exactly the same for a man, but there must be a bodily change for the...uh...emissions and such to...to work. Yes. One has to wait." He sucked in a deep breath and bit his lips together over the outrageous lie. "For the next cycle, you see." He lowered his head and shook it in frustration. "It's very complicated."

"You lucky fellow!"

"Lucky?" he asked. His head came up smartly. He caught her slumberous gaze and watched it travel down to the buttons below his belt.

"Mmm-hmm," she cooed with a knowing smile. "Your cycle seems to have...extended itself."

Laura bit back a laugh at Sean's distressed expression. His mind and body were at such odds, he had lost his usual equanimity. He obviously wanted her, but had decided she was not up to lovemaking because of her recent spell of sickness. If he only knew how gloriously energetic she felt right now. Excited.

She watched him with one brow cocked, her eyes traveling from his face to his groin and back again, curious as to how nimbly he would account for that blatant erection of his.

He didn't disappoint. "Swelling," he explained. "Too much recent activity, I suspect," he explained somewhat breathlessly, still frowning down at his errant member.

"Sean?"

His head came up with a guilty jerk. "Yes?"

She gave him a pointed look. "I'm not sixteen anymore. My women friends who are long married have been rather vocal about what's involved. And, believe it or not, I can read, as well. Now tell me what has prompted this absurd fabrication of yours? Are you teasing me?"

The pained look on his face wiped away all the humor in the situation. He wasn't making sport of her inexperience at all. "Or is it my illness?"

Laura watched him carefully as he exhaled a protracted sigh. "In a way, it is," he admitted softly as he trudged to the bed, turned around and sat down heavily beside her.

"You're disgusted by it? Afraid of it? What?"

"No, no, nothing as simple as that," he said as he caught up one of her hands and kissed it. He clutched it against his chest where she could feel his heart thumping hard against her wrist. "I'm falling in love with you, Laura." A long pause ensued while she digested that before he added, "And I don't want to."

"I don't blame you," she said with a wry laugh. Laura plucked at the edge of the sheet with the fingers of her free hand. "Surely you realize what's making you think this could be love. We've only known each other for three days. All this seems romantic to you, and tragic. You are a very compassionate person, Sean."

"No, that's not it. Something sparked the moment I first saw you. Before I knew about—" He stopped a moment, obviously unwilling to put her problem into words. "And then, of course, I do know what it's like. Love, that is. It can be hell."

Laura felt a sharp pang of jealousy barely tempered by compassion. She made her voice soft when she asked, "Your wife?"

He nodded.

"How did she die?" Laura had been told by her solicitor of the rumors surrounding the first Mrs. Wilder's death. She hoped for Sean's sake they weren't true, but she thought she should know.

"She fell from a cliff," he said, staring at the wall as though he could see into the past. "Ondine and I left London and went home to the house in Cornwall, where I attempted to clear the air between us. She wept that night." He glanced at Laura and then away. "You see, she confessed to an affair with Wade Halloran before we married," he stated in a flat tone. "Wade and I knew each other from Eton, and his family members were also Mother's neighbors after she moved to Cornwall. Ondine swore things were over between them. So I forgave her." Sean sighed and covered his eyes with one hand and shook his head sadly. "Then she told me...other things even more heartbreaking. Still I forgave her, though it wasn't as easily done that time. She seemed all right when we said good-night."

"When did she die?" Laura whispered.

"That next morning. Mother's steward and I searched for her when we realized she was missing. We found Wade staring down at her body as it lay on the rocks just above the surf. He suddenly ran raving mad with grief. Only by using considerable force did I prevent his leaping after her. The authorities were forced to lock him away immediately for his own safety. Poor old Wade. I suppose he still languishes there in that locked room with his lost wits and his secrets."

"Secrets? Was it...? Do you think she fell on purpose?"

Sean shook his head. "I don't know. I truly don't. Wade's wild accusation, that I'd driven her to do such a thing, certainly made me wonder. But he obviously met Ondine there that morning for a reason. It occurred to me that maybe he pushed her, but I hate to believe that. Perhaps she jumped, as Wade declared, or fell accidentally. I suppose I'll never know the truth. At any rate, she is dead and Wade ended as much a victim as she."

"Oh, Sean," Laura whispered, her heart aching for the pain he had obviously endured. "That must have been dreadful for you. Your wife and your friend. Such betrayal. I wonder how you stood it."

"Not very well, I admit. I only brought it up to assure you that I do recognize what's developing here between us. I did love Ondine at one time. I loved her very much."

"And you lost her," Laura added. "I can well understand why you wouldn't want a repeat of *that* situation."

He raked a hand through his hair and released a harsh breath. "God, it sounds so damned selfish of me when you put it that way! I do care so much for you already, Laura, but—"

"You don't want to love me and suffer a grief you've already suffered once." She patted his hand and squeezed it with reassurance. "That's just good sense, Sean. Self-preservation. You mustn't think for a moment that I fault you for it. I would feel exactly the same way in your place. You're right, of course. The closer we become, the worse it will be for you. I really don't want you to love me," she lied, keeping her eyes averted so he wouldn't guess what she really felt.

He remained silent, staring down at her hands clasping his.

"This simply won't do. I should go home," she decided with a succinct nod. "That's the prudent thing, for both our sakes."

"No!" His vehemence surprised her. "You can't do that. I won't let you."

Laura frowned with frustration. "Well, we have to do *something!* Imagine how guilty I'll feel at the end. Being left behind by someone you love has to be the worst feeling in the world." She thought of her parents' constant desertion and how it had affected her. Affected her still. "I refuse to hurt you that way," she said. "I shall leave tomorrow."

"I can't let you go," he whispered. "No matter what, I just can't."

Her hand wriggled out of his and she clamped it to the other so tightly her knuckles turned white. "Well, you'll have to eventually, won't you? For your sake we shall have to alter our relationship somehow. Or at least prevent its progressing into something more profound." She considered for a moment. "Of course, you know that. That's exactly what you have been trying to tell me, isn't it? We can simply be friends," she suggested. "Can't we?"

"That did occur to me," he said, wiping the sweat off his brow. "Yes, I think we must try."

"Fine! It's all settled then. No more of this playing at seduction, I promise. I was terribly clumsy at it anyway." Her self-deprecating laughter sounded forced, even to her, but Sean joined her anyway. His sounded worse.

"You're damned good at it, and you know it, you little minx."

"Why, thank you! How nice of you to say so," she said, preening theatrically. "I did have you going for a while there, didn't I?"

Sean simply nodded, his eyes sad, his wide smile locked in place. He didn't speak or move again for the longest time.

"I'm sorry, Laura," he said finally. "I didn't foresee this happening."

She sighed and shrugged, fighting her disappointment. Time grew too short to waste any on regrets. "Oh, that's all right, Sean. I wish you wouldn't talk on so about it."

He rose then and headed for the door. Grasping the handle, he turned and smiled. "Do me a favor, old chum?"

"Anything for a friend," she said, relieved that he had regained his composure, and determined to hang on to hers.

"Lose the perfume and try to look ugly. Maybe develop a taste for garlic? I absolutely loathe the stuff."

Laura laughed again, a real laugh this time. The rascal still had his sense of humor. And he really did want her. Maybe he wouldn't mind a little flirtation later if she kept it light and funny. Perhaps, if they had enough time to become truly good friends, he wouldn't resist a bit of superficial lovemaking.

Surely such a thing existed. Men fed these hungers all the time without getting their hearts involved. Sean, of all people, should be aware of that. Sympathy was getting in his way right now. He would get past that notion of love growing between them in a few days.

Even if she wouldn't.

During the next week, Laura wondered why Sean still insisted on sharing a room. His presence gave her comfort but made sleep an elusive thing for both of them.

Occasionally she would surprise a tortured expression on his face that mirrored what she was feeling herself. One such fleeting look could start her body pulsing in places she had hardly noticed before he came along. Each night her desire seemed to double.

He would leave the room while she readied for bed and she politely turned her back to him when he returned to undress. That chaise longue by the window barely supported his tall frame, but he wouldn't hear of her giving up the bed. Such a gentleman.

Laura ached to probe beneath Sean's studied gentleness, but for his sake she carefully restrained the urge. Living together in such close quarters seemed akin to playing with fire in a room full of explosives. And neither of them knew just when an errant spark might set things off. Every time their eyes met, Laura expected the volatile entity that was their passion to ignite.

Friendship definitely was not working. By day, it appeared to flourish, but the nights—ah, those nights—when she lay so still, pretending sleep and watching the outline of his long body silvered by the moonlight from the window. Forbidden fruit.

At times, she would wake and feel his gaze on her, as well. Perhaps he only checked to see whether she still breathed, but Laura knew that was not his only interest. The desire emanating from his makeshift bed grew almost palpable.

Those torturous six nights aside, they had truly done Paris during the daylight hours. She certainly couldn't fault Sean as a tour guide. He had pointed out all the sights promised and more. This morning they had walked for miles along the Seine, had luncheon at a café along the Champs Elysées, and then climbed the steps to the top of Notre Dame. The magnificent view of the city almost banished her exhaustion.

"I've saved the Louvre for tomorrow and the day after," he said when they descended to street level again and exited the cathedral.

"Thank goodness, I'll have tonight to soak some feeling back into my feet." She would never admit it to Sean, but the attractions of Paris dimmed in light of his own.

The grandeur of Napoleon's Arc de Triomphe, the magnificent stained glass of La Sainte-Chappelle, and the strange tower that Eiffel designed were only feasts for the eyes. Sean fed every single sense she had and a sixth one she only just discovered, an inner sense fully attuned to his hidden needs. It made her want to give him everything she was, to fill with light that dark void Ondine had left. But could he withstand another such loss when she had to leave him?

What she needed was a real distraction, something to engage her mind fully, something to displace the mind-drugging memories of their one intimate encounter the day they married.

"I wonder when we'll meet this Charles Beaumont?" Sean had sent round a message to the man. They had expected an invitation from him every evening when they returned to the hotel. "He doesn't seem to be in any rush to sell the picture, does he? Do you think he has decided not to part with it?" Laura asked as they approached rue St. Jacques where their hotel was located.

Sean shrugged. "Who can say? But I'm not in any great hurry. We've been here for a week now and he has my direction. It's his move. Would you like an ice before we go back?"

She rolled her eyes and grinned. "Good Lord, Sean, you've already had two since breakfast! I'm beginning to think that's the only reason you accepted this assignment."

"It's very warm today," he said, looking a little petulant, "and you nag like an old nanny."

"I'd hate to have been *your* old nanny. You were a right little monster, I'll wager. A nasty little scupper."

His eyes narrowed and he looked away. "Just so."

With his taciturn reply, Laura recalled that Sean had never had a nanny at all. His childhood must have been frightening and shameful, lacking any of the amenities she had enjoyed. Unlike her, he'd had his mother with him. But could even a mother's love compensate for passing one's tender years in a place rife with sin and degradation? She thought not.

He had seemed cynical about it the one time they had discussed it, the day she had proposed to him. Small wonder. Laura felt guilty now that she had reminded him even though it had been inadvertent.

Though it was certainly not of the prurient sort, she admitted to a curiosity about what his life had been like there. Perhaps if he recounted some of his early experiences, they would not appear so ghastly to him after all this time. She could point out how such adversity had fostered a strength and self-reliance in him that most men envied and women found infinitely attractive, as well as comforting. Especially this woman who had married him.

"Shall we visit your mother in Cornwall when we return from Paris?" she asked, hoping to turn the conversation happier.

"No, I never visit unless it's absolutely necessary. The memories I bring are distressing to her. And to me," he added.

"Would you like to tell me about it?" she asked gently.

The look he gave her was angry and defensive. "Not for a sure place in heaven would I relive it, even with words. And certainly not with you." With that, he strode right past the ice vendor and on toward the hotel, leaving her to follow.

Laura knew she had overstepped the bounds of their relationship. She cursed her quick tongue and wondered if she had destroyed what little progress they had gained in becoming true friends.

Hurrying her steps, she caught up to him and reached out for one of his fisted hands. "Sean? I do apologize. Please don't be angry with me."

He altered his stride so that she didn't have to run to keep up. "I'm not angry, Laura," he said without looking at her. "Not with you anyway. It is just that some subjects are not for the ears of a gently bred woman. Trust me that my existence on Gumthorne Street definitely qualifies."

Laura sighed and remained quiet for the rest of their walk back to the hotel. Sean's silent preoccupation led her to believe he must be dwelling on his past in spite of what he'd said about not reliving it in any way. How often did he do that? she wondered.

She must be very careful not to refer to it again. Somehow, she believed that his recounting it aloud might help him bring it into proper perspective, but the risk of alienating him altogether seemed too great. Perhaps, someday, he would trust her enough to bare that darkness in his soul.

If there was time. She accepted the fact that she would die soon. The certainty troubled her still, but strangely enough, the occurrence of death itself bothered her much less than the things she would be forced to leave undone. Important things like loving Sean as completely as he deserved.

Laura squeezed the large hand that encompassed hers and placed her other over the top of it. Sean turned his head, looked down into her eyes and smiled. "Tell me I haven't spoiled the whole afternoon."

"What's past is past," she said as brightly as she could manage. "Right now is all that counts."

Chapter Five

"Monsieur…Monsieur Wilder!" A thin voice greeted them from behind the desk as they entered the lobby of the Lenoir. "A letter for you. And a parcel."

Sean excused himself and accepted the envelope and small package from the clerk. He tucked the letter into his pocket and the book-size package under his arm for their trip up the narrow staircase.

Laura preceded him, wondering how she could make up for the gaff she had made in bringing up the awful memories of his youth. She decided the less said about the previous topic, the better. To apologize again would only make things worse. Better to go on as though nothing out of the ordinary had happened, and hope that he would simply dismiss it from his mind.

Immediately she unbuttoned her shoes and stretched out on the settee. "Ah, home at last. The cathedral was grand, wasn't it? Makes one feel small in the scheme of things. Insignificant, really. I read somewhere that's what the architects had in mind. Think so?"

"Mmm-hmm." Sean settled into the chair by the window, pushing back the curtain to catch the faint breeze. He retrieved and immediately ripped open the envelope the clerk had given him. After glancing over it, he quickly jammed it back into his pocket.

"What's wrong?" Laura asked. She couldn't decide whether their former conversation accounted for his troubled look or if the contents of the letter had caused it.

"It's nothing," he said, and took out his pocketknife and began to open the brown-wrapped parcel.

"What do you have there?" Laura asked.

"Probably a book. Burton always sends me the latest volumes on...ha, this is certainly peculiar!"

Puzzled excitement replaced his worried expression as Sean stared down at the object inside a sturdy box. From where she sat, it appeared to be a picture. He lifted it out and carefully examined all sides, pursed his lips for a moment, then laid it back inside. Laura thought she detected a hint of a smile playing round his eyes as he got up and walked over to her.

"I'm afraid this Beaumont fellow's a bit touched. A whole week to answer my message, and now this. See what you make of it." He set the box on her knees.

The crudely done landscape lay nestled in a swath of tissue. Laura ran a finger over the cheap oak frame as she stared at the garish colors on the canvas. "Well, Sean, I'm no expert on these matters, but offhand I would say this is definitely not what we came to Paris for."

"Read the note," he instructed as he joined her on the settee.

She plucked a small card from the edge of the frame and read it aloud.

"Mr. Wilder: Please present this gift to Mr. Burton with my compliments. It deserves a proper setting. Beaumont."

"This is dated a month ago," she added.

"Yes. Roughly three weeks after he contacted Mr. Burton and offered to sell the Rembrandt to the gallery," Sean explained.

Together, they stared down at the poorly executed picture.

"This is undoubtably the worst landscape I have ever seen," Laura said. "Why do you suppose he sent it? The deal for the Rembrandt is off, then? *This* is meant to compensate for *that?*"

"The package has been opened and resealed."

"Someone tampered with it? Perhaps he sent the Rembrandt and someone later switched the paintings," Laura suggested. Then her curious gaze fell on the left lower corner of the painting. "Sean, look! Beaumont did this. He signed it. It's a bit smudged, but there it is." She pointed.

Then she lifted the painting out of its rustling nest and turned it over as Sean had done. "Oh, see here, Sean, the back of the canvas looks old, but that part folded over the edge of the stretcher bars isn't!"

Sean smiled and raised his eyebrows. "Clever girl! And I thought you only a pretty face." He lifted his hand and playfully traced her cheek and chin with one long finger. "But you certainly are that, as well."

"You planned it, didn't you? You saw Beaumont already and had him send this round. You set up a bit of mystery so that I wouldn't be bored with all this." The thought warmed her, that he would go to such lengths. That he cared for her that much.

He shook his head, but Laura could see the guilt in his eyes.

"Your ears turn red when you lie," she teased.

Immediately he cupped his hands over his ears and laughed.

"You didn't have to," she said, smiling, "but it was sweet of you." She placed the painting back in the box.

"Well," he said, inclining his head, "truth be told, I didn't. No now, wait. I admit, I briefly considered something along those lines. You looked so woebegone when I explained our reasons for coming, the idea just popped into my mind. But honesty won out. I swear I haven't seen Beaumont at all and this has not been set up for your amusement. I'm every bit as surprised by this as you are."

With obvious eagerness, he pushed the box at her again, indicating she should examine it further. "You aren't yet finished with this. Get on with it!"

Laura lifted the painting again, turning it this way and that, picking at the back edge where the new white canvas lapped over its wooden stretcher. A darker linen thread stuck out from underneath. "Just as I thought. There is another under here!"

He already had his pocketknife out, prying loose the frame. Once the stretched canvas had been freed, he worked out the tacks that attached the canvas to the stretcher bars.

Gently, he lifted the top canvas off and sighed with awe. "Here she is," he whispered. "Hendrickje Stoffels, the old fellow's mistress, by God! Here she is, and you have found her, Laura. Well done of you."

Heady with excitement, she clapped her hands and giggled like a schoolgirl. It took only seconds for realization to dawn. "You knew all along the Rembrandt was there, didn't you?" Still she smiled, delighted that he allowed her the privilege of discovery.

"Strongly suspected once I saw that older canvas," he admitted. He had already located his magnifier and was adjusting the lamp.

"Is it real? Authentic?"

"As nearly as I can tell. We don't have the provenance, of course, but I would almost stake my life that Rembrandt did this. One of his later works, naturally, judging by the subject. But also by the style. Very fresh and spontaneous, probably a study for a larger work." Sean appeared enthralled as he peered through his glass at Hendrickje Stoffels's nearly bared bosom.

Laura cleared her throat.

"Luscious brush strokes," Sean quipped, turning his head to wink up at her. "Sensual."

Laura's own breasts tightened at his suggestive remark. She rolled her eyes heavenward and quickly changed the subject. "Why would Beaumont send it this way, Sean? Isn't that a bit risky? And why backdate the note? Does he expect payment for it when he calls it a gift?"

"Only one way to find out," Sean said, putting on his coat and straightening his tie. "It will probably be late when I get back. I'll try not to disturb you."

"You can pinch me and keep me awake on the way if necessary."

"Laura," he began, shaking his head.

"Leave me here and I'll follow you," she warned with a meaningful lift of her brows.

"Oh, all right, I suppose it can't hurt if you come," he said after considering her threat. She ignored the dark frown.

Laura had to admit he caved in readily enough. She had expected, and been prepared for, more of a fight. Point of fact, she had rather looked forward to one, thinking it might diffuse some of the tension that existed between them.

But Sean never fought with her, never denied her anything she asked of him, except for the lovemaking she had offered a week ago. On that point, he held firm though she had not really tested him fully yet. She had made up her mind she wouldn't.

He obviously still worried that he would come to love her if he gave way to their desires. A man's mind must work differently, requiring physical reinforcement to establish a deep connection of spirit. Or perhaps Sean held the act in more reverence than did his fellows. That would be a wonder, given his frequent exposure to it at such an early age. She supposed that his experiences could have had a reversing effect on his outlook.

Whatever his reasoning, Laura knew sex would make no

difference whatever in her feelings for him. She already loved
Sean as much as it was ever possible to love another. The
emotion permeated her every waking thought whether she
ever expressed it with her body or not.

But she would not suffer for their separation once the end
had come and gone. If she did not honor his belief about ar-
resting their feelings for each other, however, Sean likely
would suffer the worse for it. The poor man had already
endured quite enough grief in his lifetime, and Laura determined she would not add more if she could help doing so.

She needed to put all thoughts of loving out of her mind
in order to protect him. The mystery they needed to unravel
would surely help. Beaumont's curious note and package
arrived at precisely the right time. Now they would become
comrades in arms, partners in business, mates in the platonic
sense of the word.

More's the pity.

Sean shifted in the seat of the hansom cab so that his thigh
touched Laura's leg. He hadn't intended the contact, but he
noticed her jump. He wondered what had put her so on edge.
Their little mission, perhaps? "Are you nervous? Want to go
back to the hotel?"

She lifted her chin in challenge and her eyes sparkled.
"Certainly not! You're not going to get rid of me that easily.
Just you remember who found the Rembrandt!"

Laura could be rather cheeky and was being more so than
usual at the moment. He experienced an overwhelming urge
to kiss that impertinent mouth of hers. That would suit her
down to the ground, he knew. Those sly, come-hither looks
of hers—intended or not—grew more potent every time he
had looked at her. Or else his own weakening resolve
imagined them doing so.

Her persistent joy in the moment was infectious, and more than anything, he wanted to enter fully into the spirit of it. He wanted to let go of this blasted reserve between them and abandon all thoughts of the future. Live for the present and love her in every way a man could love a woman. He would caress every inch of her, follow the touch of his hands with kisses. Hot and wild and endless kisses progressing on to…no! He had to stop this now. If he didn't, he'd be unable to stand upright without embarrassing himself and her once they reached their destination.

Sean tore himself away from the bedroom fantasies that deviled him and deliberately focused on the matter at hand. He would think about the case. Only the case at hand.

"Maybe Beaumont simply decided to donate the picture to the museum. Unusual way to do so, however."

Laura raised her perfect eyebrows and pursed her lips. "Perhaps, but he could be in some sort of trouble since he sneaked it out to you in such a way."

"Great drama, isn't it? Lord, if I'd tried, I couldn't have come up with anything this ridiculous to entertain you. I shall have to buy the man a drink and thank him. You are entertained, aren't you?"

"Oh, mightily," she remarked in a dry tone. "See if you can get your mind on what you're supposed to be doing instead of worrying whether I'm a victim of ennui."

"What more would you suggest I do, then?"

They bantered back and forth until the cab slowed to a stop. Sean stepped down and surveyed their surroundings before allowing Laura to alight.

As Parisian mansions went, Beaumont's looked fairly ordinary. Though not huge, it was properly ostentatious. The facade shone pink in the twilight, sporting bas-relief half columns and the obligatory gargoyles. Something struck Sean as not quite right, however. The hansom had driven right through the open wrought iron gates, past ill-kempt grounds, and up the U-shaped drive to the front entrance. He noted no lights within, but then the evening had not yet grown fully dark.

"Place looks deserted," he mumbled as he assisted Laura from the cab and ordered the driver to wait. They traversed the dozen steps to the double doors and Sean applied the knocker. Since it was in place, he knew someone must be in residence. They waited a long while before anyone answered.

Finally one of the doors opened just enough to reveal a disheveled gray head. Sean smiled at the rheumy-eyed fellow and announced, "Mr. and Mrs. Sean Wilder to see Mr. Beaumont, please."

The man's eyes widened with surprise and then took on a resigned expression. He opened the door a bit wider. "I am Beaumont. I wish you had not come here."

"My wife and I wanted to thank you, on behalf of Mr. Burton and the museum, for the generous gift of the—"

"It is nothing," Beaumont interrupted, "just a keepsake for an old friend. Tell Burton I wish him well. You must excuse me now." Beaumont's frightened gaze kept darting past Sean and Laura. "Not decent to receive a lady, don't you see."

"Is something wrong, Mr. Beaumont?" Laura asked. "We can't leave unless we know you will be all right. You look ill."

Suddenly the older man slumped and he shook his head. "Bankruptcy," he muttered. "They have confiscated everything."

"Your collection!" Sean exclaimed. "Everything?"

Beaumont nodded and flashed a sad smile. "All but my clothing and—" he said with a rather pointed look at Sean "—my very personal effects such as my own worthless paintings."

"Ah, I see. And your home?" Sean probed.

"I must vacate within two days," Beaumont admitted.

"Have you anywhere to go, sir?" Laura asked.

"You will come to us," Sean said firmly. "To the Hotel Lenoir. You know it? We'll see you back to England. I'm certain, in view of your...friendship, that Mr. Burton will—"

Beaumont interrupted him. "No. Thank you, but I have plans. Please, just go now. I'd not like anyone to discover your little errand here."

"But, sir," Sean insisted, "you're obviously in need of funds and I can help you."

Beaumont drew himself up as though girding for a battle, but his voice lowered to a whisper. "Wilder, my creditors would pounce like a jungle cat on any remuneration I receive for anything. This paltry gift for Burton's walls is the only thing I have left to show for thirty years of effort. Do you understand? I would like to know that at least one person in the world appreciates something I have done with my life before I wrecked it at the tables. Now, if you have any compassion whatsoever, take your beautiful wife and begone from here. This is dreadfully... embarrassing."

Sean agreed and shook hands with Beaumont. "Good luck to you, sir. And everyone who visits Mr. Burton's *walls* will thank you for your gift. I promise you that."

Beaumont smiled sadly. "Good night, Wilder. Mrs. Wilder."

As the door closed, Sean felt a chill snake down his spine. He dearly hoped Beaumont wouldn't do away with himself over this. He took Laura's arm and escorted her back to the cab.

"Sean, will he really be all right, do you think?" Laura asked, echoing Sean's own worry.

"One can only hope," he replied. "Beaumont's lost it all through gambling, and then run up debts trying to recoup. There's bound to be guilt in either instance, as well as despair."

"Well, he seems a nice old gentleman. I hate to leave him like that. Isn't there something we could do to help him?"

Though darkness surrounded them now, Sean could hear

the tears in her voice. Somehow he had to banish them. He could not abide Laura's tears.

"I think I will purchase his passage to England and send round the papers first thing tomorrow. His creditors surely won't take that since it isn't cash. Mr. Burton will see to him once he gets there. Perhaps put him on staff at the museum. God knows he's had enough experience acquiring from what I've heard."

"Oh, Sean, what a marvelous idea! I knew you would think of something." She leaned over and pressed her lips to his cheek. It was all he could do not to ravish her then and there.

They rode in silence for a while, lost in their own thoughts. Sean wondered whether Laura realized how rare was her capacity for caring. She worried about an old man she didn't even know. Most people would dismiss him as a blundering fool who had only himself to blame for his misfortune.

What a big heart she had for such a small person. She even loved her negligent parents and always spoke well of them, even though they had given her nothing in the way of emotional support. Most remarkable of all, she offered friendship to a husband who was too cowardly to love her when she so badly needed love.

Laura's generosity of spirit humbled him. Was it a result of what she knew she must face in the near future or had she always been so beautiful inside?

He didn't need his powers of deduction to answer that. What he meant to do about it was another question.

"We should stop for dinner before we go back," she suggested. Her cheerfulness had returned. "How about the Chévillard?"

"Craving chocolate?" he teased, but gave in gracefully since he knew she liked the place and it was on their way.

Laura's delight in the restaurant's supposed Parisian typicality lightened his mood and by the time they had finished dinner, he felt positively buoyant. He resisted telling her that most of the café's patronage consisted of tourists out to glimpse *tout* Paris by night.

No one was about when they finally entered their hotel. When they reached the room, Sean stuck his key in the lock, realizing too late that the door wasn't even properly shut. As it swung open, he shoved Laura behind him and reached for his pistol.

"Wilder," growled the distinguished man standing by the window. "You are not getting away with this, you know. Laura, collect your things."

"Mr. Middlebrook!"

"Father!" Laura echoed.

Sean glanced down at her, not missing for a moment the way her fingers clutched his arm as she peeped around him. Rather than pleased, she looked apprehensive.

Middlebrook bore half his weight on an ebony cane and assumed an affected pose. Sean supposed the man thought it dashing, that attitude of relaxed superiority. Indeed he did look well turned out. The nasty sneer and narrowed eyes spoiled the effect. "Well, my girl, you've finally reached the heights of stupidity. Are you happy now that you have interrupted your mother's sojourn to the Trouville? Now I suppose we must take you with us. Don't just stand there gaping like a fish out of water. Get packed."

Sean ushered Laura farther into the room and closed the door behind them. "We hadn't anticipated your visit, sir," he said, determined to be amiable, "but you're welcome, of course. I'm certain Laura is delighted to see you. Would you like a drink?" He gestured toward the decanter of brandy and glasses on the table in the corner.

"Devil a drink, Wilder. You know very well why I've come.

Here I paid you a bloody fortune to do a bit of work for me and you repay me by snatching my gullible daughter. Thank God Lambdin had the good sense to wire me back directly once I contacted him. With this damned Exposition going on, it's taken me days to find you two. I'll tell you straight out, man, you'll never get a farthing of her money. This sham marriage of yours will be history before the week is out. Depend on it." For emphasis, he dented the floor with the metal tip of his cane.

Laura went to her father and rested her palm on his sleeve. "But, Father, you don't understand. I—"

"Have made a perfect fool of yourself as usual!" he said, completing her sentence. "You've quite outdone yourself this time, you little idiot. Didn't you have the presence of mind to know what the man was after? Did you think he wanted you for yourself? Are you that desperate, to believe he has a tendresse for you?" Middlebrook scoffed. "Did he tell you so?"

Tears welled up in Laura's eyes as she bit her lips together and stepped back. Sean moved toward her and draped an arm around her shoulder. "Sir, if you have no thought for your daughter's feelings, you'd best consider mine. I resent your tone, as well as your words. If you won't be civil, I must insist you leave."

The man laughed bitterly. "Insist? You, insist that I leave? Fine. As soon as the addlepated ex-spinster here gathers up her belongings, we'll be gone." He shot Laura a venomous glare and raised his cane. The brass tip poked roughly at her middle. "Get to it, girl!"

Sean's fury snapped loose. With a lightning move, he crushed the man's neatly tied cravat in one fist and backed him against the wall. "You posturing old fart, touch my wife again and you won't need the stairs to reach the street!"

"Sean, please!" Laura cried, pulling at his elbow. One glance told him she was near to losing control.

With a furious oath, he released Middlebrook with a shove and moved away. "Get out of here before I rip open that chest of yours and see what's in place of the heart you don't have."

Middlebrook patted his tie and sniffed with disdain. "You see, Laura? You see whom you've chosen? A barbarian with less manners than he has money! An opportunist, right and tight."

He leaned down so that he was nose to nose with his daughter. "What, did you think to get a child off this buffoon and deny your brother what should rightfully be his? *He* is your heir. You are to stay on with Lambdin and allow him management of your grandmother's legacy now that he is eighteen!"

"Nineteen," Laura corrected.

"Better yet! That old Ames harridan cut your mother off without a cent. 'Twas spite because she married me, but by God, she won't do my son out of his part."

"But Lamb really isn't even related to—"

He whirled and again stabbed the floor with his cane. "Your mother is waiting. Let us go."

"I'm not going with you, Father. Sean is my husband whether you like it or not. There can be no annulment, if that's what you intend." Her voice seemed steady and determined, though Sean noted her hands shook badly as she wrung them together.

He felt he had to do something to elicit whatever bit of sympathy Middlebrook might have hidden inside that cold exterior. Sean could understand a father's anger. Middlebrook thought Laura had thrown her fortune to the winds, but nothing excused the mean-spirited attack on her self-esteem.

For Laura's sake, Sean fought for patience as he attempted to set things right. "Sir, you ought to know that Laura has not been well at all. In fact, she—"

"Hush! Don't!" Laura demanded, grabbing his arm. Her eyes pleaded with him not to continue.

Then she turned to her father and took a deep breath. "I am sorry you felt it necessary to interrupt your trip. But there's nothing you can do to alter the fact that I'm wed and intend to stay that way. I am a married woman, Father, and Lambdin will never be my heir."

He seemed not to have heard a word she said, but instead remarked on Sean's interrupted words. "Not been well, eh? So you're already breeding. I should have known this jacka-napes would see to that without delay."

With a nasty curl to his lips, he turned on Sean. "Did you sweet-talk her, Wilder? Did you choke out lies about her beauty, her desirability? Ha!"

Sean stalked the man, backing him toward the door. "I'm painfully close to rearranging your face, Middlebrook. I have killed men for less reason than you've given me this past quarter hour. I strongly suggest you take this chance to vacate the premises in one piece while the opportunity still exists."

"You hear that, girl? Do you hear how he threatens your own father? Twice now! How can you stand—?"

Sean didn't wait to hear more. He jerked the door open, bodily lifted the man and tossed him into the hallway. Then he slammed the door and shot the bolt.

When he turned, fully expecting Laura to crumple with despair, she surprised him with a watery smile. "Thank you, Sean."

"My pleasure," he replied, and held out his arms. She walked into them and rested her head on his chest. For a long while, he simply held her, his lips against her hair, his hands brushing her back and halting for an occasional pat. "I wish to God I could have spared you that. Has he always been so unloving?"

"No. I don't know. He hasn't been around me all that often.

I did realize that he resented my grandmother's affection for me. But I was all she had left when my real father died. She saw that Mother received nothing following her second marriage. He protests that, of course."

"Why didn't you allow me to tell him about your illness? He might have come round a bit if he knew."

She laughed a little. "I'd much rather taunt him with the fact that he's old enough to become a grandfather, even if we aren't really related by blood. He prizes youth above everything now that his own is fading. He will have suffered abominably by the time he learns the truth. Serves him right for his greed."

"Good for you, then," Sean said, giving her a fond squeeze. "And I'll have you know that I haven't thought once of your money. I wish you would leave it all to Lambdin. He really doesn't seem such a bad sort. A bit flighty perhaps, but that's only due to his youth. He's nothing like his father."

"No," she said sadly. "Not a whit like him, but Lamb won't need the money. I want you to have mine. You have made me very happy since our marriage, Sean. Happier than I've been in my whole life."

Sean sighed and rested his lips on her forehead for a moment. "I'm glad of it. You've changed my life, too, you know?"

"Have I?" she looked up at him with a bittersweet smile.

"Seeing everything through your eyes gives me a different perspective. Everyday things I always took for granted or never stopped to consider before, take on new meaning. Sunsets, the sights of Paris, even the ices taste better with you to share them."

"What is your dearest wish, Sean?" she asked softly.

He thought for a moment. "To make you happy. See you smile. And what's yours, darling?"

"This. You. Paris. I have my heart's desire right at hand,

you see. You must not worry about what just happened. I promise you I won't."

Sean turned her slowly and began unfastening her frock. It was late and the confrontation with Middlebrook had exhausted her emotionally. When he had undressed her down to her chemise, he tucked her into the bed and lay down beside her still fully dressed. "Just rest, sweetheart. Let me hold you close. That's my wish right now. We won't worry about anything at all, and I'll keep you safe while you sleep."

He absorbed her sigh and fought back his anger at her parents for their abuse. They could have beaten her daily instead and not caused such hurt. How could they treat her so badly when she was all that was good in the world? Any father should take consummate pride in a child with such courage. Any mother should rail against having her daughter so vilified. Sean wanted to knock their heads together and curse them for the uncaring, shortsighted fools they were. Why couldn't they see how precious she was? Would they ever realize what they had lost once she was gone?

Automatically he drew Laura closer, as though his embrace could somehow prevent what would happen to her. Tears burned the backs of his eyes. "To hell with them. *I* will love you," he mouthed softly against her temple as she slept. "I *do* love you." And he knew without a doubt that he meant every word. God help him.

Chapter Six

The unusually mild autumn felt very like late spring. Paris on a day like today must rival heaven, Laura decided with a sigh. Heaven wouldn't need the odiferous public urinals on the street corners, of course. Or have the ancient grime and pigeon deposits that coated the buildings.

The heavenly thing was that, with the exception of the tourists, people never hurried here. The native-born behaved as though they were already precisely where they wanted to be. Almost to a person, Parisians exuded an *I've found it, sorry you're still searching for it* attitude. She need not envy them that, however, for she had found it, too. With Sean, the man she loved.

By unspoken agreement, neither of them had mentioned her stepfather's visit the night before. She had no desire to see Sean's handsome face darken with rage again, and he probably didn't want her to dwell on unhappy thoughts, either.

Maybe she should explain that she'd already had years to grow accustomed to her parents' lack of love for her. She had never really lived with them in a normal family situation. Her grandmother, through her letters and visits before her death, had more than made up for the lack. Her stepfather and mother were virtual strangers to her, like unpleasant and thankfully infrequent visitors to Midbrook Manor. She tried to love them in spite of everything, simply because the church and common decency said she must.

Because of their absence, she had given her younger brother as much of herself as she could. Probably spoiled him in the bargain, she thought. Lambdin might have escaped the open disdain her father had so recently heaped on her head, but he received no more real affection from him than she had.

Ah well, she would let the matter rest for now. Dark thoughts did not belong in this beautiful sunshine. If she encouraged Sean to keep up his forced gaiety much longer, it might well become real. She flashed him her most winsome smile.

Sean believed in early starts on their little excursions. The only things open to the public when they had begun their day were the market stalls along the river. He had purchased several charming little watercolors by unknowns and a posy of summer roses for her. They had whiled away all of the morning strolling vendor to vendor, examining the wide variety of treasures available. She knew he had held off as long as he could before he crossed the street to a small shop and gave in to his addiction.

Laura licked daintily at her strawberry iced custard while she waited for Sean to pay for their treats. He consumed his lemon ice in less time than it had taken the vendor to pile it on the tiny cone and promptly ordered another. "Shameless pig," she whispered, laughing.

"Don't chide me, sweetheart. Nobody's perfect." His gaze fastened on her lips as she tasted the cream. "Except you."

Laura felt her heart skip once and then thunder so loudly in her ears, she almost missed his question. "Do you want to rest for a while before we take on the Louvre?" He drew her free hand through the crook of his arm and resumed their walk along the Seine. "It will make for a long afternoon, I warn you."

"The day's too beautiful to spend it indoors. Maybe we should wait and go when it rains again. Have I thanked you yet for extending our stay in Paris?" she asked, hoping to divert the direction of her unsettling thoughts. "Will Mr. Burton still cover your expenses for the whole trip, do you think?"

"Probably. It doesn't really matter," he assured her. "This is our honeymoon and you shouldn't worry about that or anything else."

She shrugged and snuggled closer as they walked. "And our Mr. Beaumont should be fine now. You saw to that, didn't you?"

"The concierge at the Lenoir is taking care of everything. I spoke with him first thing this morning," Sean said.

His muscle flexed beneath her hand as he turned them off the path toward a vacant bench. Laura closed her eyes, remembering how smooth and faintly salty the heated skin of that arm had been under her lips the afternoon of their wedding. How elusive, here in the open air, was that spicy cologne blended with his own special scent. She drew in a deep breath to try to catch more of it.

Sensual memories assaulted her frequently and most unexpectedly. Now, even in the daytime. If nothing else, this forced abstention of their marital rights certainly made the time she had left seem longer.

"Are you unwell, Laura? You look flushed." Sean's concern dragged her back to the present. Her ice cream had melted all over her glove.

"Yes! No. I'm quite all right, but look what a mess I've made."

He quickly disposed of her cone and dabbed with his handkerchief at the sticky wetness on her glove. "Ah no, you've ruined your gown." With that, he began to rub at the spots down the front of her dimity frock. The rhythmic motion of his hand sent ripples of desire flooding through her middle.

"Stop!" she ordered, backing up several steps. "Don't!"

Sean tensed, the hand with the handkerchief still suspended, clenched as was the other. For a long moment he regarded her face carefully and then lowered his eyes to stare at her exposed neck.

She watched as the green heat of his gaze traveled downward to rest on her heaving bosom. Laura immediately held her breath.

"Let's go," he said quietly, huskily, as though he barely had his voice or his emotions under control.

"Where?" she asked breathlessly.

"Where do you think?" The words sounded promising, even without the slightest inflection.

She didn't need his abrupt change in direction toward their hotel to divine an answer to that. Laura knew exactly where they were going. And why. She required two strides to his every one in order to keep up, and it was all she could do to wipe the smile off her face. Until she recalled the reason they had denied themselves for the past fortnight.

They turned onto St. Jacques, headed for the Lenoir. With a shudder of regret, she stopped in her tracks just at the corner of the building. "This isn't a good idea, Sean. You know it's not."

He grasped her arm none too gently and growled, "You can go into that hotel under your own steam, or over my shoulder like a sack of meal. Your choice!"

"Don't be angry, Sean," she begged, knowing he might hate her more for what was about to happen than if she refused him outright. "I only want you to be certain this is what you want."

Regret softened his face as he quickly stepped toward her. A loud report rocked the silence the instant Sean moved. Blood blossomed just above his right brow.

Laura screamed.

The sound cut off abruptly when Sean's shoulder pushed into her midsection and her feet cleared the ground. Next thing she knew, they had tumbled together into the small lobby of the hotel Lenoir. "Hurry," he muttered, and scrambled up off the floor where he'd nearly squashed her. She dumbly accepted his grasping hand and managed to get her feet under her.

Laura looked for someone to send for the police, but the lobby appeared deserted.

Blood poured out of the wound on Sean's head, coated his cheek and dripped off his chin. He swiped at his eyes and cursed.

"Get upstairs," he ordered, giving her a rough shove. "Go! I'm right behind you."

Laura forced her feet to move forward. Once she got them underway, they seemed to take on a life of their own, stumbling in their rush to lead Sean to the safety of their room. Once there, she wheeled around to lock the door behind him. Her fingers fumbled and the key dropped to the floor. "Oh God, oh God!" she sobbed frantically as she scrambled to find it.

"I envisioned hearing that from you again, but not exactly under these circumstances," he said with a wry grunt, peeling off his bloody gloves. "Catch your breath and come help me, will you?"

"Oh, Sean!" Laura felt so faint she had to lean against the door for a second. She couldn't collapse now. Sean was bleeding to death. Pushing herself into motion, she dashed to the washstand and grabbed a hand towel.

When she turned, he was sitting on the edge of the bed with a gun in his hand, trying to load it by feel. "Just get the damned blood out of my eyes. I can't see what the hell I'm doing."

"Lie down, you fool!" she ordered in a shaky voice. "For goodness' sake, you've just been shot!"

"And don't intend to let it happen again if I can prevent it. Damn and blast, I should have taken those notes more seriously," he muttered.

Sean continued shoving ammunition into the pistol's cylinder and finally snapped it shut. "It's just a graze, Laura. A direct hit and I'd be lying on the street out there. Wet that towel and have a look at the damage." He held out the gun. "Here. Put this on the table there, will you? My vision's still a bit blurry."

She took it with both hands and laid it down. His calm assessment of the calamity helped steady Laura's mind, but her body still shook with the shock of what had just happened. The gash on the side of his forehead oozed red. She blotted it firmly with corner of the towel. "It's quite deep and has three corners! What do you make of that?"

He grinned up at her. "Square bullets?"

Laura burst into tears.

"Ah, here now, love, don't! You've done so well thus far," he chided, pulling her onto his lap.

The wretch had the gall to laugh. Laura punched him lightly in the shoulder with her fist. Not that it had any effect. "How can you joke about this? Someone tried to kill you! Shot you!"

"Shot *at* me," Sean corrected, holding her closer so that her head rested on his left shoulder. She sobbed one last time and wiped her tears on his lapel. His steady voice rumbled in the ear she placed against his chest. "I think the bullet must have hit the building and popped off a piece of brick. That's probably what got me. I'm all right, just a bit woozy. You'd better get yourself in hand, however, or I shall be doctoring you."

"You know who it was, don't you?" Laura demanded. "What notes were you speaking of just now?"

Sean found her hand and laced her fingers through his. "Warnings. Probably from some ne'er-do-well I sent to prison a while back when I worked for the Yard. Whoever it is must have tracked us all the way from England. I got one of the damned things the same time we got Beaumont's package. There were a couple of others before we left London."

"He'll try again, won't he?" Laura demanded, sitting upright in his lap.

"Probably wait us out, try to waylay me again when we leave the hotel."

A tap on the door interrupted them. Then a deep voice spoke in French, *"M'sieur? Madame?* I was just going downstairs and I see fresh blood on the floor here. You require a physician? May I enter?"

"Un moment," Sean called out. Then he whispered, "I don't like this."

Laura reached for the pistol he had just loaded and placed it in his hand.

"You keep it," he murmured. The heavy thing hung there, dead weight, as she stared at it.

He tugged lightly on her gown. "Listen to me, Laura! Hide this in the folds of your skirt and stand over there out of the way. It won't fire unless you pull back the hammer. This is the hammer, see?" His fingers brushed over the weapon, halting to tap on the part he identified. "From here on, we trust no one. If the good doctor has any surprises for us, you're to raise this, cock it, and pretend you know what you're doing. If you're threatened, point and pull the trigger. Don't hesitate. Understand?"

"But why can't you—?"

He propped one foot on the bed and reached into the top of his boot. With a wink, he flourished a derringer and then closed his palm around it.

Laura nodded, biting her lips together and taking a deep breath. "I'll unlock the door." She did so, standing ready and determined to protect Sean.

"Enter," Sean called out.

A tall, slender dark-haired man carrying a black case entered and executed a negligent bow. He wore a languorous air and moved with a casual, unhurried grace. Laura had immediately stepped directly between the stranger and Sean.

He stared at her clothing. "Are you hurt badly, *madame?*"

Laura glanced down and saw that the front and side of her dress were saturated with Sean's blood. She looked up. "No, it's my husband's."

He moved toward the bed where Sean sat. "I am Dr. Eugene Campion, at your service, sir."

"Camp?" Sean asked softly, "Is it really you?"

The doctor almost dropped his bag when Sean faced him fully. "Sean? Wild man?" He grabbed Sean by the shoulders. "It is you, by God! Ha! I do not see you in two long years, and now you turn up in a scrape. Ah, and with a beauty in tow. I might have known. What has happened to you?" He began examining Sean's wound.

"Someone shot at us just outside the hotel. I think I was hit by a sliver of dislodged brick."

"Hmm. It is rather deep and beginning to swell," the doctor remarked. He peered into Sean's eyes for several long seconds. "Vertigo? Nausea?"

Sean shrugged without answering. Laura watched silently while the doctor tended the nasty wound. Once he had applied the sticking plaster, he rummaged in his bag and set a small vial on the night table. "Use this to prevent infection when you change the dressing. You need to stay abed for a few days until your equilibrium returns. If it does not, you must let me know. I shall summon the gendarmes now."

"No, Camp, don't bother with that," Sean said quickly. "They would only ask tons of questions for which I have no answers. Perhaps someone's gun discharged quite by accident in a nearby building. Who knows?"

The doctor glanced at Laura. "Are you certain you are not hurt, *madame?*"

"No! I mean yes, I'm certain. I'm fine," she answered.

"She's just shaken up a bit," Sean assured him. "This is my wife, Laura. Laura, Eugene Campion, a very old friend of mine."

Campion stood and executed another of his informal bows. "Madame Wilder, it is my great pleasure to meet you. Anyone who can tame the wild man must be extraordinary, indeed. Are you two here on holiday?"

"Honeymoon," Sean answered curtly. "And stop flirting with my wife, Camp." He turned his head toward Laura. "Beware this rake, Laura. He has the rovingest hands on three continents."

Campion laughed merrily, his broad shoulders shaking. "Speaking of that, I must go. Lisette sent me down for coffee and she will think I am dallying with one of the maids."

He paused with his hand on the door handle. "Will you two join us for supper? We could order up. You and I have much catching up to do, my friend. I am certain the ladies will not mind if we reminisce. Ah, the tales I could tell you, my dear," he said to Laura with a mock leer.

"Perhaps tomorrow?" Sean suggested. "Maybe then I can see what I'm eating." He reached into his breast pocket and drew out his wallet.

Campion's eyebrows rose as the corners of his sensuous mouth turned down. "I sincerely hope you're not going to offer to pay me for this, Sean."

"Don't get your hopes up. You still owe me thousands of pounds from our last game of poker. I thought I might buy your lady an excellent *vin* to go with her dinner."

Campion reached out and scooped up one of the bills. "I shall let you, too. We are just down the hall in the corner room if you should need me. I cannot tell you how happy I am to see you, Sean."

"Likewise. Thanks, Camp." He tossed the wallet onto the bed beside him.

"I shall stop in later on and see how you are." The doctor looked pointedly at Laura's hand, the one that held the poorly concealed gun. "Wise to be cautious." He inclined his head, smiled at her and left, closing the door quietly behind him. They listened to his footsteps echo down the hallway.

A moment later the door burst open, trapping Laura behind it just as she moved to lock it. A man entered, a gun held ready against the side of his leg. When he raised it to aim, Sean rolled off the bed. Laura cocked and fired.

"I've killed him!" she cried, horrified.

"Let's get the hell out of here!" Sean struggled to his feet and groped for her hand. He took the smoking pistol from her and turned. They ran straight into Eugene Campion, who stood in the doorway.

He glanced past them at the crumpled form of the man Laura had just shot. "Come with me. This whole floor will be a madhouse in seconds."

"We're leaving," Sean declared, trying to push past him.

"Idiot! You're in no condition to flee, and your wife looks set to faint. Come to my room until we straighten this out." He looked again at the still form of the man on the floor and back at Sean. "He may have friends outside."

Laura moved first, frantic to leave the room. Campion rushed them three doors down to the end of the hallway and ushered them inside his chamber.

A beautiful, ebony-haired woman wearing a lacy white peignoir sat at the escritoire writing. She looked up as they entered, her dark eyes round with questions.

Laura could imagine what the lady saw, her husband busily locking their door, a bandaged brute brandishing a pistol in one hand and a derringer in the other, and a wild-eyed woman covered with blood. She knew very well the doctor had not had time to explain about them.

"Monsieur et Madame Wilder, Lisette," said Campion.

Sean tucked his derringer back into the top of his boot and laid the pistol on the table by the bed. Then he bowed over Lisette's reluctant hand. *"Madame."*

The woman swallowed hard and squeaked, *"Enchanté."*

Laura collapsed laughing. Her entire body shook as she knelt on the floor. Helpless tears poured down her face. God in heaven, she had just shot a man and here they were exchanging pleasantries! Somewhere in the back of her mind, she recognized the hysteria but couldn't seem to control it. Sean lifted her and the bed frame squeaked as he lowered her to it. The sound prompted a fresh wave of giddy mirth. Why couldn't she stop this?

"I'll get a syringe!" she heard the doctor say.

"No!" Sean said. He jerked her to a sitting position. The shock of his light slap stilled Laura immediately. "No sedative," he added for Campion's benefit. "I promised her."

"But after all she has been through?"

"Give her a moment. She'll be fine," Sean said in a soothing voice. His words were meant for the doctor, she supposed, and the tone for her. Laura absorbed it like a thirsty sponge. He held her firmly against his chest and stroked her head. "Calm down, sweetheart. Be calm." She felt so tired, exhausted. A man was dead at her hand. She had killed someone. Taken a life.

"Everything will be all right now. It's all over," Sean whispered.

For long moments, he held her. All Laura wanted to do was escape this madness. She had simply had enough and could not seem to think anymore. With her head buried in Sean's shoulder, she struggled to block everything from her mind.

"It is not all over," Campion declared. "Your wife just shot a man. Though it is a clear case of self-defense, the authorities will want to question her."

Sean narrowed his eyes and tried to assess Camp's determination through his faulty vision. "I have no idea who wants me dead. There's nothing I can tell the police. All this came right out of the blue. We can't stay here and put you and Lisette in danger while the law blunders about trying to sort things out. We have to go now."

Campion threw up his hands and sighed. "You *need* my help! Listen, wait here with Lisette. Whether you approve or not, I must see whether the man still lives and, if so, give him medical attention. Later I will help you both to leave if you wish."

Sean decided he couldn't very well fault a man for living up to the oath of his profession. "All right, Camp. If you wouldn't mind, bring a change of clothing for us. We can't very well traipse about covered in my gore."

"Very well." Campion switched to rapid French, informed Lisette about what had happened, and left to see to the man Laura had shot.

While they waited for his return, Sean checked Laura's pulse again and then brushed her hair back off her brow. He had just finished unbuttoning her dress when the doctor returned. Sean grabbed his pistol and whirled toward him.

"Take care with that thing, will you! The man is gone. Disappeared. Judging by the dearth of blood on the floor, I do not believe he was mortally wounded."

Campion dumped a pile of clothes on the foot of the bed and tossed Sean's leather folder on top of it. "Apparently robbery was not his motive. This lay in plain view where you left it."

Sean laid his pistol on the night table again and shrugged out of his coat. The shy Lisette quickly turned to face the wall.

When he had changed all his ruined outer garments, he began undressing Laura.

"Steady, darling. Let's just get you out of this."

She grabbed the bodice to her breasts and stared wide-eyed over his shoulder at the doctor. "Sean?" she whispered. "He has a gun."

Slowly Sean turned. Sure enough, Camp stood there holding a pistol, though he had not yet aimed it. Of all the people in the world, this was the last one he would have expected to turn on him. "What do you want, Camp?"

"A bit of *trust* would not be out of place, old man. Here," he said, reversing the pistol and handing it over to Sean. "Your intruder dropped this when your wife shot him and it slid under the bed. I suppose he did not tarry to look for it."

"Thank you," Sean said, trying to examine the gun as an excuse to disguise his shame and his profound relief. He refused to apologize for suspecting a man who waved a pistol in his direction, no matter how well he knew him or how benign the reason.

"I should insist you stay here for a while, Sean. You are a trifle concussed, given the way those pupils of yours look. However—" He glanced meaningfully at Lisette, who sat frozen in the same position she had held when they first arrived.

"No, we must leave as soon as possible. I have friends who will put us up."

"Yes, well, getting to them without collecting a bullet might present a problem. I will have my coach brought round to the back entrance. My driver can take you wherever you need to go."

"That's generous of you, Camp," Sean said sincerely. "If I can ever return the favor—"

"Idiot," Camp said, dismissing the nicety with a wave of his hand. "I took the liberty of locking your door. Is there anything else you need from your room before you go?"

Sean considered asking him to retrieve the painting from the hotel safe, as well as more of their clothes, but decided a speedy exit was more important. The shots fired had no doubt prompted some of the guests to summon the law. Involving them would not help at this point. In his experience, the French police were not terribly effective under the best of circumstances. He and Laura would be required to remain available for questions and he had damned few answers.

"After we leave, would you ask your cousin to hold my room for me and to keep it locked? I will send for our things and pay him within the week. He has a valuable painting of mine in the hotel safe and I would appreciate his keeping it there for the time being."

"Done and done," Camp agreed. "You cannot see, can you, Sean?" he asked pointedly.

"Yes I can," Sean lied. Though he could distinguish objects and their colors, everything still appeared blurred. The dizziness had not abated completely, either, but he could function well enough. He must. "Are you all right, Laura?"

"A bit light-headed, but it will pass," she assured him. "Let's go."

They followed Camp down the narrow servants' stairs across the hall and waited in a small anteroom while he arranged for his conveyance.

Sean turned to Laura when they were alone. "Help me watch when we go out. We don't want to be followed."

"You really can't see, can you?" she whispered in a trembling voice.

"Not well," Sean admitted. He hated to frighten her, but he couldn't trust his eyes. "Can you watch our backs for the time being? I'm certain I'll be fine once I've had a good rest."

"Of course I can," she answered, sounding very determined. Stronger, as though she suddenly thrived on his confidence in her.

Once the coach drew up near the back door, Sean lifted Laura inside and gave brief instructions to the driver.

"Keep in touch with me, Sean. I shall be here at the Lenoir for the next few weeks. Look after him Laura," Camp said. *"Bonne chance."*

"We could use a bit of good luck," Sean muttered as the carriage rolled through the alley to the main street.

Laura scoffed as she drew her head in the window of the coach. "I heard that! You really shouldn't be so ungrateful, Sean. You are about the luckiest person I know."

"Oh well, pardon me. You're right, of course. I must have imagined someone spraying bullets about our heads during our morning constitutional. That fellow you had to shoot must have been a figment of my sorry dementia. Looking at the world through this damned fog is just a dream, isn't it?"

Her hand grasped his and squeezed hard. "No, but you are alive, Sean! We have escaped." She sighed and leaned against his shoulder as the coach rocked over the cobbles. "Where are we going?"

"I suppose leaving the country won't solve anything. That's probably what we'll be expected to do. We shall stay in Paris, but will have to go to ground. I'll call in a few favors and try to discover who's looking for me. When I find out, I'll set a trap and bring him to me."

"Make a stand," she reiterated. "Yes, I like that idea."

"You would," he said with a grunt of frustration. "This is not a lark, Laura. Still hungry for adventure?"

She laughed, a little unsteadily. "I have certainly had enough for today. I'd welcome a safe haven until you get your head straight and your eyes uncrossed. It *is* just the concussion, isn't it? You don't think there is any permanent damage?"

He heard the tremor of fear in her voice. "I'll be fine after a good sleep. I had the same reaction after a blow from a cricket bat once. Give us a little quiet now and let's get our wits together."

Sean silently blessed her for obeying him this once. His head was fit to burst and he could feel those lemon ices he'd had earlier getting ready to make a return trip.

By all rights, he should send Laura packing back to England and that feather-witted brother of hers. Unfortunately, there was no way he could determine whether the wretch who had invaded their room might go after her for a little revenge. She had shot the man. Even if that didn't make her the primary target, whoever it was might think to get at Sean through his wife. No, she would be safer where he could keep an eye on her. If only one eye or the other could see clearly.

Camp's driver halted the coach at the Pont de la Concord where Sean quickly exited and helped Laura alight. With a brief word of thanks to the driver, he urged her toward the Palais Bourbon, which was now crowded with a noisy gaggle of afternoon tourists.

"Do you see a cab free?" he asked, despising the need to ask for her continued help.

"Yes, there are several lined up along the river. Come on." She tugged on his hand and he followed obediently.

He gave directions to cross the Seine and head north along rue Royale toward Montmartre. Once they were settled in the rickety two-seater, he settled as far back as he could and urged her to do the same. No one could see their faces now without coming close and peering inside. He heard the driver, who stood high on the back of the conveyance, crack the whip over the top of the buggy.

Safe. For the moment.

Sean shuddered to think what he must expose Laura to in

the next few days or weeks. But if, by some chance, she still craved further adventures, he was certainly taking her to the right place.

Chapter Seven

They followed a circuitous route all the way to Montmartre. Sean signaled the driver to stop near a row of small shops in Place du Tertre. When they exited the cab, he pulled out a bill to pay their fare and Laura hurriedly took it away, replacing it with another she pulled from his wallet. He mumbled his thanks and drew her close to his side.

"We'll go along Lamarck toward the cemetery," he directed. "Watch for Carriere and turn right. It isn't far. How are you doing?"

"Better than before. You?"

"Can't see worth beans and my head feels as though I've just come off a weeklong tear, but I'll do."

Silently they walked at a steady clip, her hand gripping his elbow and guiding him along until they turned on rue Carriere. "What am I to look for now?" she asked.

"A two-storied shop with blue shutters."

"Just there, but it looks closed for business," she said, and hastened her pace. "There's no sign, either."

He sighed and pulled her to a halt in the shadows, leaning his back against the rough stone of the building. "We need to talk for a moment before we go in. Laura, this little undertaking may generate some disgust on your part, but bear with me. My primary goal right now is to keep you safe. Please keep an open mind."

"Of course. I always try to do that."

"Louise Weber is a laundress," he said carefully.

"My acquaintances were never limited to people of means, Sean. I knew the washerwomen in our village. We got on quite well."

Sean pursed his lips and looked away. "Well, this one doesn't actually wash clothes."

He heard her quick intake of breath. "Oh. I see."

"Just so. Well, Louise is good-hearted, but you must prepare yourself. She's rather, uh, forthright. Spirited." He had to laugh a little at his understatement. "They call her *La Goulue.*"

"The glutton?" Laura gasped. "That's perfectly awful! Why?"

"She eats life the way I eat ices," he explained ruefully.

"Then I think I shall like her very much! Is she a *good* friend of yours?"

Sean knew exactly what Laura was asking. Her jealousy, subtle as it was, pleased him. "Not an intimate friend, no. We've crossed paths frequently in the past two years. I had an assignment that involved one of her employers, an artist for whom she modeled. As a result of that, she recommended me to another of her friends who needed my help, a wine merchant. It's this man I wish to find if he's still around. I believe he will help us."

"Hide us, you mean, until we're ready to take on that villain when you set up your trap?"

"Hiding is what we need to discuss. If we are to remain in Paris incognito, we must blend into an entirely different society than you are accustomed to. I mean really *different,* Laura. There will be things you might consider terribly indecent," he warned.

She clapped her hands and sounded delighted. "Truly? But that's marvelous!" She fairly danced with anticipation and Sean wished he could focus well enough to see her eyes. They always sparkled when she became excited. "I have always heard there's this delicious freedom from convention that only the real Parisians embrace! Why, I believe I even sensed it in your friend, Campion. He is from Paris, isn't he?"

He smiled. "Yes, but not of this small world where we have come. Here, freedom from convention as you call it, is the law of the day, not the exception. Some of that is surface glitter. Pretense, mostly. However, there are some astonishing deviations in Montmartre after dark. You've only walked this arrondissement on Sunday afternoons when it's relatively tame. Nights here will probably shock you right out of your knickers."

Laura threaded her fingers through his and he could hear the suggestive smile in her voice. "The last time I got shocked out of my knickers, I had a rather glorious time of it."

"Lord, I've created a monster! Come on, then, and take care not to choke when La Goulue turns the air blue around you."

In a way Sean regretted having to expose Laura to the underground life they were about to encounter. In another, he knew she would revel in any new experience, however bizarre. In her own genteel way—and for vastly different reasons— Laura seemed as hungry for life's feast as La Goulue herself.

He knew he couldn't simply provide his wife with a fork and stand back, however. Constant vigilance would be necessary to ensure that she didn't bite off more than she could comfortably chew.

Laura stared with disbelief at the figure that answered Sean's knock. The woman appeared draped in a robe of frayed chinese silk. Blond hair frizzed every which way out of a pointed topknot and framed a round, baby-pink face. That face color proved to be the only thing babylike about La Goulue. Her generous breasts nearly spilled out of the loosely lapped blue garment that was cinched with a man's leather belt. Her legs were naked from the dimpled knees down to the dirty, bare feet.

"La! Eet ees Shun Wildair!" the woman shrieked, then threw both arms around Sean's neck. Laura watched while her husband accepted loud, smacking kisses on both his cheeks. A stream of colloquial French followed, which the woman punctuated with further familiarities.

Eventually—and none too soon for Laura's part—Sean disentangled himself and made the introductions in flawless and unaccented French.

"Ah, your wife!" the woman said, beaming as though he'd brought her a bouquet of flowers instead of a rival. "But she ees sweet, *non?*" Laura almost fell backward when Louise Weber grabbed her by the shoulders and treated her to the same greeting Sean had endured. The woman must be mad.

Laura forced a happy grin, making an effort to switch her thinking to French. "Life's a carousel, Mademoiselle Weber! Here's the old hob come round again." She cuffed Sean on the shoulder and laughed. "He wanted me to meet all of his friends."

"You must call me Lou Lou. And you shall be *Le Petite Cygne,* our little swan. Ah, Shun, how graceful she looks! A *danseuse, non?*"

"*Non,*" he answered promptly. "She is not a dancer." He used the first break in Lou Lou's dialogue to change the subject. "I'm looking for Valentin Renaudin. Do you know where I might find him?"

"In disgrace you find him! We were to meet last night at the Elysée. When he did not come, I had to dance alone. So much for him!" With a rude finger gesture, she turned on her heel and headed toward the back of the shop. "You come and have a taste, eh? Wine, absinthe?"

"No, thank you," Sean said evenly. "Perhaps another time."

Laura noticed how his energy had flagged. He needed a bed and soon. "Pardon me, Lou Lou, do you know where we might find a room for the night? We are exhausted."

Lou Lou whirled, showing a vast expanse of white thigh as she did. "The night? Never sleep at night! You must replace that English blood of yours with vin, Cygne Cygne. The daytime is for sleeping."

"We had a tiring trip," Laura explained. "And Sean hurt his head."

"Ah, well then, you must stay here. I am out till dawn. Take my bed. Through here." She curled her fingers and led the way. "Tomorrow night," Lou Lou promised, kissing the tips of her fingers, "we make up for lost time, eh? We find Valentin, empty a few bottles, dance till our legs ache!"

"You are a treasure, Lou Lou!" Laura exclaimed, fascinated with their exotic hostess. "Isn't she, Sean?"

"Mmm-hmm," he agreed, and stretched out on top of the jacquard coverlet. "*Merci*, Louise."

During the next half hour, an intrigued Laura perched on the edge of the bed where Sean had collapsed and watched Lou Lou don her evening garb. First came a dingy white chemise, knee-length ruffled knickers and black silk stockings. Over it all she drew on a tight crimson blouse and a gay red-and-white-striped skirt, belting it tightly with a tasseled blue sash. The effect looked as festive as fireworks.

"You have yet to experience the *chahut*, eh?" Lou Lou asked, carefully daubing pot rouge on her bee-stung lips.

Laura knew the word, roughly translated, meant noise and rambunctiousness. Lou Lou must be referring to the general ambience of Montmartre evenings. "Perhaps tomorrow night?"

"*Every* night!" Lou Lou announced in an exaggerated whisper. "I am away now. See what you can do for thees husband of yours, eh? He ees becoming an old man before my very eyes!" She rolled those eyes and sighed. "Sleeping at *night!* Whoever hears of such a theeng?" With that, Louise departed for the evening, husky laughter trailing behind her like the scent of her cheap perfume.

Sean hadn't moved since he lay down. Laura loosened his tie, unbuttoned the top three buttons on his shirt and slipped off his boots. She just managed to catch the small derringer when it slipped free. Carefully she removed the other handgun from his belt and laid both weapons on the table beside the bed. He never stirred.

Tiptoeing to the door, Laura noticed Lou Lou had not extinguished the oil lamps in the front before she left. The room boasted little furniture, appearing more like an underfurnished parlor than a shop of any kind. The bedroom, directly behind it, was probably where La Goulue did most of her business, Laura thought with a wry smile.

She opened another door off the sleeping quarters and located the small kitchen. Cupboard doors stood open, revealing several bottles of spirits and a cloth-wrapped half-round of cheese. Further exploration turned up a crusty loaf of bread and a length of hard sausage. Laura made herself at home, plying the knife left on the table to slice off a small portion of each offering.

"No rules here!" she whispered to an orange tabby who peeked at her from behind the small coal heater that probably served as a stove. She had never talked with her mouth full in her life, even to a cat, but the whole atmosphere of La Goulue's abode seemed to impart a sense of licentiousness. Sort of like throwing her corset aside and kicking off tight shoes, Laura thought as she munched. Not a bad idea, that.

She hooked her toe on the opposite heel and gave her half boot a shove. Then she pushed the other off and wiggled her black-stockinged toes. Still uncomfortable, Laura laid down her chunk of bread on the table and slipped off her dress. "Now we're cooking," she told the tabby. Clad only in her loosened stays, chemise, ruffled drawers and stockings, Laura leaned back in the chair and lifted her legs, crossing her ankles on the tabletop. How marvelously wicked she felt. "C'mere, Tab. *Ici!*"

The feline leapt to her lap and accepted a pinch of the bloodwurst. Adopting Lou Lou's nasal intonation, Laura began to practice her schoolbook French on the cat with decidedly more dedication than she ever had for her old tutor.

The bedroom—despite its handsome occupant—held no appeal for her at the moment. All in one day, she had narrowly missed being widowed, saved Sean from the villain, and escaped with her true love to the naughty, fascinating, uninhibited center of frou-frou. Who could sleep, and why ever would she want to? Here was adventure that surpassed even her wildest dreams.

Sean woke to an off-key humming of *"La Marseillaise."* He didn't know how long he had slept, but he felt rather back to normal and supposed it had been long enough. Silently he slid off the bed to confirm who he thought was busy fracturing the French national anthem.

He could focus quite clearly now and the sight in Louise's kitchen arrested him at the door. Sean's breath caught and held. Laura sat tilted back in a chair, her long dark hair tumbled loose along the back of it. When he peeked over her shoulder, the high curves of her breasts were clearly visible right down to their rosy tips. Cascades of lace fell back from her knees, baring several inches of creamy flesh above her blue-gartered stockings.

Her song wound down to a discordant finish. *"Paris, à nous deux!"* she declared in a lascivious growl as she nuzzled a huge, sleepy-eyed cat.

"So it's 'between you and Paris now,' is it?" he asked.

Laura's feet flew straight up from their perch on the table. Sean caught her flailing arms as her chair toppled backward. "Good Lord!" she shrieked. "You scared me to death!"

"Such decorum, *ma chérie!*" he chastised, hauling her upright. "And here I thought La Goulue might offend *your* sensibilities."

Then he noticed the bottle. "Oh, no!" He snatched up the container from the table and quickly sampled the contents. "White wine. Thank God."

"Lou Lou offered," she reminded him, wrinkling her nose, "but it isn't very good."

Sean shook his head and blew out a huge sigh of relief. "I dare say it's better for you than absinthe."

"I'm not drunk," she said dryly, "or drugged."

"Just depraved," he suggested, deliberately leering as he took a hefty swig from the bottle. He knew he had never seen such a heady mixture of innocence, effervescence and pulchritude. Absolutely mouthwatering. Deliciously disheveled. And all *his*.

Sean forgot every reason he had ever concocted for keeping his distance. All he could remember was how her skin tasted like the sweetest cream, her lips like berries warm with sunshine. How the scent of her enveloped him in a fog that blinded him to everything but his overpowering need to possess her.

"Laura," he whispered, and suddenly she was there in his arms, flush against him with her hands in his hair. His mouth opened over hers and all sense of reality fled. Walking backward through the door, half lifting her, still plundering the depths of her mouth, he felt the backs of his legs touch the bed. He tumbled them onto it and rolled her beneath him.

As eager as he, Laura tugged at his clothes, interrupting her efforts to slide a hand inside his shirt and press her palm to his heart. Her small fingertips dug into his chest and splayed over him in frantic kneading gesture. "Please," she murmured into his mouth. "Love me, Sean."

Sean tore away his coat and shirt in one motion and reached for the buttons on his trousers. Her hands met his and together they wrestled away the remainder of his clothing and began on hers. Finally, he thought, finally together as they writhed in a heated embrace. Her lips were everywhere at once, dragging hot kisses across his shoulder, down his chest. Now he would have her. *Now!*

"So!" boomed a nasal voice. "This is how you repay me, eh?" Sean leapt off Laura and scrambled for his weapons.

"Wilder?" asked the voice in a hushed tone of disbelief.

"Renaudin?" Sean returned, abandoning his defense.

"You gutter-reared bitch," the man accused Laura, who had yanked the rumpled coverlet up to her eyes. "How dare you seduce my friend!"

"Wait, Valentin! She's not—"

"I know who she is! Is Louise not enough for you, Yvette?" Valentin snatched away the covers. Laura screamed and yanked up a pillow to hide her nudity. Sean pinned Valentin's skinny throat against the bedpost.

The tableau froze for a few seconds as Valentin realized his mistake. "Oh." He looked wide-eyed at Sean and then at Laura. "Do pardon me." His gaze drifted back to Sean's naked arms. Then he shrugged and began to laugh. The tinny sound cut through the silence and finally sputtered out. "My mistake. I do apologize most profusely. Who is this *mignonne,* my friend?"

Sean released Valentin, scooped up his discarded trousers and began to dress. "This *mignonne* is my wife. Laura, darling, meet Valentin Renaudin, also known as *le Désossé,* the boneless one. He dances, you see, as though he has none. And if he doesn't get out of this room before I get my breeches buttoned, you can watch me tie his rubber legs in knots. All three of them!"

"I am going. I am!" Valentin said, retreating. "I shall await you in the kitchen, eh?"

Laura threw the pillow the moment the kitchen door closed. "This is the man who's supposed to help us? This outrageous caricature?"

"In a word, yes." Sean decided she might as well get accustomed to the night crawlers now. Valentin was probably the least debauched of the lot. At least he was the only one who didn't insist on getting paid for his antics. "Better get some clothes on if you want in on the discussion."

She wriggled into her knickers, still huffing and panting with anger. Sean suspected her fury was mixed with more than a little frustration. His own certainly was.

Since the night of their return from Beaumont's house, when Sean had decided to abandon his reservations about loving Laura, precious little opportunity had occurred for any physical expression of it. First her father's cursed visit had exhausted and unnerved her. Then yesterday morning, after her eager response to his touch sent them hurrying back to the Lenoir, the shooter had effectively destroyed his intent. Valentin's rude, predawn interruption might be an occasion for laughter days from now, but Sean felt nothing in the way of amusement at present.

He ached with denial and he imagined—even hoped—that Laura felt the same. With a stab of conscience, Sean realized he felt angry with Laura. He knew he ought to be directing that anger at fate and circumstance instead of his wife. It certainly wasn't Laura's fault that she hadn't a future to offer him. But he couldn't quite forget that she'd chosen him out of thousands of other men to share her tragedy. Why the hell hadn't she picked the village vicar?

Perhaps it would have been better had the gunman not missed his mark, Sean reflected. Life would have ended with Laura's face the final thing he saw, loving her the last thought in his mind. He would not have been the one left behind to grieve. God, the dread was too much to bear.

"Sean?" she whispered, tugging at the sleeve of his half-buttoned shirt. "What's wrong?"

He looked down at the beautiful face lined with concern, and guilt pierced his heart. "Forgive me," he pleaded as he drew her close and buried his lips in her tousled hair. "I am so sorry, Laura. So very sorry."

She pushed away and giggled. "Get rid of that boneless wonder in Lou Lou's kitchen and you won't be!"

Sean sighed and shook his head, not even minding the throbbing pain behind his eyes that the motion generated. He deserved that and more. He would make it up to her. Even though she would never know how unworthy his thoughts had been, he promised himself he would grant her every wish from here on. Anything Laura wanted, he would provide. Anything she wanted him to do, he would arrange it. Anything she wanted him to be, he would be. *Please, let there be time enough,* he prayed silently.

Laura nibbled cheese and stroked the tabby while Sean explained their dilemma and his plans to Valentin Renaudin. Even though their French was rapid, she had no problem following either that or their current conversation concerning possible housing arrangements.

The dancer exhibited a reasonableness she hadn't suspected him capable of, given his earlier outrage. From the discourse between the men, she gathered that Valentin was a respectable wine merchant, despite his secondary profession as an entertainer. They mentioned his brother, the notary, whom Sean had met during their former business dealings. Laura couldn't help but wonder what brother Dominic did in his leisure time.

They considered and agreed upon the upstairs over Valentin's own wineshop as temporary living quarters.

"Use it as an *atelier,* perhaps? After all, you must have an occupation. Something not out of the ordinary," Valentin suggested as he turned to Laura with an assessing eye. "This one has the makings of a model," he said with a sardonic quirk of his lips. Laura blushed, recalling that he had certainly seen enough of her to judge her attributes.

"Considering what passes for art these days, you might even make a franc or two daubing her likeness," he continued. "Once we change a few of your outer trappings, Mr. and Mrs. Wilder will simply disappear. At least until we learn enough to set our snare for your huntsman."

Sean leaned forward on the sturdy table resting his chin on his hands. The long, considering look he gave her made Laura squirm. Did he not think she'd qualify as an artist's model?

After a moment, he settled his thoughtful regard on Valentin and began questioning him about their prospective quarters.

The man's replies suggested the accommodations were little better than Lou Lou's.

Laura mentally reviewed the contents of her reticule. Playing at decadence was all well and good, but the idea of forgoing her daily bath definitely did not appeal. At least the hotel where they had been living accommodated the English eccentricity for personal cleanliness. Judging by this place and the state of La Goulue's hygiene, Laura could just imagine having to clean herself with cheap wine.

"Come, come," Valentin urged, "we will go now before Louise returns. She will be put out with me again for my neglect. Unless you wish to witness a beating, we should be away."

"Never tell me you strike her!" Laura gasped.

His high-pitched laughter sliced the air. "*Non, mignonne,* I would never tell you that! La Goulue is the one with the wicked temper and the meaty fists."

Shocked to her toes, Laura allowed Sean to escort her out into the foggy dawn where they traversed lower Montmartre to their temporary home.

The large, open room was surprisingly clean. It contained a wide, lumpy bed, two sturdy tables, one overstuffed chair and a rather garishly painted armoire. The faded, floral wallpaper bore marks of things thrown against it and the lacy curtains sported larger holes than their maker had intended. Regardless, the place possessed a certain well-worn charm. Perhaps that stemmed from the fact that she would be sharing it with Sean, Laura thought with a smile. "It's lovely," she remarked. "We shall be very happy here."

"Trying to convince me or yourself?" Sean muttered as he opened his wallet and withdrew all the money within it.

Valentin accepted the funds with a small bow. "I shall convert this to coin for you. Paper won't do, you know, especially English paper, though it is worth more than ours."

He held up a long-fingered hand when Sean started to protest. "You may pay me once this is finished, my friend. I know this is all you have at present. You could be seen if you go to the bank for more. Wait here until I return with some clothing for you. Louise will help me find something appropriate. We must take her into our confidence anyway, so she will not give away your identities."

"Thank you, Valentin," Sean said.

"You saved my brother, *mon ami.* This is the very least I can do. Besides, you will be suitably grateful when we succeed, eh?" Renaudin flourished the English bills and danced backward out the door.

"What an unusual man," Laura said under her breath.

"A fairly regular bloke for this part of the world. Be warned, La Goulue herself is more in the way of normal in this particular quarter." He chuckled. "If, indeed, *anything* is normal here."

"They are lovers?"

"Sometimes. Theirs is a unique relationship that even I find hard to fathom. He obviously loves her. She loves herself." He quirked a brow and smiled as he began to examine their new surroundings more thoroughly. "As well as other women at times. Try not to remark on the strangeness of it all if you can avoid it. I realize this is all very new to you."

Sean sat down on the bed and leaned against the headboard. "Come here," he said, opening his arms.

Laura scooted back onto the bed and settled herself against him, reveling in the feel of his strength surrounding her.

"Have you spent much time here in the past?" she asked.

"Some. Over a year ago, I got involved in a political case that brought me to Paris. Valentin's brother, the accountant we mentioned, was set up to take the blame for one of his employers. Very nasty business that could have gotten Dominic executed."

"You saw that he was exonerated, didn't you?" She leaned her head back on his shoulder and looked up at him.

"Yes," Sean admitted. "He was innocent, after all. The man responsible was the one who hired me in the first place. I lost my fee on that one, but I gained some friends here."

"And enemies?" Laura ventured. "Could the shooting yesterday be related to that?"

"No. The word would have gone out beforehand to make an example of me for my interference. Everyone, especially Valentin, would have known about it. As far as I can determine, all the guilty parties are either dead or securely locked away. We certainly wouldn't be here right now if there were the slightest possibility they were not. No, because of those notes, I know this current trouble followed us from London."

Laura pushed out of his embrace and sat up with her back to him. She didn't want to voice the other possibility that suddenly occurred to her. Her first thought after the incident had involved her stepfather. Was he above having Sean shot? She truly didn't know him well enough to guess whether he had murderous inclinations.

He had made it very clear how much he wanted Lambdin to have control of her inheritance. To effect that, Sean would have to die. And so would she unless she agreed to give everything to Lambdin outright.

What if her brother had already told him she hadn't long to live? Unless Sean succumbed before her, Lamb hadn't the smallest chance of securing her fortune. All of the money would go to her husband and then on to his heirs, whoever they might be. She knew Sean's mother still lived. There could be any number of his relatives alive to claim whatever became Sean's after her own death.

Somehow this theory made much more sense to Laura than suspecting some faceless, nameless criminal who had been rightly judged and jailed in the past and now freed to exact revenge.

Should she suggest her suspicion to Sean? Perhaps he had already considered it and refrained from saying anything to spare her feelings. That would be so like him. If she had put him in danger by this marriage, she ought to admit it and see what she could do to prevent a reoccurrence.

Laura turned to face him, her hands clasped together to stop their trembling. "My stepfather may have arranged to have you killed. There, I've said it."

Sean laughed and captured her again, drawing her against him and giving her an affectionate squeeze. "Well, that's certainly what I would do if some slick-fisted bounder came along and wed my daughter for her money." He kissed the top of her head and nuzzled her hair, making light of his words. "Someone threatened me before we were married, however, so I doubt your stepfather's involved in this."

Laura still feared he might be. "I obtained the license immediately when I arrived in London. Perhaps he somehow found out. Oh, Sean, I am so sorry," she said in a small voice.

"No need. You have no control over his actions. Besides, I doubt he had the time to set a contract on my life."

But Laura sensed the false assurance in his ready reply. It could very well have been her stepfather's idea to have Sean shot. How long could it take for a man to arrange to have another killed? Such a transaction could take place in no time at all when one had connections all over the city, as no doubt her stepfather did. She felt sick at heart.

"Whoever it is will find us, won't they?" she asked dully, but it wasn't truly a question. "Eventually they will come and try to kill you again."

"I'm counting on it," Sean admitted softly while he stroked her arms and slid his hands down to capture hers. "But this time we shall be surrounded by people who will warn us. Information travels at the speed of light in this society. If the shooter is English, he'll be spotted immediately here. Any local murderer for hire off the streets will be automatically suspect and therefore watched."

"But how will your friends here know? There must be hundreds passing through these streets every day."

He nodded thoughtfully as he played with her fingers. "True. Paris may be crowded with all manner of strangers, but Montmartre has the advantage of a small community. Everyone knows everyone else's business as surely as they must have in your village back home. If an unknown comes among the locals asking questions, they are all too ready to speculate with each other about the stranger's business. We will know of any potential threat well before it becomes a reality. That's why I decided we would come here instead of some faraway place where I know few people."

"You know everyone here, then?" she asked.

"Of course not everyone. I wasn't here long enough for that, but Valentin does. They squabble among themselves like dogs at a butcher's door, but when trouble threatens one of them, they band together like family. I saw that happen when Dom Renaudin was accused. Their defense grew damn near rabid."

Laura smiled into his eyes and squeezed his hands. "And you were their hero when you saved him, weren't you?"

He ducked his head and kissed her ear. "Something of the sort, I suppose. They threw me a hell of a party."

Feeling aroused, yet unwilling to take the love play any further, Laura quickly sat up, twisting around to face him. "Tell me about it! I want to know everything!" she demanded, leaning close and wriggling with excitement.

"If only I could recall enough of it to tell," he said laughing. "I remember we began at L'Elysée-Montmartre. How the champagne flowed! Dancers were three deep on the floor, kicking higher than their heads. I viewed more underwear that night than a merchant dealing in the stuff. Later, we progressed to Moulin de la Galette."

"What else? What then?" she begged, trying to picture it all in her mind.

"The *chahut* got truly out of hand. From that point on, everything's a whirling blur. I woke up under a table with some dancer's petticoat round my neck and no notion how it got there. Haven't had above one flute of champagne since then."

Laura laughed out loud with delight.

"Lou Lou mentioned *chahut*. What is that, exactly?"

"It rather defies description," he answered enigmatically. "But I expect you shall see for yourself tonight."

Chapter Eight

Sean's hands had traveled up Laura's arms and were busy playing at the buttons securing her collar. His lambent green eyes concentrated on her neck. She knew she should put a halt to this. "Sean, I...don't think we should risk—"

A loud, rhythmic knocking accompanied a singsong greeting. "Grab up the covers, *mes amis*. We are coming in!"

Laura jerked away from Sean as the door swung open and a parade of three trooped into their room. Lou Lou, the herald, dumped a huge pile of white ruffles and bright-colored clothing on the foot of the bed. Valentin followed suit with what looked like one of Sean's smaller valises left in the hotel.

"Pinched right from your room at the Lenoir. The only one petite enough to fit through the window," Renaudin commented as he unsnapped the familiar case and threw it open. "You would be too hard to fit off the shelf, but *Madame* should not need her things while you are here." He turned to a man who looked very like himself, only younger and less emaciated. "Dominic?"

"Your livelihood," the stranger announced and deposited a scarred, paint-smeared folding easel and a leather case against one wall. "Whatever else you need, I shall bring when you have made your list." He smiled sweetly at Sean and then cocked an interested brow at Laura. "Madame Wilder, I presume? I am Dominic Renaudin, at your service." He made a low, graceful bow.

"How do you do, M'sieur Renaudin," she said, holding out her hand. He took it, jerked her into his arms and kissed her soundly on the mouth. His lips felt thin and hard against hers. Stunned at his audacity, Laura stood frozen as he released her. "Mmm, she is *worthy!*" he announced with a wicked smile. "Can she kick, though?"

She came to life at the impudent question and answered it with a swift toe to his shin.

Raucous laughter, Sean's included, echoed off the walls as Lou Lou's high-pitched voice gave benediction. "La, she is one of us! Hail, Cygne Cygne!"

The *swan,* Lou Lou called her. Laura couldn't help thinking of a long-necked bird roasted to a turn, bedecked in its own plucked feathers and served up as the centerpiece at some bacchanalian feast.

Well, she had bargained for excitement. Sean seemed determined to give her her money's worth.

"This is a madhouse!" Laura cried out over the noise. "I knew I would love it!"

Sean tightened his grip on her waist as they were pushed and shoved through the gregarious throng. Late Wednesday evening L'Elysée teemed with the working people of Montmartre come to break up the drudgery of their week. The few swells from town who had arrived to taste the dark side of Paris stood out like curse words in a sermon.

A bony, long-fingered hand tugged his arm. "Over there," Valentin directed, and led the way. Sean followed him, guiding Laura through the milling merrymakers to a table near the edge of the dance floor.

Apparently they were expected. The moment they sat down, a henna-haired woman hailed them like old friends and slid two glasses of wine past her companion. Sean nodded his thanks and blew her a kiss. Laura laughed, bouncing in her chair as she snatched up her wine and raised it toward their self-appointed hostess.

Sean couldn't seem to tear his eyes away from the sight Laura made in her borrowed clothes. The low-cut blouse revealed almost half her firm breasts, which rose dangerously high with every excited breath she took. The snowy ruffle that edged the garment barely covered the rosy peaks he remembered all too well. She had piled all that luxurious hair of hers on top of her head in the same loose knot La Goulue affected. Dark tendrils, dampened to encourage curls, danced saucily against her forehead and cheeks whenever she moved. A wide black ribbon surrounded her swanlike neck at the very place he most wanted to taste. Well, why not? He snaked one arm around her and buried his lips just below the velvet band.

She drew back and gave his chest a playful shove. "Sean!"

He leered shamelessly and let go with a torrid stream of gutter French he felt certain she wouldn't comprehend. Apparently she got most of it, for she blushed bright red and comically rolled her eyes. If he had ever in his life seen anything or anyone more enchanting than Laura at the moment, he couldn't recall it. His blood raced.

The band initiated a brassy waltz that would have set Strauss's teeth on edge. "Dance?" he asked, eager for any excuse to hold her close.

She downed another sip of her wine and nodded eagerly. Sean swept her past the swaying mass of bodies, out of the bright lights and into the surreal shadows. He held her much closer than was proper anywhere within the limits of civiliza-tion. But Paris at night, at least in this sector, was anything but civilized.

Something inside Sean altered as they waltzed. He could hold this moment, make *this* the reality. Forever carefree. There would be no past, no future. Just this glorious present with Laura. Sean allowed himself to believe he was exactly what he seemed, an indigent artist seeking inspiration in the nightlife of Montmartre and the arms of his voluptuous model, the boisterous Cygne Cygne.

Suddenly cymbals crashed and loud whoops erupted all around them. Sean grabbed her hand and made a dash for their table.

"What? What's happening?" she shouted over the din.

"Chahut!" he explained. *"Regardez!"*

The music rose to a deafening level, accompanied by raucous squeals and peals of laughter. In a flurry of whirling skirts, La Goulue and a half dozen of her cohorts roughly cleared a section of the dance floor. They formed a ragged circle and leaned forward, grasping their hems and kicking back toward the center.

With screams of pure exuberance, they came upright as one, baring petticoats, knickers and legs that seemed to pivot at the knees. Down again and then up, each dancer holding one ankle suspended above her head as she bounced in time to the blaring music.

Sean stole a look at Laura and laughed aloud. Her mouth hung open and her eyes blinked as though she couldn't believe they worked properly. "My lord!" she mouthed as a wide smile blossomed. "Oh, look!" She clapped in time, curling her lips into a shrill whistle.

Sean, startled for a moment, recovered and joined her with an enthusiasm he hadn't felt in years. Shoving back their chairs, they stood and edged their way through the hooting melee to get a closer look. Before he could stop her, Laura twirled into the uneven circle of dancers and picked up the rhythm. In awe, he watched his wife lift her skirts and treat the lowlife of the city to a prolonged glimpse of her underwear.

"You are drunk!" he accused when the dance ended and she fell breathless into his arms.

"Drunk on life!" she admitted with a gasp and a wide grin.

Life. The word hit him like a punch in the gut. The reminder burst his bubble of pretense. How could he have forgotten, for even a moment, how precarious was her very existence? How brief a time she had left?

Sean sucked in a deep breath and clenched his eyes shut as he drew out her chair for her. God, how was he to get through this night when all he wanted to do was take her back to that seedy little garret of theirs and hold her close to ease his desperation? To ward off the inevitable.

No. He must not drag her back to reality just yet. No matter how hard the act, he had to maintain it for her sake. With an effort that nearly made him ill, Sean pasted on a wide smile and shouted for a round of cheap champagne. Everyone at the table cheered them, him for the free drinks and Laura for her game attempt at cancan. Their rowdy toasts to her bravery almost did him in.

If they only knew. His Laura was the soul of courage.

Laura figured it to be about half-past three when Sean steered her up the stairs to their garret over the wineshop. Exhausted and sticky with sweat, they collapsed simultaneously on the lumpy bed. He groaned theatrically, one large hand covering his eyes.

"Lou Lou is right, you are becoming old," she said in her sultriest French. She thought she had the nasal tone down to a science.

"Spare me your criticism, please," he begged, "and that god-awful whine. Lord knows I'm ready for a good dose of English. Till tonight I'd forgotten why I left Paris."

"Couldn't have been the company. That was excellent."

He laughed wryly. "Then it must have been the wine. I think I may be sick. Wasn't it awful?"

She rolled over next to him so that her face hovered only inches from his. "Perfectly, wonderfully awful, every bit of it! I've never had such a glorious time in all my life." Her lips touched his, briefly and gently, wishing she could do more. "Thank you, Sean," she whispered.

"And you," he replied, returning her kiss in kind. "I can't recall ever having had so much fun. You were superb, you know? They all love you." He trailed a finger down the side of her face. "And I love you."

Abruptly Laura shoved herself away and sat up on the edge of the bed. "You mustn't do that! We decided against it."

"Too late, I'm afraid. Far too late."

She turned and regarded him carefully. He looked as though he meant it and she couldn't see an iota of regret in his eyes.

"Fool." She sat up on the edge of the bed, her back to him.

He sighed and smiled. "I expect you're right, but nevertheless—" His hand cupped one of her shoulders and massaged it lightly.

"I can't promise you tomorrow, Sean. I could die tonight," she warned.

"So could I," he replied, rising to sit beside her. His eyes were earnest as he attempted to explain. "Look, we have the moment, Laura. It's really all anyone has. Until I met you all I thought about was my future, piling up wealth so I would never have to worry, avoiding any kind of relationship so I wouldn't be responsible for anyone other than my mother. And even her, I leave in someone else's care. I dared not risk betrayal again."

He smiled, the expression bittersweet and endearing. "I never thought of the *now,* you see. I plowed through every day, always thinking I would have time to enjoy my life once I accomplished everything I had set out to do. That never happens. One never gets it all done. Sometimes now, I wonder whether I even cared if the day ever came. You, dear heart, have made me see what I was missing. You take such joy in life."

She scoffed and dropped her gaze to her hands, nervously smoothing her borrowed skirt. "Only the threat of its ending made me that way. I had more in common with you than you can guess."

Somehow she had to make him understand the guilt he was fostering in her. "Sean, I cannot…leave untroubled, if I know you will grieve. You must get over this or I can't bear it!"

He took her hands in his, probably to stop them wringing together, she thought.

"Laura, I want to make you forget. To make you happy. Now. Tonight."

She shook her head, withdrew her hands and rose to put distance between them. "No! I know how strongly you believe that making love is just that. *Making* love!"

Sean followed her to the window and placed both his hands on her shoulders. "Not just that, sweetheart. I don't deny that I want you, but my need is much stronger than mere desire for your lovely body. I'd like a chance to make this a real marriage for whatever time we have."

"You set the rules yourself," she reminded him, angry now that he would tempt her so. He must feel how she trembled whenever he touched her. "We agreed to be friends."

"And so we are, but it's not enough. Not for me and not for you, if you'll only admit it. You need me, too, Laura."

She turned and looked him in the eye, using all the fortitude she could muster, and lied. "No, I don't. I've made my peace with this, you see? I have it all worked out in my mind. Whole hours go by without any dread at all. You speak of your wants, but do you give a thought to mine? I want to go to my rest with no one the worse for it. I want no one to weep over me, especially not you!"

"I wish I could grant you that, but I cannot. I will weep. I will want to go with you."

"Oh, God!" Laura tore away from him and flung herself across the room. "How cruel you are!"

"No, no, I didn't mean it, Laura," he vowed, rushing to her, embracing her so firmly she couldn't move. "I never intended to say that, it just came out. Don't cry. For God's sake, I don't mean to make you cry!"

"Promise me," she demanded, grasping at his shirt. "You promise me, Sean! You'll never think such a thing again. Ever!"

"I do. I promise. It was a stupid, thoughtless thing to say. I'm sorry."

"Well, you should be! Now turn me loose and get away from me before you do something we'll both regret even more."

She watched him retreat and her heart sank at the profound expression of sadness in his eyes.

Maybe he was right. Perhaps it didn't matter whether or not they were intimate. She knew it would make no difference in the way she felt about him. But she suspected it would change and strengthen what he felt for her simply because he believed it would.

She wanted him every bit as desperately as he seemed to want her. Her blood sang in her veins every time he smiled, every time he touched her. Even a look would do it. If he already loved her anyway, what difference would it make? Had he come to the same conclusion?

Still she didn't call him back when he opened the door to leave. Of course it would make a difference. And probably not

just to him. Laura could just imagine herself cursing God at
the end, bargaining with the devil, madly struggling with
every cell in her body to live. To have one more hour with him,
one more moment. Then again, she very well might do that
anyway. With a groan, she closed her eyes and fought the tears.

Sean felt little better after his exercise. He had walked the
streets, railing like a madman until his frustration finally
subsided. His own cowardice had created this situation with
Laura. He had been afraid to love her and then lose her.

How stupid ever to think avoiding the physical act would
save him. All he had accomplished was to pass his fears along
to her in the form of guilt. Now, however, he was bound to
honor her wishes as best he could.

Just then he passed Valentin's and noticed a light in the
window. Louise hadn't left with him tonight, but the man
must be entertaining somebody. The urge to pay Valentin back
for interrupting his and Laura's lovemaking that first day was
simply too great. Sean lifted a fist and pounded on the door.

But Valentin had no woman with him. And the welcome
Sean received offered no satisfaction. None at all.

An hour later, Sean opened the door and slipped back
inside their *atelier.* Laura had not gone to sleep as he had
hoped, but sat staring out the window. The gas lamps from the
street threw weak highlights across her shadowed features.
The effect was at once moving and surreal.

He immediately thought of capturing her that way on
paper, of saving the poignant sight so he would always have
it. But did he really want to remember her this way? No, he
decided. Better to record the happier moments. Laura
laughing, dancing madly, teasing.

"Are you all right?" he asked, carefully keeping his distance.

"Yes, I think so." She turned toward him and her face was lost in the shadows. "Are you?"

"I'm through pouting now," he said, and tossed his hat onto the bureau. "You can relax."

"I worried about you wandering the streets, Sean. It's hardly safe to do that with someone out there trying to kill you."

"I'm not likely to forget the danger. Especially not now."

"Tell me the truth, Sean. Do you think it might be someone my stepfather hired?"

He shook his head. "Perhaps. But I don't think so."

Sean shrugged out of his coat and began removing his shirt. "There is something I have to tell you, Laura. I stopped by Valentin's while I was out and he had some distressing news. There's no point in keeping it from you, much as I would like to. You're sure to hear about it sooner or later."

"What have you found out?"

"Beaumont is dead. You remember I told Valentin why we were here in Paris, about the Rembrandt. He knew about this all night, but hadn't a chance to tell me, what with the crowds and everything. Also, he was waiting for more details from his friend who is a gendarme. He was getting ready to come here and tell us when I arrived at his place."

"Oh no," Laura gasped. "That poor old man!"

Sean took her hand and led her to the bed where they both sat in silence for a few moments, thinking of their meeting with Beaumont.

"He died night before last, the night we were at his house," Sean said. "He was found late yesterday afternoon in his study with a nephew of his who had just arrived from Alsace. Only relative he had left, so the police said. Both were shot."

"A robbery?" Laura asked.

Sean shifted, reluctant to explain. "No, Laura. Beaumont had nothing left to steal. It could have been a disgruntled creditor, I suppose, but I don't think so. They were fired on through the window. The younger man was of my coloring, height and build. The murderer probably didn't see his face since the bullet entered the back of his head. Perhaps the murderer arrived just after we left, mistook the nephew's identity and meant one of those bullets for me."

"You?" Laura's eyes were huge, worried and full of tears.

"Perhaps. Our *ears* at the Lenoir reported to Valentin that a man came asking for me not long after we left for Beaumont's. The desk clerk must have overheard us discussing Beaumont's collection as we departed, because he told the man he thought that was my destination."

"That could have been my stepfather. He was waiting for us when we returned."

"Maybe. If not, that someone could have gone to Beaumont's and arrived there just after we left, as I said."

"Perhaps it was someone who wanted the Rembrandt."

Sean inclined his head as though considering it. "It is a valuable piece."

"Then why shoot Beaumont? Why shoot you, for that matter? If they were only after the picture, why not simply steal it from Beaumont, or you once you got it?"

"Well, think. What with Beaumont's bankruptcy, he certainly would have had it secreted away before I came to get it. And a priceless painting such as that would have been locked away in the hotel safe once I had it."

"Then why try to kill you on the street the next day? The fellow might have been angry that he'd shot the wrong man, but what good would it do him to shoot you then?" Laura asked.

"If I were dead, then you, as my widow, would have taken all my things and headed straight away home to England for the burial, right? Child's play to relieve you of it en route while you were immersed in grief."

"A far-fetched notion, to be sure."

"But worth consideration. However, the threat could still be someone from my past. Someone after revenge. Killing Beaumont may only have been a tactic to disguise his real motive."

"What about those notes? They never mentioned the picture, did they?"

"There's the puzzle," he admitted with a shrug.

"Show them to me," Laura suggested. "Let me see what I can make of them."

"And get you all upset to the bargain. You wouldn't sleep a wink tonight."

"It's morning already and I won't sleep anyway."

He got up and fetched his coat, sliding a small packet of folded papers out of the breast pocket. "Here. They are in order. I'll light the lamp."

When he'd done so, she moved the chair near the light and began to read aloud.

"You deserve worse than death."

She shifted the first page aside and went to the second.

"You bastard. I will destroy you."

Laura looked up and quirked her expressive mouth to one side. "Not very loquacious, is he?" Then she read the next.

"Prepare to die."

"He meant you to suffer awhile, I suppose," she said, perusing the last a few seconds before she slowly formed the words it contained. *"Your time has come."*

"Well, he does get right to the point. They came, when?"

"The first, a couple of days before you came to me and proposed," Sean said with a wry smile. "The second one, the morning of the day we married. The third, at my rooms, the day after that. The last came to the hotel, the same time we received Beaumont's package containing the Rembrandt."

"This isn't my stepfather's handwriting," she said with obvious relief. "And unless someone notified him that I had applied for the marriage license, he had no reason to issue threats to you before we married."

"What about your brother? You never told him what you intended?" Sean asked.

"Of course not! He would have stopped me."

"Don't you keep a journal of any kind, Laura? Most women do, don't they?"

"A diary, of course, but Lamb would never intrude on my privacy. No, I'm inclined to agree with you now. This has the markings of someone who believes you've wronged him somehow. I can't tell you how relieved I feel that it isn't anyone in my family doing this!"

Laura sighed and folded the letters together again. "Well, we aren't likely to solve this immediately, are we? I suppose we should try and get some rest."

"You're absolutely right. I vote we dismiss the subject altogether until we have more information to work with. Look, the sun's well up already."

"So it is," Laura said softly. "Another day. A mild autumn, isn't it. Ordered up just for us, I expect." She moved to the folding dressing screen in the corner and began to dress for bed.

Sean noted well her weariness as Laura tried to make light conversation. All he could concentrate on were the articles of clothing she began draping over the edge of her flimsy barricade. "Will you begin painting today?" she asked.

"I thought I'd set up down by the small fountain. Do quick sketches of tourists and pick up a few francs. You should stay here."

"And miss your first day on the job? Not likely. I'll hang about and collect your francs. Then I'll spend them for you at the chocolate shop."

"And in no time I'll have a round, rosy model that would do Ruebens proud. I shall love to paint dimpled fat."

She laughed merrily as he'd meant her to and came to join him on the bed. He shifted to make room for her and welcomed her into the curve of his arm.

Words of love rushed to his lips and he bit them back. Instead, he kissed her lightly on the head and spoke into the softness of her hair. "Would you pose for me here, later tomorrow? I would like to paint you."

"Of course. How you flatter, suggesting a picture of me would sell!"

"I'd sooner sell my soul as part with a likeness of you. No, I want it for myself."

"I can't think why you would. Surely there are prettier things to hang on your wall." She looked up, her small pink tongue worrying the edge of her teeth.

Sean felt himself lose every vestige of control at the provocative sight. He grasped her chin and kissed her, tasting that sweet pinkness and reveling in her quick response. For a delicious space of time he abandoned all thought except to have her.

Reason returned only when she began to struggle in earnest, her cries of protest breaking through his sudden fog of passion. When he released her, she bolted upright with a palm flattened against his chest. Her breath issued every bit as ragged as his own. She shook with the same need. Why? he asked himself. Why did she continue to stop him? Laura wanted this as much as he did. But in his heart he knew. It was him, not herself, she protected.

"All right," he whispered. "No more."

Her shoulders sagged with either relief or frustration, a bit of both, he supposed. Did it matter, anyway? With a harsh expletive, he heaved himself off the bed and went to the chair by the window. "Go on to bed, Laura. I won't bother you."

Without another word, she curled into a ball, drew the tangled coverlet over her shoulder and ceased to move.

Still he could feel her tears like rivulets of fire, burning furrows through his soul.

Sean leaned forward and buried his face in his hands. The threats to his own life seemed trivial at the moment. He would catch whoever meant to kill him sooner or later. At least he stood a fighting chance and never doubted he would succeed. But he could do nothing to save Laura's life. Never had he felt so powerless. Even in his early years, during the darkest and most frightening hours of his abuse, there had been at least a small spark of hope deep down for escaping despair. Now he had none.

Not one, but two physicians had signed her death warrant. He could hardly bear to recall her words. Not for the first time since she'd told him what to expect, Sean forced himself to think long and hard of what it would be like. He must prepare for it.

Sometime in the very near future there would be no Laura. He would lay her in a cold stone crypt, grieve himself hollow, and wish for her sweetness every day that was left to him. She would die, a fact she had already come to grips with. How he envied her acceptance of it all.

Sean raised his head and glared out the window into the new morning. "Why her?" he demanded, knowing even as he asked, that he was not the first man to ask the question in anger. He also knew he would not find an answer.

He had never believed in a grand master plan or that everything happened for some unfathomable reason. He had never believed life fair or that justice would be served in the end. But always before, he had been able to twist the chaos of his own life into some kind of order. He could think of no way to fix this, no way to save her.

Holding his breath, Sean rose quietly and quickly let himself out of the room. He sought solitude downstairs in the back of Valentin's wineshop and gave vent to his anger and grief. Later, when he returned to their room, he slid beneath the covers and drew her sleeping form against him. He rested a palm beneath her left breast simply for the comfort of feeling her heart beat.

"Please," he mouthed silently into the darkness to whatever deity would listen. "Please."

Chapter Nine

For the next six weeks, life in Montmartre settled into what Laura laughingly called a routine. She noted that even the wild and disorderly inhabitants there fell victim to habit. She and Sean rose just after noon each day and joined some of their new friends at the small Café du Tertre down the street for a breakfast of coffee and croissants. Then the two of them returned to the room over the wineshop where Sean painted.

This life-style suited Sean, Laura thought. He had totally discarded his carefully attired businesslike demeanor and assumed the casual nonchalance common to their Montmartre neighbors. The language sounded natural on his tongue and obviously came easily to Sean. He confided to her that one of the *girls* in the house where he'd been born had taught him French as a child. While Laura's parlance in the tongue might be improving beyond her old tutor's expectations, she still spoke as little as possible except with their close friends.

Sean seemed to know exactly what he was doing. She wondered whether he had ever considered a career as an artist. Valentin had placed several of Sean's paintings, which he had signed simply as *Sauvage,* in a gallery over on rue Lemercher.

Two of them had sold immediately. Tourists had purchased a few right off the easel he set up each day by the fountain.

In private, he continued work on her portrait, which he seemed rather desperate to finish. She knew why, of course, but they never discussed it. Why dwell on it, when simply living from moment to moment made more sense? If Sean had set out to make her forget all that was to come, he very nearly succeeded. Sometimes a whole day passed without her thinking of it.

No further threatening notes arrived to disturb their happiness. No word on the street indicated that anyone sought their whereabouts. Sean seemed content to put the matter of the death threats and Beaumont's murder aside completely. Though she suspected he might only be postponing his pursuit of it for the duration of his time with her.

Valentin, Lou Lou and Dominic wandered into their studio-bedroom at will without even knocking, dragging other acquaintances along as the mood struck them. Privacy in the quarter was a foreign concept. The lack of it certainly aided Laura's resolve to prevent intimacy between herself and her husband. Late afternoon and the very early morning hours, which they usually had to themselves, offered the greatest temptation.

When daylight faded, Sean put away his paints. He hauled water upstairs where they took turns at the hip bath behind the screen. Dressed in what served as Montmartre evening clothes, they threw themselves into the nightlife at the Club Elysée.

Laura traded jokes and insults with Lou Lou and the other women while Sean argued politics and painting techniques with M'sieur Lautrec, Valerian Quinet, or the odd fellow they knew only as Georges. The wine, the lively exchanges and the raucous dancing always left them pleasantly exhausted. Laura wished it could last forever.

If only she and Sean hadn't loved each other, life would have been perfect. Fantasies played constantly in her head and wreaked havoc with her body. She knew he entertained a few of his own, given the heated looks she caught on his face at odd times. Like now.

"We don't really want to go out tonight, do we, Laura?" he asked.

Sean's long, sun-browned fingers abandoned the buttons on the shirt he'd just donned. Damn him, he must realize how the sight of his bare chest excited her. Tactile memories almost overtook her.

Laura hesitated in answering his invitation to remain in the garret. She feared staying in with Sean, considering the mood he was in. It could precipitate an argument very like the one they had suffered two weeks ago. If she could even bring herself to protest again. More likely she would succumb to him without a fuss, and that would be even worse than a confrontation.

He wanted to make love to her again. Though he had said nothing about it, the constant hunger in his eyes said it all. She couldn't be sure of putting him off this time. Her own will had weakened dangerously.

Her doubt must show, she thought, as he approached.

Instead of embracing her, as she half feared, half hoped, Sean passed by her, smiled and sank into the chair near the window.

He braced his elbows comfortably on his knees. "Goulue's right, I am getting old. Or jaded, maybe."

"Tired?" Laura asked. Unable to resist, she moved forward and ran a hand through his damp hair. He nodded, and for a time they both remained quiet, staring out the window at the gathering darkness.

Finally Sean reached for her hand and drew her down to his lap. It was the closest prolonged contact they'd attempted since that night they had quarreled about it.

"How are you really, Laura? Do you feel well? You look wonderful, you know. Henri remarked on it just last evening. There are roses in your cheeks. Your eyes sparkle." He ran a hand over her waist as his gaze fell on the low neckline of her blouse. "Beignets and chocolate become you."

She laughed and slapped playfully at his hand. "And your ices have likely put a roll around your middle if I dared to check. It's the good life, isn't it, Sean? Eat, sleep and play. I've never enjoyed anything so much."

"Haven't you?" His eyes glowed with hot, green fire.

Laura tried to escape his hold but he tightened his grip. "Don't let's go through all that again, Sean."

"All right," he agreed, but he still held her.

His expression changed from sensual to thoughtful. The words he spoke seemed carefully chosen. "Laura, do you think it's possible that you might be recovering? I know I've never seen a woman so blooming with health. I pray for it, you know." Dark lashes fell, and she could no longer see his eyes. "And I'm not much on supplication in any form." His voice dropped to a strained whisper, his large hands cradling her ribs. "I so want you to be well."

Laura embraced him, pulling his head against her chest and burying her face in his hair. "Most of the time I feel fine," she said. That was true enough. He didn't need to know the rest right now. How could she tell him about the dizziness, the nausea that had begun to plague her? Though not nearly as debilitating or enduring as she had experienced when they'd crossed the channel, the bouts of sickness had increased in frequency over the past few days. She must hide the fear.

Suddenly his arms tightened like bonds around her and his lips found the hollow of her throat. Hot, whispered words fell against her skin like tears. "I want you, Laura. Please don't deny me this. I need something to hold on to. I need to know that you love me, too. I swear to God that nothing we do or do not do will change what I feel. I love you so much, nothing could increase it." She felt his shivering breath against her ear. "Nothing, I swear!"

His mouth sought hers and a fiery rush encompassed her whole body, burning away any thought of denial. Her need for comfort and communion and release from the damnable tension overwhelmed her. *He* overwhelmed her.

The scent of clean, male heat enveloped her. Her skin tingled and tightened as his hands slid beneath her clothes, touching, grasping, soothing, pleasuring. A harsh sound, more demand than plea issued from his throat as his lips claimed hers again. She opened, eager to taste his hunger, show him her own. Beneath her, she could feel the hard probing of his body, pushing delicious memories aside to make way for more. He slid from the chair and, in one movement, lowered her to the threadbare carpet beneath the window.

Past caring where they came together, Laura pulled away his shirt and ran her hands over him, glorying in the swift rise and fall of his chest. He stripped off her blouse and chemise with one motion and worked her skirt over her hips in frantic haste. "Don't say no," he demanded, "Don't."

She nodded once, adding her hurried efforts to his as he began tugging at the flap on his trousers. When he sprang free, she ran an eager hand over him and reveled in his groan of frustration.

"Bed?"

"No!" she said, unwilling to wait. "Here." With that, she grasped his hips and drew him to her. He entered with a harsh groan, and held still, trembling with the effort. He loomed above her, braced on his hands, only their lower bodies touching, joined.

Laura, suffused in pleasure, watched his eyes close, his

nostrils flare, his lips tighten, as though he battled some inner demon. Seconds later, he released a breath and looked directly into her eyes.

Slowly his mouth descended to take hers so gently she wanted to scream for more pressure. She felt his hand glide down over one breast, her ribs, her belly and settle where his body claimed hers. His fingers burned like liquid fire. He made a low sound of encouragement, stoking the flame higher.

She moved against him, seeking more. He gave it, then withdrew and gave again. Laura cried out as ripples of pleasure danced over her nerves, growing into waves of pure feeling that mounted higher and higher until she felt engulfed, lost, found.

He drove into her, retreated and plunged again. And again. Rhythmically now, increasing in fervor until she once more felt the fire ignite, glow fiercely as he took her mouth and explode in a burst of glorious white heat. His primal growl echoed through her as she felt their souls meld in his deep, final thrust.

With a long, shuddering release of breath, he rolled to his side, his palms holding her fast against him until they rested side by side. Neither spoke as they settled into sleep.

Laura woke in bed later that night, unable to recall when he had put her there. His long muscular leg rested over both of her legs. One arm lay across her chest, his fingers tangled in her hair. She smiled and snuggled closer. Replete and willing to lie there forever, she closed her eyes and slept again.

"Ah, God!" Laura cried, struggling to free herself of his hold.

"What? What is it?" Sean demanded, certain she was in the throes of some nightmare. He tried to calm her even as she shoved him away and scrambled off the bed. The grogginess of sudden awakening slowed his reflexes so that it took him a moment to follow her behind the screen.

He found her retching pitifully and already on her knees before the chamber pot. Sean quickly knelt and held back her hair, one hand to her forehead for support. The moans cut into his heart like blades thrown one after the other.

When she finally sat back on her heels, gasping for breath, Sean held her gently. "I'm putting you back to bed now. All right? Will you be all right?"

Laura nodded and he proceeded to lift her in his arms. Her entire body felt limp and spent against his chest.

He cursed his thoughtlessness of last night. How could he have been so bloody stupid? She had seemed perfectly well when he'd loved her and now she was so dreadfully sick. If only he had known it would affect her so. Now he recalled her illness on the ship. Perhaps their intimacy after the wedding had prompted that, as well. No more. He would never risk this again. Please God, he hadn't shortened the time she had left.

A rapid knock cut through his thought. "Thank God, someone's come. I'll send them for a doctor."

Sean placed Laura on the bed, hurriedly pulled on his trousers and jerked open the door.

Valentin handed him a letter addressed to Laura. "Jeanne-Marie maids at the Lenoir now. She picked this out of your box when the clerk was away from the desk." He glanced past Sean at Laura and then stepped back onto the landing, beckoning Sean to follow. He whispered, "This other was stuck under the front door downstairs. I just found it as I came in."

Sean frowned at the envelope bearing only his name. They had been found.

Whoever had sent the other notes threatening him knew exactly where they were. The protection of their adopted community somehow had been circumvented. He opened the missive and read it.

Do you love her? How appropriate. She will die first.

Valentin gasped as he read the words over Sean's shoulder. *"Mon Dieu!"*

Sean crushed the paper in his hand. "Laura is not to know about this, do you hear?"

"I cannot understand how the devil has found you without our knowing he made enquiries. But you must tell her, my friend. Since he delivered this note here, he could easily get to you anytime he chooses. You will have to take her away!"

"Not possible. She's ill, Valentin. Will you fetch the physician for me?"

"Oui, maintenant! It is serious you think?"

Sean nodded. "Go to the Lenoir. My friend Dr. Eugene Campion is staying there. Ask him if he will come. No, don't ask. Just bring him."

"He will come if I must drag him here," Valentin declared.

"Tell him to bring what I left in the hotel safe, will you?"

"Oui."

After a massive attempt to steady himself, Sean tucked the note into his pocket and went back in to Laura. She lay as he had left her, pale and shaken.

"Was that Valentin?"

"Yes, it was. I sent him to the Lenoir to bring Camp to see about you." He placed the other letter in her hand. "He just brought this for you. It's from your brother. Shall I read it for you while we wait for Camp to get here?"

She shook her head and pressed the envelope to her chest. He brushed her hair off her forehead and rested his palm on her cheek. "There's no fever," he said gently. "That's a good sign, isn't it?"

"I wish we had tea," she murmured, and then sighed. "I miss tea, don't you? And biscuits. Those shortbread things, you know?"

Sean swore under his breath. "I'll send for some the moment Valentin comes back. We'll storm the English consulate if we have to. There is coffee downstairs. Shall I fetch you some?"

"Yes, thank you," she said, smiling bravely. When he made to rise, she clutched at his arm. "Sean? You're feeling responsible for this upset, aren't you? You must not!" she said vehemently. "Promise me you don't regret last night. Promise?"

He leaned down and kissed her in reply. Then he held her troubled gaze and pressed her hand where it rested on his forearm. "I'll treasure last night, darling. Always." Then he left before she could see his tears.

Valentin and Campion arrived before he got the water hot.

Only then did Sean question his faith in his friend; he had no earthly idea whether Camp was any good at what he did for a living.

Even as he considered this, Sean urged him toward the stairs. "Hurry!" he demanded. "She's very ill."

He followed, but Camp turned and blocked his way. "Best wait down here. Privacy will ensure her candor, most likely. Women usually downplay their ills if husbands are present. I shall speak with you as soon as I have seen to her. I shan't be long about it, I promise." He smiled comfortingly at Sean before resuming his climb.

Sean started to argue, then thought better of it. In his present frame of mind, he might give Laura the idea that he didn't expect her to recover. Instead, he retreated to Valentin's kitchen and proceeded to finish the coffee.

"She will be all right," he chanted between sips of the bitter brew. "She will be all right."

Valentin extended a few words of agreement to that effect, excused himself and left sometime during Sean's continued litany.

A half hour later, Campion descended, humming merrily to himself as Sean met him at the foot of the stairs.

"Well?"

"Oh, yes, she is perfectly well, Sean," he said, smiling.

Sean lowered himself to the bottom step and rested his face in one palm. "Lord, Camp, I feared she was dying."

Campion threw back his head and laughed aloud. "It is frightening, isn't it? Especially the first time. But I assure you, your lady is in no danger. None whatsoever."

"She's not going to die now?" Sean asked, barely able to catch his breath. "Do you promise, Camp? Are you certain of it?"

He laughed again and inclined his head. "Well, wild man, we are *all* going to die sooner or later. But I'd venture to say your lovely wife has at least a half century to worry about that. She is as healthy as the proverbial horse."

"But what about the disease? The one caused by the insect bite? She has overcome it completely? Can you be so certain?" Sean waited for further reassurance, for definite verification.

"My dear friend, I have no idea what you are talking about. I don't know what absurdity your little minx concocted to explain her morning sickness to you, but believe me, she is a blooming example of expectant motherhood. Why, if I had to choose a woman who—"

"Pregnant?" Sean shouted, jumping straight up from his seat on the bottom stair. "Laura is *pregnant?*"

"Yes! Congratulations, old man!" Campion popped his bag open and took out a small package. "And here is what you asked for. I have to get back to Lisette. She's determined to get me to the opera tonight and I only have hours to dissuade her. I must be off. You owe me champagne, this time! *Bonjour, Papa!*"

Sean's knees buckled and he nearly fell. The swell of exultation he had felt at Laura's reprieve from death crashed down like a giant tidal wave. In its wake lay suspicion. Then underneath, the gritty sand of certainty. Laura was not going to die. And she had known that all along.

She had not even mentioned her sickness to Camp. Because she hadn't dared! A real doctor would have exposed her in a minute.

"Damn her for a lying…" He couldn't think of a word strong enough, foul enough, to describe Laura Middlebrook. No, he corrected himself with a sneer. Laura *Wilder*. She had suckered him with the oldest, dirtiest trick in the book. Conned him into giving his name to her bastard. So that's why she "needed a husband immediately," eh? Her very words in his office that afternoon. Well, bugger that! He wasn't about to let her get away with it!

Sean stormed up the stairs and slammed into the bedroom. She looked up, wearing an excited grin. He wished for a moment he were capable of violence toward a woman. If he ever were, it would certainly be this one. Choked speechless with anger, he tossed the wrapped painting onto the chair and approached the bed.

"Isn't it wonderful, Sean? Did Dr. Campion tell you?"

"Oh, he told me all right," Sean finally muttered. "He told me everything! Pack your bags. I want you away from me before I do something I might very well hang for."

"What…what are you saying?" she asked, looking so prettily confused he wanted to slap her silly.

Oh, what innocence, he thought bitterly. Exactly like Ondine's innocence all those years ago. Deceitful bitches, both.

He backed away, against the wall to trap his fists there. "How do you do it, Laura? Such convincing lies. So many false tears."

"But, Sean, listen! It's all here, the misunderstanding's clear," she said, shaking the open pages of the letter he'd given her before he went down for her coffee. "It was my mare, Cleo, whom they thought would die, you see? But when I overheard Lambdin and James—"

"That's what gave you the idea?" he snapped. "How creative you are."

"I knew the moment I read Lamb's letter it wasn't me they were talking about at all. But Campion came in before you returned, and there wasn't time to tell you—"

"Oh, give it up, Laura! You arranged the marriage to give your child a name. And I will not, under any circumstances, claim your bastard. Had I known you were pregnant, I'd never have married you, and you knew it. You fabricated that atrocious lie about a fatal illness to gain my sympathy. Well, you certainly had that for what it's worth. In spades." He glared at her with all the hatred roiling in his gut. "You made me weep. You made me pray, for God's sake. You made me *love* you, damn it!"

"Sean, it is your child! You know it is. You know that I never—"

"I *know* you were already pregnant when we crossed the channel. No one could pretend nausea like that. No one," he shouted. "And it stretches the imagination more than a bit to think a pregnancy of one day would cause it!"

He began to pace, then whirled again, projecting the full impact of his anger toward her. "I haven't the faintest how you faked virginity, but if I'd had my wits about me, you'd not have fooled me then!"

She lowered her wet-eyed gaze to her lap. "I never tricked you, Sean. Never, not once! I really believed—"

"Don't you cry, Laura! Don't you dare. You have money. Your parents are here. Just get the hell out and go find them! I don't ever want to see you again."

Her chin came up with a snap and she stared directly into

his eyes. "Fine," she said in a tight voice. She sat up and slid her legs over the side of the bed.

Sean quickly looked away from the smooth ivory limbs he had taken such pleasure from mere hours ago. "I'm leaving for one hour. Be gone when I get back," he ordered. Before she could reply, he strode through the door and slammed it so hard a hinge came loose.

Laura stared at the door. For a long moment she sat in shocked silence, unable to move. Emotions careened inside her, struggling to separate themselves. Absolute relief that she wouldn't suffer an early death. Anger at herself for jumping to such a ridiculous conclusion after eavesdropping. Awe that a child grew inside her and she hadn't once suspected. Red-hot fury that its father would suspect her of such a foul deception. After a few moments, the fury won hands down.

Laura snatched up the traveling case Valentin had brought from the hotel containing Sean's clothing. She dumped the few articles he had left inside it onto the floor, scattered them with a kick and began filling the case with her own belongings.

She hadn't much to pack, one change of borrowed clothes and a few toiletries. Huffing and cursing under her breath, Laura pulled on the same things she had worn last night and ran a brush through her hair. Sean's brush, she noticed, and flung it against the wall.

Tears ran down her cheeks and she swiped them away with the back of her hand. "I won't cry over you, you rotten scoundrel," she growled with a determined sniff. "Stupid, cork-brained idiot!" Her shoelace broke as she yanked it. "Pompous foul-minded fart!" She sniffed again, her rage doubling. "High-handed beast! Who needs you anyway?"

With a groan of frustration, she slammed the gaping suitcase shut, stalked out of the room and down the stairs.

When she opened the door to the street, Sean stood there

blocking her way. He wrestled the bag from her and pushed her back inside. "You can't go," he said.

For a moment, her heart fluttered with relief. Then she noticed that nothing had really changed. His scowl looked every bit as hostile as when he'd stormed out not a quarter hour past.

Laura scooted around him and headed outside. "Just watch me, you wretched bully!" His hand closed on the back of her blouse and her feet nearly left the floor when he jerked her back.

"Sit down!" he thundered, and proceeded to back her toward the stairs. She plopped down onto the second step. "Read this," he ordered, and threw a wadded paper into her lap.

Laura had to squint to make out the words in the dim light. When the message registered, she gasped and looked up. "Me? He wants to…to kill me first?" Her voice squeaked and she shuddered.

"He's found us. We'll have to leave immediately." Sean refused to look at her now. His body visibly quivered with suppressed rage.

"But…but where will we go?"

"To England. I'll have to find a place to hide you while I discover who's behind all this. I should have done so by now, and would if I hadn't been so concerned about my poor, dying wife!"

"You would leave me somewhere? Alone?" she asked in a near whisper, huddling her knees to her chest and grasping the dreadful paper in her fist.

He blew out a harsh breath and pinned her with a hateful glare. "Dear heart, I'd leave you on the street outside if someone wasn't after your hide! But I won't have your death on my conscience. As soon as I find this madman and deal with him, you and your little surprise package are on your own."

Laura reached out. "Sean, the baby is—"

"*Not* mine," he finished emphatically, and leaned down to

grab her elbow. She managed to get her feet under her as he pulled her up. "And don't mention the little mistake again if you know what's good for you. I don't relish a reminder of my stupidity every time you open your lying mouth. You have my protection for the duration of this situation, and that is all you're going to get."

She jerked her arm out of his grip. "I don't want your protection or anything else from you. I'll go to my parents, thank you very much." Again she tried for the door.

Again he snatched her back. "Don't be a worse fool! Middlebrook may be the one who wants us dead. Suppose your sainted brother *did* read your diary. Suppose he wired your stepfather what you planned to do. In that case, all of the notes could have come from him. He admits he wants your inheritance for his son."

"I don't need the money!" she shouted.

"You'll change your mind quickly enough when you don't have any," he shouted. "Believe me, I know! When you're out in the cold with that little bastard depending on you, you'll welcome every tuppence you can lay your hands on! When creditors start beating down your door demanding last month's rent. When your friends drop away like dead leaves off a tree, fearing you'll ask a handout. When your clothes grow threadbare and the nappies run out. Yes, you'd see then how handy a bit of blunt can be. I almost wish it on you since you're so goddamned hungry for adventure. How would you like to feel real hunger, Laura? How would you like to hear a stomach rumble with lack of food? A stomach you are directly responsible for filling? It's a thousand times worse than your own pangs, I can assure you!"

He turned away so quickly she almost missed the anguish that flashed through his outrage. Sean had known the life he described. A frisson of compassion and understanding rippled through her, dislodging her fury for a moment.

"It's all yours, anyway. I promised you the money if you married me," she said quietly.

His eyes met hers and his lips drew tight. When he did speak, his voice was soft. "That's right, so you did. If I denounced you, divorced you and cited my reasons, that loving family of yours would have no cause to welcome you back. You'd have nothing." Would he really do that to her? The thought chilled her blood.

"I would have my child and the hope of a long life," she stated evenly. "That's more than I had when we began this farce."

"You had both before we *began this farce* and well you know it." He snatched up the lightly packed travel bag. "Now, stay here while I get my things."

Fear generated by the threatening letter prompted her compliance. Laura tamped down her ire with the realization that Sean might prove her only protection. At least he didn't want her dead. Much as she hated the thought, she certainly couldn't say the same for her stepfather.

The picture Sean painted of her future looked bleak, indeed. She would be cast out on her own without funds to support her. There would be a baby to raise and educate. Public censure resulting from a divorce would hamper her ability to gain employment. What would she do?

The logical part of her mind understood how Sean had misconstrued everything. That did not nullify her anger or exasperation, but it did justify his a little. Perhaps once he calmed down, he would regain his rationality. He was basically kind. Maybe she could propose a compromise of sorts. But she doubted she would ever convince him he had fathered this child.

When he returned with the now bulging suitcase, he jerked

open the door and ushered her out. She started to speak but he silenced her the moment she opened her mouth.

"Hush! If you're wise, you'll keep that tongue between your teeth. Your untimely death is still a grave possibility, but it won't be at my hands unless you continue to provoke me."

Laura didn't doubt it for a moment. She accompanied him down the street where he hailed a passing hack. All the way to the Gare du Nord he stared at the passing scenery while she ruminated over her dilemma. No words passed between them as he bought tickets and settled them on the train that would carry them to the coast.

Once aboard, she turned her face to the window and ignored Sean's silent wrath. Just outside, a couple hugged a goodbye and parted at the last possible moment. Laura bit her lips together in empathy as the woman burst into tears at being left behind.

A tall, bearded man dashed after the train just as it picked up speed. Too late, she thought when he slammed his hat on the ground. Everybody had problems today. She only wished her own as trivial as missing a train.

Paris—its centuries-old grandeur layered with dirt and pigeon droppings, stinking of poor sewerage, mildew and unwashed bodies—rolled by the window, passing into the faded, mottled gold of the late autumn countryside.

The sparkle of France had dimmed completely, and England seemed a world away. If she had learned anything at all during this misbegotten adventure, it was to live for the present. But she had a future now, and that must be considered. Perhaps by the time they reached England, Sean would be ready to listen to reason.

Chapter Ten

〜∞〜

Waves heaved the ship in an undulating dance that had even Sean gripping the rail. He worried in spite of himself about the trip's effect on Laura. Seclusion in that cubbyhole of a cabin, and probably retching her insides out, couldn't be good for her in her condition. Still, topside would be worse, he thought as he pushed away and headed inside. Maybe he would just check to see if she needed anything. Dressed as she was, none of the other passengers would care whether she lived or died.

He shouldn't have brought her aboard looking like a doxy off a dance hall stage. Why hadn't he requested that Valentin's friend sneak at least one of Laura's dresses out of the hotel as she had done with his clothes? Well, what was done, was done. There's no way he could have guessed they would be forced to flee on the instant. Laura would simply have to make do until they reached Dover. Served her right.

She moaned as he opened the door. Curled in a ball, her knees to her chest, her body hardly took up a third of the tiny bunk. Pity swept him, more powerful than one of the cursed waves they rode. He noted no stench of sickness, but then she hadn't eaten anything since well before they left Paris. He couldn't even recall her taking a drink on the train. The little fool would suffer dehydration!

Sean rushed to her side and ran a hand over her shoulder and arm. "Laura, can you stomach a bit of water?"

Her tortured negative groan squeezed his heart. She dug her face into the mattress and trembled under his palm.

"We're almost there, you know? Less than an hour, I think. I have seen the Dover cliffs already."

No answer except another, more violent tremor.

He sat down on the bunk, scooped her into his arms and braced his back against the wall. "You're like ice. Here, I'll warm you. Try to relax and think of something pleasant."

She chuckled at that. Or sobbed. He couldn't tell. His arms tightened around her even as he cursed the compulsive protectiveness and frustration he felt. Why should he care so much? Why should he agonize with her? The little wretch had ruined his life, interrupted all his plans for the future and made him feel things he had sworn never to feel again.

He ought to dump her on this misbegotten excuse for a bed, go back up for fresh air and leave her to suffer. Instead, he brushed his chin over the mass of her tangled hair and inhaled her special scent.

"Try to sleep for a while," he said gruffly. "This will be over soon. Very soon now."

When they finally disembarked, Sean had to carry her ashore. Her weakness did not abate even after he had bedded her down in the nearest hotel and brought her food. He could see that her attempt to recover was genuine. She forced herself to eat and drink and then promptly lost it.

"Lord, what am I to do with you now? I should get a doctor again." He started for the door.

"No," she said quietly. "I will be fine. Just let me sleep for a while."

Sean nodded and watched her snuggle into the downy comforter. Maybe she was right. He decided to leave her to rest while he made arrangements for their trip inland. That shouldn't take above an hour and if she hadn't improved by then, he would summon a physician.

Laura seriously considered feigning sickness even after the horrible nausea abated. It would be dishonest, yes. But if it prevented Sean from returning to beastly behavior, it might be worth trying.

By the time he returned, however, she had decided not to settle for his temporary compassion. A pretense on her part now would make her almost as guilty as he believed her to be. They might as well get on with whatever he planned for them.

"Well, I see you're back from death's door. Yet again," he commented lazily, leaning back against her door. In the mirror, she watched his gaze travel over her.

Laura swiveled from the small vanity where she sat brushing her hair and faced him directly. "I should like some tea and a light meal. Then I wish to return to my brother at Midbrook Manor."

"What you wish means absolutely nothing to me," he said. "Your food will be up shortly, however. I took the liberty of ordering for you. I felt certain you would recover whenever it suited you."

He had looked in on her once since they'd arrived at the inn, noted curtly that her color had improved. Laura knew he had been drinking since then. She could smell the liquor, his voice sounded laconic, but he seemed sober. And quietly furious.

Perhaps if he became angry enough, he would send her to Lambdin. She badly needed to be away from Sean just now. At least until he came to his senses. "I suppose I should be happy that you haven't decided to starve me. Or your child," she added to provoke him.

"If you possess one whit of self-preservation, Laura, you will refrain from mentioning your bastard in my presence. I'll not tell you again!" He had raised his voice, but not by much.

"Are you threatening me, Sean?"

He sighed. "For all you have visited on me, lady, I could set you on the street without a farthing. I am tempted, so you had better pray that I don't."

"Why? Is that what happened to your mother?" she asked, resorting to outright cruelty, hoping to make him see how heartless he had become.

The green gaze darted away for a moment. His lips tightened to a thin line and he exhaled sharply. When he looked at her again, he seemed thoughtful. And so sad. "Yes," he said, "that is exactly what happened."

Laura wished she had not asked. Small wonder. She'd had no right to dredge up what must have been horrible times for him. "I'm sorry," she muttered. And she truly was.

"Are you now? Perhaps, I'll tell you the story. Show you just what you and your little baggage might have had to look forward to were I a lesser man. Want to hear it?"

"No," she said. Pleaded, really.

Someone knocked on the door.

"Put the tray outside and go away!" he ordered in a sharp voice.

His parody of a smile made her shiver. "Now then, where were we? At the beginning, I believe."

Laura watched him draw a deep breath. His tone became conversational but with a strong undercurrent of bitterness. "My mother was sixteen when a baron's second son seduced her. You know, one of the fellows who inherit nothing but the family charm? My grandfather put an end to the affair and sent him packing. Afterward, she traveled unescorted to the young lord's flat in London to present him with the exciting news of

OFFICIAL OPINION POLL

ANSWER 3 QUESTIONS AND WE'LL SEND YOU
2 FREE BOOKS AND A FREE GIFT!

0074823 ||||█||█|||| ||||█||| ||||█||| FREE GIFT CLAIM # 3953

YOUR OPINION COUNTS!

Please tick TRUE or FALSE below to express your opinion about the following statements:

Q1 Do you believe in "true love"?

"TRUE LOVE HAPPENS ONLY ONCE IN A LIFETIME."
- ○ TRUE
- ○ FALSE

Q2 Do you think marriage has any value in today's world?

"YOU CAN BE TOTALLY COMMITTED TO SOMEONE WITHOUT BEING MARRIED."
- ○ TRUE
- ○ FALSE

Q3 What kind of books do you enjoy?

"A GREAT NOVEL MUST HAVE A HAPPY ENDING."
- ○ TRUE
- ○ FALSE

YES, I have scratched the area below.

Please send me the 2 **FREE BOOKS** and **FREE GIFT** for which I qualify. I understand I am under no obligation to purchase any books, as explained on the back of this card.

H8GI

Mrs/Miss/Ms/Mr _____ Initials _____

BLOCK CAPITALS PLEASE

Surname _____

Address _____

_____

Postcode _____

DETACH AND POST CARD TODAY!

The Reader Service™ — Here's how it works:

NO STAMP
NEEDED!

THE READER SERVICE™
FREE BOOK OFFER
FREEPOST CN81
CROYDON
CR9 3WZ

If offer card is missing write to: The Reader Service, PO Box 676, Richmond, TW9 1WU

NO STAMP
NECESSARY
IF POSTED IN
THE U.K. OR N.I.

my impending arrival." Sean strolled across the room and stood by the window, looking out at the heavy fog. "He was already betrothed. Laughed and told her to go home."

"Did she?" Laura asked, curious in spite of herself.

"My grandfather was a peer. He would not have had her back in her condition. She knew that. So she panicked and ran. Ran and ran until she could run no more," he said, his voice grown soft and melancholy.

Laura knew Sean had forgotten her presence entirely. He was seeing that sixteen-year-old whose life his conception had ruined. Her heart went out to him, even though she knew he would never welcome her sympathy.

"Two women from Ruffles House rescued her," he continued. "Their madam took pity on her for a while, let her sew and clean for the women. Saved by her needle, she used to say. Humph. Then I came along. Darling of the ladybirds. Named *Sean* for a strapping Irishman who was Madam's favorite lay, and *Wilder*...well, just because they figured that I might be a wilder sort someday. Mother stuck in the *Cavendish* to remind her of home."

For a long time he stood silent. Laura had decided that was all he would say, when he turned all of a sudden. "But that's neither here nor there, now is it? You want to know what really happened! Of course you do. Everyone in London wants to know. They speculate like playwrights, and I let them. I even add a line or two when it suits me. But you, sweet lying wife of mine, get the true story! The blood and guts of my early existence, so you will know what you and yours might face should you find yourself alone."

Laura tried to stop him then. "Sean, please don't. This isn't necessary."

"Oh yes, yes it is. I had to earn my keep as soon as I was old enough. Your little beggar would have to learn quickly,

too, if we were to part company." He stopped to light a
cheroot, something he seldom did in her presence, and never
before without asking permission. An insulting stream of
smoke enveloped her. She swallowed a sickness only half-
related to the acrid cloud.

"I walked the gents' horses while they dallied, ran
messages for the girls, listened at their doors for sounds of
trouble, and summoned Big Jack to stop it when there was.
Lifted a few purses. Placed bets. Spied. Informed. Danced and
sang. Anything for a coin.

"That was the life I led. Until one night Madam decided
to diversify. This new customer came in, very wealthy and
with, shall we say, eclectic tastes? She offered him me. Only
not just for the night. She sold me outright." Sean smiled
again, that terrible, icy expression. "So, you see, you are not
the original owner, I have been purchased before."

Laura gasped. "No! He didn't…?"

"No, he didn't, as a matter of fact. But not for lack of
effort, I assure you. He knocked me senseless and then took
me home with him to play."

"Oh, Sean! What did you do?" Laura asked, hurting for
him even now. She stood and started to go to him. More than
anything, she wanted to take him in her arms and make his
past retreat. He stopped her with a look of warning.

"When he bent down to remove his boots, I coshed him over
the head with a decanter full of whiskey," he said, throwing his
cheroot on the hearth and crushing it with his shoe.

"You killed him?" she whispered, half disbelieving, half
hoping he had.

"No. Merely knocked him out as he had done to me." Sean
paced slowly then, not meeting her eyes, as he finished. "I
escaped and went back to my mother and she hid me."

"How…how old were you?" Laura asked.

"Ten. Mother wrote to my grandmother the next day and begged her mercy. We were in luck, Grandfather had died. She arrived within a week and took us away." He shook his head and clucked his tongue. "Unfortunately, your grandmother has passed on, hasn't she?" He cocked a burnished brow. "Who would rescue you, I wonder?"

Laura felt weak, shocked, but not really afraid. She knew Sean would never harm her physically. But she feared the coldness inside him had taken over completely. His anger at what he thought she had done may have destroyed any faith in humanity he had left. There remained little evidence of it now.

"Oh, I almost forgot!" he added with false cheerfulness. "My mother's lover, you recall I mentioned the chap at the beginning?"

Laura simply nodded, afraid to hear it.

"Seems about eight years ago, some civic-minded citizen alerted all his investors to investigate possible fraud on his part. Pity. The rascal was forced to flee the country in all haste, without a pence to his name."

"You?"

He inclined his head and pursed his lips in a thoughtful attitude. "Well, patricide's a bit much, even for me. The punishment really should fit the crime, don't you think?"

"Why, Sean? Why are you telling me all this?"

The glittering eyes leveled on her and held her still. "Because I want you to understand exactly who you are dealing with, Laura. Forgiveness is foreign to me, especially for something of this magnitude."

"Did you relate all this to Ondine, Sean? Is that why she leapt to her death? For fear you would take revenge for her affair with your friend?" She almost believed it. How could she have loved this man? How could she love him still when he chilled her to the core?

"Perhaps she did," he said quietly. "At least she had the grace to feel guilty and admit what she had done. But I cannot expect that from you, can I?"

She returned his glare with one just as steady and placed both hands over her middle. "I told you the truth as I knew it when I sought you as a husband. Do your worst if you hate me so much, but this child I carry will still be yours, Sean. Nothing you can do or say will ever change that fact."

For a long moment, he stood there silently watching, waiting for her to look away. She never even blinked.

Finally he left her without another word. Only then did her knees give way.

He would never believe her. His eyes betrayed the cold certainty that she had tricked him. Would he truly turn her out to fend for herself and the child as his mother had been forced to do?

If he did, she could contact Lambdin and he would come for her. Sean surely knew that. But what if, aware of that option, he left her without enough coin to send word to Midbrook Manor? Abandoned in London, she could contact her grandmother's old solicitor, or the judge for that matter, and be rescued. But suppose Sean left her here in Dover, where she knew no one at all?

Suddenly panic made her rush to the door, to hurry after him and plead at least for fare to London. With her hand on the handle, she realized she had no idea where he might have gone. How long had she sat there on the floor, grasping at possible solutions? He could be in the next room or miles away already.

Laura opened the door anyway and spied the tray of covered dishes beside the wall where the maid had left it. She picked it up and carried it inside where she placed it on the rough-hewn table. She might as well make herself eat, she thought. This could very well be her last meal for a while.

If worse came to worst and he had left her here, she could always steal a horse. Turning thief certainly seemed preferable to wandering the streets until she faced Sean's mother's fate.

The chair in the corner of the inn's public room provided poor accommodation, but Sean doubted he would find comfort anywhere tonight.

He felt sick to his soul. Betrayed. No other person in the world could have hurt him as badly as Laura had done. How had he let himself completely abandon his guard that way? To tumble madly in love as though he had never found cause to do otherwise?

The first time, with Ondine, he could chalk it up to youth and inexperience with nice women. Ha! *Nice?* The lowest whore at Ruffles had more scruples than his two wives combined! With Laura, he had never even questioned whether she might be lying.

Those wide gray eyes projected such innocence, he had never suspected her scheme. Not once. And act? Lord, she had missed her calling. How many times had she brought tears to his eyes? Made him laugh with glee? Conjured up such bittersweet feelings that just the memory of them embarrassed the hell out of him. And, worst of all, she had made him pray! He, who had never even admitted there was a God, at least not one who paid any attention to him. Even now, if he thought there might be the smallest chance that she told the truth…

No, he must face the facts and God knew them as well as he did. Laura had undone him right and proper. She had even reduced him to threatening her, something he had not even done with Ondine. But he had let Laura think he had. Just to frighten her, to punish her.

He felt soul-sick that he had laid out his sorry life like a warning. *Here, but for the grace of Sean Wilder, go you!* He didn't want her to know all that about him. No matter what she had done, he would never consider for a moment putting her through what his mother had suffered. But hadn't he, then? Somewhere in the dark recesses of his mind, had he not wondered how she would survive it all?

Sean rubbed his hands over his face, scrubbing at eyes that felt gritty from lack of sleep. If he had any compassion at all, he would go back up those stairs and reassure Laura that he had only been ranting, wallowing in heartbreak and disappointment. He should tell her he meant none of it, so she would at least be able to sleep without worry. But how could he do that without admitting he still loved her in spite of everything? He couldn't.

Determined not to soften his stance one iota, Sean finally leaned forward on the table, rested his head on his hands and closed his eyes. *Let her worry. She deserved it.*

Tomorrow he would relent, if she would simply admit what she had done. That's all she had to do, confess her guilt and apologize. He would insist on that. Then he would suggest they begin again and try to work something out between them. Her child would be a problem. Maybe he could bring himself to accept it eventually. Maybe he would even forgive her. But only if she showed a bit of contrition. Only then.

"*Mon ami?* Wild man!" a voice urged playfully as a hand pounded his shoulder. Sean struggled to force his eyes open, knowing very well who he would see when he did.

"Camp? Where the hell did you come from?" As much as he needed a friend right now, the fact that Camp had found them so easily worried Sean. "I hope this meeting is coincidental."

Campion grinned, beckoning the recently arrived barkeep to the table. "Two coffees, my good man. With sugar. Have you any of those, ah—" he made a little circling gesture with one hand "—those little flat things? Ah, biscuits. I have been away too long, eh?" He reached to pound Sean again.

"Will you kindly stop your assault and tell me what you're doing here?"

"Why, I brought the remainder of your things from the Lenoir, of course. I returned with them to your *atelier,* but you were gone when I arrived. Did you realize you left that lovely little portrait of Laura behind? I brought it with me as well, by the way." He held up a hand to forestall Sean's intended reprimand. "Be still! No one followed. I made certain of it. As I was saying, I collected your things—after all, your Laura looked in dire need of apparel—and when I found you gone, I surmised that trouble must have found you again. Not difficult to deduce that you would return home. I sent Lisette on alone to Cannes and followed you. There you have it. Ah, here is the coffee! Pay the man, would you?"

Sean dug a few coins out of his pocket and tossed them onto the table. When they were alone again, he leaned forward over his cup, inhaling the strong scent before speaking. "Camp, I can't be responsible for you, too. Someone is after us, determined to kill Laura first and then finish what he started with me. Now you take the next crossing back to your pretty wife and stay safe. I promise to visit when this is all straightened out."

"Lisette is not my wife," he admitted with a shrug. "But I will grant you she is pretty. A bit feather-witted, but that has its advantages, *non?*"

"I'll drink to that," Sean said dryly, wishing Laura were not so damned canny. He downed his coffee all at once and set the cup down with a thunk. "What were you doing in Paris in the first place?"

"Well, I gave up my practice in Lyons and decided last month to return to Paris. I missed it. Good thing for you, is it not? Fate has a way—"

"Camp, go home. I don't need you to watch my back."

"*Bien,* I shall watch Laura's back. It is a much nicer back, I might add," he said with a mock leer, "and I have seen them both."

"I can't get rid of you, can I?" Sean asked wearily, rubbing his aching brow.

"No, I expect not. I owe you a great favor, Sean. Allow me to repay it, will you?"

Sean rolled his eyes and sighed. "For God's sake, Camp. You could hardly stand there with a bullet in your leg. All I did was haul you away when the damned Dervishes broke through the line. Any man next to you might have done the same. That young Chadwick, the lad who covered the both of us to the rear guard. Now there's the bloke you should find and repay. Met him in London recently, quite by chance. I'll give you his direction and you can go and devil *him.*"

"Eventually. But for now, you are the object of my affection, like it or not!"

Sean hauled himself up. "I suppose I've no choice in the matter. Let's roust Laura out of her comfy bed and begone from here. If you found us so quickly, who knows how close on our heels the danger might be. I'll explain the situation later."

Campion shot him a wicked grin. "Will you also explain what you were doing out of her comfy bed and snoring on that table there?"

"Not on pain of death," Sean said darkly. "And if you ask Laura about it, I will do you worse than those Dervishes might have done."

"At least tell me where we are going!" Laura demanded as Sean hurried her into the hired coach. When he didn't answer, she asked his friend. "Dr. Campion?" He only shrugged and smiled.

As soon as she was settled and the luggage loaded, they climbed in behind her. Sean took a seat beside her, putting as much space as possible between them, and the doctor sat on the seat opposite. He looked curiously from one to the other of them as though he expected the answer to a question he hadn't asked. Silence reigned.

Laura couldn't stand it another moment. "Have you business in England, Dr. Campion?"

"Oh, do call me Camp. May I call you Laura? I know I should wait to be invited to do so, but we are already familiar." Laura gasped. Was he referring to his examination of her? If so, his crudeness surpassed even Sean's.

He must have guessed her thoughts. "I meant that your husband is my best friend, *chérie*. That alone breeds familiarity."

"And familiarity breeds contempt. Trust me," Sean mumbled, keeping his gaze trained out the window.

They both stared at him and then at each other. Laura noted Camp's barely suppressed grin. Then he winked and said in a loud stage whisper, "Sleeping on tables does this to him."

Delighted to discover that Sean had spent an even more uncomfortable night than she had, Laura replied, "A medical opinion, sir?"

"Only an observation. Does he indulge in the habit often?"

"Not to my knowledge. Though I do recall his reclining on the floor once for the better part of a night. However, that seemed to improve his mood considerably." Laura risked a glance at Sean, who remained impervious to her outrageous reminder of their lovemaking.

The doctor stifled his laugh with a cough. She smiled at him simply because she liked Campion. He always seemed in good humor, as were most of the Parisians she had met. She knew he'd been educated in England, since Sean said they had attended school together. His French accent was negligible unless he chose to emphasize it, which he usually did while flirting. As he certainly was doing at the moment.

"You do seem in excellent form this morning, *chérie.* But then you did say you have been fine since we found you to be *enceinté.*"

"She lies. She nearly expired during the crossing," Sean growled, still not deigning to look at either one of them.

Campion nodded, all sympathy. "Ah. Some people are disposed to suffer *mal de mer.* I expect your condition exacerbated it, *non?*"

Laura agreed, feeling rather green at the mere mention of her sickness. "It did seem worse this trip."

Sean grunted with ill-concealed disgust and they all fell silent. The carriage rattled along at top speed, its motion shifting her to and fro. A sudden bump in the road bounced her clear of the seat. Sean's arms caught her fast and lifted her into his lap.

His voice rang rough against her ear. "Damn! We should've taken the rail. This can't be good for her." Laura soaked up his concern. He cared. In spite of all he had said, he did care for her.

Campion rapped on the ceiling of the coach and stuck his head out the window. "Slow the thing down!" he yelled. When he resumed his seat, he offered Laura a smug and endearing half smile as if he had read her mind. Had Sean told him everything? If so, Campion had apparently decided to champion her cause. Maybe with an ally, especially a physician, she might eventually convince Sean to believe her.

The hope continued to grow when Sean still held her, even after the road smoothed out and the coach assumed a calmer pace.

"That's so much better," she remarked. "Will you be traveling with us for a while, sir?" she asked, trying to prevent her desperation showing.

"*Mais oui!* My one goal in life is your continued good health."

"Cease trifling, Camp. Now!" Sean ordered, his face stern and his voice gruff.

"Well, if you insist." The doctor settled in the corner of the coach and pulled his hat down over his eyes. "Do let me know if you get tired, old son, and I'll hold her for a while."

Sean's growl, barely audible over the coach's rumble, vibrated through Laura like an inner caress. She buried her nose in his lapel and smiled. No longer did she fear abandonment.

Chapter Eleven

Sean had abandoned her! Laura gripped the borrowed bed robe together across her breasts as she stared out the third-floor window. Sean, mounted on a huge black horse, thundered across the small bridge at the end of the drive. When she could no longer see him, Laura let the curtain drop and returned to the bed. At least he hadn't left her penniless on the streets of Dover.

When they had arrived at this place late in the night, she had not awakened enough to notice it properly. It appeared to be a rather grand country house. The room where Sean left her was very well appointed, indeed.

The maid who had attended her the night before had not returned this morning. Instead, Sean had arrived to shake her awake just after dawn.

"You are to stay here," he had ordered in a clipped voice.

"Where are you going?" she asked.

"London. Golfindle House is the safest place I can think to leave you. Blake Tyndale is still in the city. I shall speak to him as soon as I arrive and advise him that we are imposing on his hospitality."

Laura protested. "But Sean, we can't just come here without invitation! What are you thinking? The owner is a peer?"

"I know him well or I wouldn't presume a welcome. He won't mind at all. That's not your concern anyway. Just remain here and keep to your room. If there are visitors—and I mean anyone who arrives—you are to lock this door and answer to no one but Camp. I'm leaving him here to guard you."

"Guard me! Are you saying that I'm a prisoner?"

He groaned. "No, of course not! Remember the note we received? Whoever wrote it has probably followed us from France. He is planning to kill you first, in the event you forgot. Now stay put and do not argue about this."

"But why are you leaving?"

"To deliver the Rembrandt to Burton and then visit the Yard. Maybe the record of arrests there will give me some idea of who our pursuer might be."

"Please, Sean, take me with you."

Though he had shown a measure of gruff kindness during the crossing and the day before in the coach, Laura could see that Sean's hurt and anger had not abated. How could she ever convince him of her truthfulness if they were not together?

"I do not want you with me," he'd said in a flat voice that belied the stormy expression in his eyes. With no elaboration, he had abruptly turned and exited the room.

Now, not ten minutes later, Laura watched him ride away with no idea when, or even if, he would return for her.

Well, of course he would come back, she chided herself. He couldn't simply leave his own wife in a stranger's house and forget she existed. And he had assured her that Campion remained here. To guard her, as he'd put it. As much as she liked the man, Laura had no inclination to accept the good doctor or anyone else as her watchdog.

It would take awhile for Sean's note writer to discover

their absence from Paris. Who knew how long it would take him to find out where they had gone from there? Highly unlikely that he would be after them this quickly. Renaudin would never give them away and he was the only one who knew that they had returned to England. She was safe enough in that respect and Sean knew it as well as she. The only reason he had left her here was to punish her.

She would do as she pleased. Dr. Campion wouldn't stop her. She would borrow a horse and follow Sean to London. They would never settle things between them if they were apart.

Laura found her cases that Camp had brought from the Hotel Lenoir and shook the wrinkles out of her riding habit. No time for neatness, she thought as she slipped it on. If she hurried, and Sean was not riding hell-bent, she might catch up to him.

Campion stopped her in the hall. "Laura, you cannot go out."

"Watch me," she replied and pushed right past him.

"No! Sean says you must remain here. The danger is great, *mignonne.*"

"Save your pretty French. The danger is nonexistent at present and you very well know it. Now leave me alone. I want to catch Sean before—"

His long, slender hands gripped her upper arms and guided her forcibly into a small parlor. He pushed her down onto a brocade settee and stood over her like a schoolmaster. "Listen to me! You must stay where your husband put you!"

"Sean is only after retribution. He's not afraid for me! He only wants me to sit here and worry about what he plans to do with me. I have to go to him and try to make him understand that I didn't lie. Don't you see?"

Campion sank down beside her on the settee and gripped her hands in his. Laura felt the act was more to restrain her than to offer comfort. He verified it. "I see quite well. He told me after we arrived last night all that you have done. Sean does not want you in London, therefore you will not go."

When she lifted her chin to argue, he shook his head and continued, "It is true, he does not believe what you say, but he does fear for your life. Why else would he charge me to keep you safe?"

Laura looked deeply into his clear brown eyes and noted the mistrust, and the distaste, which had not been there yesterday. "You don't believe me, either, do you?" she asked.

"No, to be honest, I do not. How you ever convinced Sean is a mystery to me. An insect bite?" he scoffed. "A lingering death with no symptoms at all? There is none such. Still, Sean might have been flattered by your unusual ruse. That you would go to such a length to have him might have amused him, once he got past the anger. But, unfortunately, there is your pregnancy. Your attempt to pass off another man's child as his own, he will never forgive."

With a heaving sign of defeat, Laura nodded. "Very well." Campion allowed her to withdraw her hands from his grasp. "I suppose he will still see that as a lie, even if the child comes exactly nine months from our wedding night?"

Campion inclined his head in thought for a moment. "He might rethink things if by chance such happens. However, he must know—and if he does not, be assured I shall tell him—that firstborn children frequently arrive a few weeks early. I should not pin my hopes on that were I in your place."

Laura realized the futility of arguing her case with Sean's good friend. Of course, he would take Sean's part, and she did admire his loyalty. But they were buffleheads, the both of them.

So she was on her own. Nothing she could do would change things. Especially lounging about as an unwelcome guest in a stranger's home, waiting for Sean's promised retribution.

She rose and he followed her out of the parlor. "May I go to the library? Perhaps a book will help to pass the day."

"Certainly. Lord Tyndale should not mind if you avail yourself. If you wish breakfast, it is laid in the dining room, just there." He pointed toward a door down the hall.

"Thank you, Dr. Campion," she said, assuming her most formal tone and manner. "You are too kind."

"Not at all," he murmured.

Laura agreed. She moved slowly down the hall to the dining room, turning as she went in so that she could judge Campion's destination. *Up the stairs.* Well, he might not be so kind, but he certainly was accommodating. And stupid, as well, if he thought she meant to stay here. She hurried back to the parlor with its floor length windows and quickly slipped outside.

The stables weren't hard to find, and were luckily unattended at the moment. There were only three horses. Presumably this Lord Tyndale had most of his cattle in London with him. She chose a small mare who looked rather sturdy and quickly located a sidesaddle and tack.

Laura led the saddled animal out the back toward the pasture, keeping the stables between herself and the house. She paused a moment to think and glance up at the morning sun. If Sean had been riding toward London, then this place lay west of it. She must ride northeast to Midbrook Manor.

But did she really want to go there? Now that she no longer took life for granted, could she submit to the mundane existence she had endured for the past twenty-five years?

Laura now knew her stepfather must be behind the discouragement of her former suitors. Not that she would marry again even if Sean divorced her, but the thought of Mr. Williams turning away all future possibilities made her livid.

Lambdin would welcome her home, she knew, but he would soon marry Jillian Fortesque. Midbrook Manor would have a new lady of the house. Where would that leave her? A poor relation, of course, now that Sean owned every pound her grandmother had left her. Laura had no desire to languish as a poor, cast-off relation with a child on the way, a subject of scorn and ridicule.

In view of that circumstance, her old home held very little appeal, especially now that she had experienced life away from it. And going there would be a cowardly thing to do, wouldn't it? Running away. No, she decided, she could not return there. Not yet. Not while the smallest chance remained that she could make things right with Sean. London, it was, then.

But how far must she go to reach it? Sean had carried no valise with him for an overnight stop, therefore the city must be within a day's ride. She should have taken a moment to look for maps in the library. That had been her purpose in asking if she might visit it. However, another opportunity to escape might not have presented itself. As it was, she might hope for an hours-long head start before Campion realized she was gone.

With that reassuring thought, Laura urged the mare to a trot, making a wide circle around the grounds within the tree line so she would not be spotted from the windows. When she reached the road Sean had taken earlier, Laura clicked the mare to a gallop, putting Golfindle House and her watchdog behind her.

Taking charge of her life this way restored her courage and her hopes. Somehow, she would make Sean listen, listen and believe her. She needed him and he needed her, whether he realized it or not. There had to be a way to salvage all that they had found together. The alternative did not bear thinking about.

"What the devil do you mean, she's missing!" Sean leapt to his feet and rushed around his desk. He grabbed Campion by the front of his coat and shook him. Just as quickly, he let go and began to pace, ramming one fist into his other palm. He kicked aside a small rubbish bin that stood in his way. "Damn it, Camp! He's got her. Perhaps she's already—"

Campion leaned over to catch up the rolling bin and set it right. "No one has her, Sean. She took a mare from Tyndale's stable and ran away. I should have guessed she would try something such as that. Devious little witch! She turned up meek as any lamb when she came downstairs this morning. I thought her resigned to staying. The moment I discovered her gone, I came directly here to London."

Sean pinned him with a menacing look. He wanted to knock his teeth down his throat. "What time did she leave?"

Camp chewed his lip for a moment, thinking. "That is part of the problem. You see, I did not miss her until time for luncheon. The maid took her a tray and then could not find her. Laura might have left anytime after we spoke, which was shortly after you departed."

"Did you look for tracks to determine her direction?"

"Why should I? She intended to follow you to London, or that is what she said when she came downstairs. Of course I refused to allow it. Later, when we discovered her gone and the mount missing, I logically assumed she had come after you."

Camp slumped down into one of Sean's armchairs. "She was nowhere along the way. Once I arrived, it took me awhile to locate your office. I had to ask directions, since you had only mentioned it to me in passing. I stopped first at Scotland Yard and then the National Gallery to see if she'd been there looking for you and no one at either place had seen her. I had truly hoped to find her here with you."

"You don't see her, do you?" Sean thundered. He took a deep breath, fighting to regain his calm. But he hadn't experienced calm in so long, he feared he wouldn't recognize it if he did find it. "Think!" he ordered himself. "Where the devil would she go?"

In spite of what Camp had said about her intentions, Sean did not believe Laura would seek him out. Not after he had told her he didn't want her. And to think, he had faulted her for lying. He wanted her more than his next breath.

Pride had forced him to postpone his plans to offer her another chance. He could not bring himself do that yet. "She practically begged to come with me. Why? To what purpose?"

"Be damned if I know," Camp answered, alerting Sean to the fact that he had spoken his thoughts aloud. "Most women caught in such lies would simply take their leave and search for another mark. Perhaps she has done so."

"I am not a *mark!*" Sean declared.

Camp laughed bitterly. "*Non?* She wears your ring, my friend. She wears your name! You treated her to Paris, city of love and light. She spent your money. Enjoys your protection. Tell me again that you are no mark!"

"Some protection, when I don't even know her whereabouts! And the name's certainly nothing to brag about. She is no opportunist. Laura has her own money." But she could not get it, he recalled. It was now *his* money, and he had been quick to tell her so.

"She bought the ring herself." How much could she get for it if she found herself without funds, he wondered. The little fool had no means to travel. What had she been thinking?

"Well, then," Camp said pleasantly, as though nothing at all were wrong. "What's the worry? You obviously wanted rid of her. Now she has gone. *Voilà!* Your problem is solved."

"She is in danger, you idiot. Have you forgotten someone is out to kill her in order to punish me?"

"Well, if we cannot find her, neither can he."

Sean prayed Camp had the right of it. Ah damn, now he found himself praying again. He blew out a harsh breath and gave his head a shake. He needed help with this. "I'm going back to the Yard," he announced. "You coming?"

Sean knew that Camp felt guilty that he had carelessly trusted Laura. That innocent look had fooled everyone. He would have to watch that in the future. If, indeed, they had a future.

Since they had both stabled their horses for the evening, Sean hailed a hansom and they headed toward Trafalgar Square. Maybe the chief inspector would help him organize a search for Laura. MacLinden had always had a soft spot for him, even when Sean had been a little street urchin deviling Lindy on the Whitechapel beat.

He pulled out his watch, checked the time and frowned. "He probably won't be there this late. We'll try his home."

As it happened, MacLinden was not there, either. A red-haired youngster greeted them at the door and advised Sean that the inspector had gone to Havington House for a musical evening.

"You can catch him there, sir, if it's important," the lad offered. "He's gone to hear Gran play and my da sing."

Sean smiled and thanked the boy who looked so much like his grandfather. The little fellow must be the same babe old Lindy had bragged about just before Sean resigned from the Yard.

"Thank you, Tobias. If I miss finding him there, would you tell him that Sean Wilder called?"

The boy's eyes grew wide and his mouth made a perfect *O*. "Cor, *the wild one!*" he said under his breath.

Sean laughed. His reputation had filtered down to this generation already, eh? Well, it was good for business, he supposed. He thanked the little carrot-topped fellow and said goodbye.

After hurrying down the steps of the MacLinden's modest town house, Sean climbed into the waiting coach. It was time to call in a few favors, he decided. And this couldn't wait until morning. Even now, Laura might be wandering, lost and afraid, somewhere between Golfindle House and the city. He needed help to find her.

The gathering inside the Havington mansion sounded lively when Sean and Campion arrived. Since they hadn't an invitation, the butler ushered them into a small parlor near the entrance to wait while he summoned MacLinden.

Sean sneaked a glimpse of evening finery at the end of the hallway where the double doors to the ballroom stood open. He had been here before, of course, when he had escorted his former fiancée, Camilla Norton, to the fete celebrating the Earl of Lyham's marriage to her old school chum.

Sean did not miss the pomp of these affairs any more than he missed the social-climbing Camilla. He could not imagine why he had ever desired attending either one.

"Inspector MacLinden will be with you shortly, sir," the butler whispered. "Mrs. MacLinden is to perform in just a moment. Shall I leave the door ajar? She is quite wonderful to hear."

Sean nodded. Camp fiddled impatiently with his hat.

In the next few minutes, Sean could not credit what happened to him. Music never moved him, but the sounds emanating from the ballroom stirred his very soul. Visions of Laura grew more vivid than reality. His mind's eye saw her with the wind in her hair, her eyes alight as she ate strawberry ice, then laughing wildly as she danced cancan at L'Elysée. He pictured her in the throes of passion, totally abandoned to pleasure. The images changed with each measure played, and enveloped his senses to such a degree that he felt bereft when the music drew to a close. As though he had lost her somehow, which indeed he had.

A protracted sigh near at hand reminded him to breathe.

"Damn!" he mumbled, bewildered that he could be so affected by a mere song.

Camp offered much-needed sympathy. "Ah, Sean, I see by the pain on your face that you are a lost man, aren't you?"

"Yes," Sean admitted. "Apparently so."

They said nothing else, just stood there bemoaning Sean's fate. No listing of Laura's faults, or praise of her virtues would change a thing and they both knew it.

MacLinden joined them, beaming with pride over the extraordinary performance of his wife and son. Graying red hair and a slight paunch had not altered much the man he had once been. Sean treasured the stern affection MacLinden had offered him when he needed it so badly as a youngster. And the special attention later when he had come to the Yard as a recruit.

"Sean, lad! I wish I had known you were coming!" He shot Campion a curious look.

Sean shook off his melancholy. "Chief Inspector MacLinden, my friend, Dr. Eugene Campion." Without waiting for any further amenities, he hurried on. "I really need your help, Lindy. My wife is missing."

"Ah. You didn't mention a wife when we spoke earlier! I thought Miss Norton—"

"No, no. Not Camilla. I married Laura Middlebrook. You wouldn't know her. Remember the fellow I was searching the files for this morning? The one sending the notes? I'm afraid he might have caught up to us—to her, actually." He grasped MacLinden's arm. "Lindy, I'm desperate!"

"Then let's get on with it," the inspector said. "Allow me a moment to make my excuses and then we'll see what's what. I can round up about twenty lads who'll be glad for the extra duty. It will cost you," he warned.

"Money's no object," Sean assured him. "I just want my wife back. Alive."

* * *

Laura's borrowed mare pulled up lame just as she left the outskirts of a small village. It seemed she had been riding forever. If she hadn't taken that wrong turn just after noon, she might have reached the city by now. Heaving with exhaustion and frustration, she walked the animal back to the smithy shop she had passed. Cursing her luck wouldn't do, she knew. The situation definitely could have proved worse. At least she hadn't far to go to ascertain the problem.

"Good ev'n to ye, ma'am," the brawny smith said in greeting. Without bothering with the obvious question, he drew the mare forward into the lantern light and lifted a hind hoof. Drawing a pick from his pocket, he gouged at an embedded stone. "She could do with a bit o' rest, y'know," he said, patting the mount's hindquarter gently as he lowered the hoof. "By the looks of it, ye could do with the same."

"What is this place called?" she asked, ignoring his suggestion.

"Barnswallow, ma'am."

"How far to London?"

"Nigh on six leagues." The smithy nodded in the direction she'd been traveling. "Not so far."

Six leagues might have been six hundred, but she had no money for a room to rest even had there been a suitable inn nearby. "Could we beg a drink of water, my good man?"

"Aye," he assured her, smiling. He seemed a pleasant sort, much like the smithy in the village back home. A gentle giant with a kind voice. She dismounted, followed him to the shed and accepted the dipper full of cool water he offered. While she drank, he led the mare to the trough at the side of his building.

"'Tis full dark now. Oughtn't to be out," he said. When she did not comment, he offered, "Ye got trouble, ma'am, say th' word. I'll do what I can. Name's Owen Stod."

Laura smiled up at him. "Thank you, Mr. Stod. I do appreciate it. There's no trouble at all, but I must make London tonight."

He led the mare around in a wide circle, noting her gait. "She'll do, I'm thinking. But I don't like to see ye ridin' away this time o' night. Ain't safe."

"I will be fine," she said, hoping it was true. Surely she could make it six more leagues. "I hope you trust me, Mr. Stod. I shall send payment for this as soon as I reach my destination."

"Don't think of it, ma'am. My deed fer th' day and all that. Just you have a care, eh?"

"I shall," she told him as she mounted with his assistance. "And thank you again. Goodbye."

As she rode away, Laura felt better. There was at least one gentleman left in the world, if not according to his social designation, then certainly by his inborn manner. She had begun to doubt it was so.

A bright harvest moon relieved the darkness, and Laura had no difficulty finding her way. If not for her weariness and hunger, the ride would have been rather pleasant.

She realized how she had missed seeing the stars since she had left her home in the country. They had been visible over Paris, of course, but their brightness had been dimmed by the constant film of smoke that hovered above the city. London would be even worse. The little roan plodded on, thankfully without a limp now that the smithy had removed the offending stone from her shoe.

Suddenly the sound of pounding hooves behind Laura wrenched her attention away from the road ahead. She guided the mare aside to allow the hurrying rider full access to the roadway. Instead of passing, however, he pulled up beside her and snatched her reins away.

"Aha! Caught you," he crowed. "Tell me I ain't been

living right! You don't give a man much of a chase though, do you, lass?"

Her heart thundered so hard Laura thought she might faint. The very size of the man unnerved her. His features were not visible in the near darkness, but her imagination filled them in all too well. The voice sounded hard, cruel and pitiless. If he so much as scented her fear, she suspected he would strike like a snake. She struggled to stay rational. "Unhand this horse immediately!" she demanded.

"Or what, love? Will you deafen me with a scream? Scratch out my eyes," he taunted. With a lithe motion, he dismounted, leading his own mount and hers away from the road and into a copse of trees.

She didn't have to be a genius to figure what came next. Laura kicked free of her stirrup and slid to the ground at a run. Only his reluctance to let go of the horses gave her a head start. Her sturdy half boots ate up the ground at a pace that amazed even her. She headed for the roadway, knowing the packed smoothness of the ground would aid her speed.

He was a large man, too large to be very swift, she thought. The loud explosion took a moment to register. A gun! He had a gun and was shooting at her! The man from Paris! It must be!

Who else would want her dead? Not a highwayman. Were he that, he'd want her money, her horse or her virtue. Killing her wouldn't help one of that ilk. On and on she ran, a sharp pain in her side threatening to bend her double in the midst of the road. At any moment, she expected to feel a bullet tear through her body.

Laura tasted defeat, resisting it, willing it away. She could do this. She could outrun him. All the way to Barnswallow if need be.

Chapter Twelve

Sean allowed MacLinden to divide up the groups of searchers while he studied maps of London's surrounding roadways. He could see only three possible ways in which Laura might have gone off the main track from Golfindle House to London.

In little over an hour, all twenty of the men set out on hired mounts. He, MacLinden, Camp and two other fellows would follow the most direct route. The other three teams intended to split off the main party as they reached Laura's possible detours. Then they were all to meet at Golfindle once their searches were complete.

"I should have brought a coach," Sean remarked. He suffered a sudden vision of Laura lying cold and still beside some out-of-the-way ditch or hedgerow. "She might not be able to...if we find her, she may be—"

"We'll find her all right," MacLinden promised. "And I'm willing to bet she will sit a horse better than you do."

"Well, she would not need much proficiency to accomplish that!" Camp said with a wry chuckle. "Wild man here hates the beasts! Never could ride worth a damn."

The chief inspector laughed. Sean wondered if these two

were as absolutely unfeeling as they sounded, or if they were only trying to boost his wavering hope of finding Laura alive.

"Aye, I remember," MacLinden said. "We tried to put him on mounted patrol when he first came to the Yard. One of the least favorite moments of his brief career, I can tell you."

"Hell, I've already spent my entire morning on one of these knacker-baits," Sean grumbled. "If God meant us to have callused backsides, He would never have provided us the wheel!"

Camp tried to soothe him, "We can better cover the off-road areas with the horses. You agreed that we could."

"That only proves I'm not capable of rational thinking at this point. How the devil am I supposed to get Laura back to London if she's—"

"She is perfectly fine, Sean, I am certain. Comfortably tucked up at an inn somewhere enjoying her supper, no doubt. It is very probable that I passed right by her haven on the way," Camp said.

Sean did not reply. He knew Laura had no way to pay for an inn's comfort, or food or assistance if she needed it. Lack of proper transportation was the very least of his worries at the moment, but he could not give voice to the greatest of them. He stumbled over the very thought.

Before the roads forked, the entire search group reached Barnswallow village, a small burg of no consequence at all. Except that in passing through it, Sean noticed a crowd milling around the well-lighted smithy shop. "What do you suppose is going on there?" he asked MacLinden. "Let's stop and ask if these people might have seen…oh my God! There she is!"

Sean jerked his horse to a halt and leapt down. He tore into the midst of the villagers and grabbed Laura by the shoulders. "Where the hell have you been?"

Laura murmured something inaudible over the rumbling of the surrounding crowd.

Someone grasped Sean by the back of his coat and jerked him away from her. "You know this man, ma'am?"

"My husband," Laura answered.

"Damned right," Sean affirmed, "And just who the devil are you?" He whipped around, breaking the man's hold on his clothing.

If the giant answered, Sean didn't hear it. He now noticed the bloody body draped over the horse standing just beyond Laura's new protector.

MacLinden, ever the man in charge, stepped in and parted the crowd like a plow. "Chief Inspector, Scotland Yard. What's happened here?"

The villagers must have known very well that the Yard had no jurisdiction this far out. But no one looked inclined to question Lindy's authority. Having nearly a score of mounted horsemen behind him did not hurt MacLinden's case, Sean decided.

Laura's mammoth protector, obviously the smithy by his size and apparel, assumed the role of spokesman. "Name's Stod, sir. That bloke what's dead there be a highwayman. Set upon the young lady, sir," he said. "Tried to shoot 'er."

Sean moved to Laura's side and put his arm about her shoulders. She looked as though she needed support to remain standing. Then he noted the darker splotches on her skirts. *Blood?* "Are you injured, Laura?" He tipped up her chin to see her face in the lantern light. "Answer me! Did he hurt you?"

She shook her head. He felt her shudder and drew her closer, wrapping both arms around her. Her current scent of horse, sweat and lilacs provided a combination as divergent as his emotions. At once, he needed to upend her for a sound thrashing and comfort her tenderly as one might a panicked child. Would she even tell him if the worst had happened to her?

"Mr. Stod," Sean said, feeling profoundly grateful and

relieved, despite his warring inclinations, "if it was you who killed that miscreant, I'd like to thank you for saving my wife."

Stod shifted from one foot to the other and glanced warily at MacLinden before speaking. "The bloke rode by here soon after she left. Clear he was on th' chase. I thought she might be a runaway wife and he was after 'er. Didn't appear they matched up, if you take my meanin'. Him a rough lot, her a fancy. I thought I'd best see what was what."

"So you followed?" MacLinden asked. "The truth now, Mr. Stod, did you shoot him?"

"I met her hurryin' down the road afoot." Stod said, ignoring the question, his eyes trained on Laura. "If I was you, I'd set th' lass down somewhere afore she falls."

Sean immediately lifted Laura into his arms and sat down on the bench by the shop's opening, holding her on his lap. She felt tense as a coiled spring against him. And cold. Her forehead against his neck was like ice. Must be shock, he thought, considering the mildness of the evening.

"I did it," she announced in a loud clear voice. "Mr. Stod only found me and caught the horses. He didn't—"

"Shh, let him tell us. You don't have to," Sean murmured.

"But he did not kill the man," she insisted, pushing herself to a sitting position in his lap. She faced MacLinden as though he were judge and jury and about to order Stod hanged for murder. The villagers grew quiet, obviously spellbound by Laura's defense of their neighbor.

"I passed through here late," she said. "Mr. Stod warned me it wasn't safe to go on, but I did. I had to go on!" She turned her wide-eyed gaze on Sean. "Everything was fine. It wasn't so very dark. I wasn't afraid. Then he came riding up." She pointed at the body on the horse. "He snatched my reins and tried to make off with me, but I got down and ran. He shot at me. I heard it. I kept running as fast as I could."

She paused then and brushed a hand over her mouth. "He caught up." Sean felt the catch in her breath, a stifled sob. He clutched her tighter, cursing under his breath.

Laura continued. "He'd stuck the gun back through his belt. To free both his hands, I suppose. I felt it there," she said, one hand pressing to her middle. Her voice sounded strained, but somehow growing stronger with the telling, Sean thought.

"My hand was trapped between us," she explained. Another deep breath. "I got the hammer thing pulled back and found the trigger." She looked up, her eyes bright with tears, her lips trembling. "It pointed downward, Sean. I only thought to shoot him in the leg so I could get away. I didn't mean to kill him."

Sean slid his fingers through her hair and pressed her head to his chest. "I know. I know. It's all right, dearest."

He knew very well what Laura suffered. Taking a life, any life, for the first time, distressed even a grown man. He could just imagine what it did to a young woman. He recalled her shock when she had shot the man in Paris and thought him dead. Seeing this dead body, and knowing without doubt she had killed him had to be unnerving. Especially in one who had recently faced death herself. Then he remembered. She hadn't really faced death at all. Well, at least not until tonight.

For a moment, he had completely forgotten her lie. All he had recalled was her courage. Pretended courage. But she'd gone past pretending in this instance. She was falling apart and there was no one to put her back together but himself. The fact that he relished doing so angered him a little.

But what did her dishonesty matter when he had nearly lost her? Sean sighed and embraced her more fully, trying to shield her from the cooling night air and the colder waves of shock that permeated her small frame.

"Got him in the thigh. Bullet hit the artery," MacLinden declared. He and one of his off-duty officers had dragged the body from the horse and laid it out on the ground. "Bled to death right quickly, I should think."

"He could be the one," Laura said, drawing her head away from Sean's chest. "The one from Paris. The one I shot before."

Immediately Sean, Camp and MacLinden gave her their full attention. "Are you certain of that?" Sean asked.

Laura looked off into the night as though reconstructing the event.

Sean broke into her reverie, overly anxious to ensure that threat was behind them. "I was half blinded from the concussion and the blood, but you saw the man who came to our hotel room, Laura. Is this the same man?"

Slowly Laura pulled away from him, glanced quickly at the body and swallowed hard. Her voice dropped to a whisper. "I don't know. He…he's big. Dark beard. I never looked carefully at his face that day. It happened so quickly, all I could see was his hand pointing the gun at you."

Camp stepped closer to the body and peered down at it. He motioned to one of the villagers holding a lantern to come nearer. "This could very well be the same one. He was lying on his belly that day, and I only saw the side of his head. He is of the same size and coloring."

"His name is Simms," MacLinden said, motioning for two of the others to replace the body on the horse. "One of our old friends who did a year or so in Fleet. You recall him, Sean?"

Sean studied the bearded face, which wore the grimace with which it had greeted death. "One of my earlier arrests while I was still in uniform. Robbery down by Wonderland, wasn't it?" He almost never forgot a face. This one had aged and appeared almost unrecognizable with his heavy beard. Also, the scum looked a good stone heavier, but it was Simms all right.

"Sergeant Brogden brought him in again a few months

ago for a theft in Clapham Park, but there was not enough proof to hold him," Lindy said.

"He must be the one!" Laura exclaimed. "He did say something about a chase."

Camp nodded, toeing the corpse's foot with his boot. "Laura is right. Why else would he try to shoot her? Even if they intend to do away with their victims, wouldn't a simple highwayman usually fancy a bit of sport first?"

Sean glared. "Kindly keep such thoughts to yourself. Can't you see she's upset enough!" He cradled Laura closer.

"Oh. Right. Well, I expect you'd best get her somewhere more agreeable than a smithy's shop so she can recover," Camp advised, glancing at Stod. "Sorry, no offense."

"None taken," Stod muttered. Then he pushed past Camp and stood directly in front of Sean and Laura. "Lady, ye're welcome to stay and rest in my room fer the night. Ain't much to speak of, but it's clean enough." He glared at Sean with a threat in his eyes. "Yer husband can rest on the 'prentice's cot in the back. He 'pears to need a bit of coolin' down afore he sees to ye."

Sean tempered his outrage at Stod's presumptuousness only because the man had Laura's best interest in mind. "Kind of you, Stod, but I shall take her on home." He stood and lowered Laura to her feet. "Be assured, I shall keep her safe from here on."

Stod was a common smithy, a good man who had gone well out of his way to see to Laura's welfare. But common or not, Sean recognized a man secure in his own worth when he saw one. He grudgingly admitted that the fellow had cause to be proud of his looks, as well as his imposing size. That, however, was not what sparked his jealousy.

When questioned, Stod had not denied shooting Laura's attacker, and had been willing to take responsibility for the deed. The man had sought to spare Laura that. Sean felt guilty that he himself had not protected her better. Stod should never have had occasion to make such a gesture in the first place.

Guilt over that fact had somehow gotten tangled up with the jealousy. He hated that some handsome, anvil-pounding, rough-edged chevalier had flown to Laura's rescue while he himself had nothing to offer but an uncomfortable ride home.

Devil it all, Laura looked at the man with such gratitude, he wanted to clamp his hand over her eyes and boot the fellow in the crotch.

Nothing for it, but to get her away from here, he decided. Sean marched over to his waiting mount, practically dragging Laura along with him.

Damned horse. He would have given his left arm for a well-sprung carriage. With a disgusted sigh, he set Laura in the saddle and climbed up behind her. He didn't relish the next six leagues at all, but they were a vast improvement over the last six he had endured.

He settled her back against his chest, carefully supporting her as he reined the horse around and headed back toward London. Campion, MacLinden and the others secured Simms's body on his horse and followed, quietly discussing all that had occurred. Sean ignored them, riding ahead a ways, seeking solitude and hoping Laura could sleep.

At least she was safe now. Safe in his own arms, away from that proprietary smithy, and free of the threat against her life. That cur, Simms, had to be the writer of the notes, the man who had chased them to the Continent and back. Something about that conclusion bothered Sean. Probably because he had nearly convinced himself that it was George Luckhurst, a wilier fellow, and a likelier candidate for revenge than Simms. That Sean had arrested Simms once, plus the fact that the man had fired at Laura tonight instead of merely trying to rob or abuse her, proved too much of a coincidence to think otherwise. Simms had to have been the one after them.

Now that all that was behind them, perhaps he and Laura could construct a normal life together. Tomorrow, he would have her confession and apology for all she had done. Then he would forgive her for everything. It made no sense to hold a grudge.

He was a fair man and could understand to a certain degree why she had done what she had done. Women must use what means they had to make their way in a world ruled by men, he supposed.

Some rake had seduced her, played on her naiveté, then left her to deal with the consequences alone. Laura had erred seriously there, as well as in the trick she had employed to snare a husband. But how else could she have avoided scandal and ruin?

Sean admitted that he had executed some rather nefarious schemes himself. Too many for him to judge Laura as harshly as he had done. Yes, he believed he could excuse her everything, once she understood that she must never lie to him again. Marriage must be based on trust. He must make her fully aware of that.

Laura experienced a profound desire to do this man bodily harm. She shouldn't, given that her memory of the highwayman's death remained so vivid. She had not meant to kill that one. She did not want this one dead, either. But if she thought for a moment her hands would reach around his neck, she would squeeze it until his eyes bulged. Until he begged her for mercy and swore he would not utter another word.

They had returned to Sean's rooms, where they had discovered such joy after their wedding. He had rapidly supplanted that memory. Where he slept, she had no inkling, but for the third morning in as many days, Sean had called her on the carpet like a misbehaving child. Each time, he demanded that she acknowledge her wrongdoing. Then, he said, he wanted a sincere expression of repentance and her promise that she would never again lie to him.

He had been tender that first day, but firm. She had remained calm, steadily answering him with a recitation of exactly how things had come about. His fury erupted so suddenly, she had no time to react to it before he stormed out cursing. Laura had wept.

Yesterday he had approached her again, red eyed and disheveled, more than a bit worse for the strong drink he had obviously consumed during his absence. Laura decided to remain silent and aloof in the face of his renewed accusations. Eventually he gave up, exasperated and red in the face, and left again. This time she did not cry, but resigned herself to reality. Sean would never allow himself to believe her. And she thought she knew why.

Now, this morning, he seemed even more determined to extract her obeisance. And proved a lot more forceful about it. He had railed at her for a good quarter hour already. "Your stubbornness will be your undoing, girl! I have had enough!"

Laura nodded and struggled against thoughts of mayhem. "I can see that you have and so have I, Sean. Get out of here now before I do something less than ladylike."

"Lying is not ladylike in the least and you had no qualms about that, did you?" He paced back and forth, head down, hands in his pockets as though to keep them from striking something. Probably her.

The calmness of defeat descended, almost extinguishing her anger. "We should end this travesty now. Apply for your divorce and you will be free."

He halted midpace and his gaze flew to hers. "What?"

"End it all now. You do not want to be married to me!" she declared, her voice growing more heated in spite of the fact she fought to control it. "You never wanted a permanent commitment, Sean. That was the only reason you agreed to marry me in the first place. Because you thought I would be dead in a few weeks. Oh, it made you feel the grand knight, didn't it? Sacrificing a bit of your precious freedom to play the hero to a dying damsel?"

She reveled in his fleeting flash of guilt.

"But then I did not die! So now, you cannot reconcile yourself to the fact that you are bound to someone for life! You trust no one! Every wrong ever done you, you heap on my head because you cannot bear to think I might be telling you the truth. If you admit that to yourself, you will have the obligation to care not only for me, but for a child you do not want to love. Your child, Sean. *Yours!* And if you expect me to cave in and fabricate a false confession just to salve your stupid conscience, you need a cell in Bedlam. Because you are *mad!*"

On the last word, Laura stomped her foot and then flung herself across the bed facedown.

"You *want* a divorce?" he asked, his voice soft and rife with disbelief.

"You want one!" she shouted. "You said so in Paris!"

"No! Then I was…I've decided against it!"

With supreme effort, Laura pushed herself to a sitting position on the edge of the bed, ashamed of her tantrum. She could barely recall the last fit of this sort when she was seven. It had been just as ineffective then.

Clearing her throat, she summoned what would pass for a reasonable tone. "You needn't arrange for a settlement, if that is your worry. You clearly provided everything I paid for. I will not haggle with that. My inheritance belongs entirely to you."

"Bugger your inheritance!" he shouted. "I never wanted your money! I don't need it!"

"Nevertheless, you shall have it."

He resumed his pacing, but he watched her all the while, whipping his head back and forth each time he changed direction. "You have no grounds for divorce," he said, almost a warning.

"Perhaps *you* do, if you choose to claim that I deceived you. You believed the marriage temporary. You expected I would die." How it hurt to think he wished that she had.

"Get this right out of your mind, Laura! You are my wife and you will remain so. Till death do us part, remember? And you are not, nor ever have been, ill!" He looked ready to leave again and she hoped to God he would hurry before she disgraced herself further with tears. The tantrum had been bad enough.

"Well, I won't die just to please you!" she cried. "Not that you or anyone else would care, but I am glad not to die at twenty-five! Glad not to die, and beyond glad to have a child to look forward to. If it inconveniences you, my unesteemed stepfather, and the entire population of the civilized world, I don't care. Do you hear? I mean to live. And I don't intend to do it with a self-righteous lack-wit who names his own child a bastard. And you will never goad me into doing away with myself no matter how mean you become. Now get out of here!"

He looked stunned as the sudden silence lay thick around them. "Do away with yourself?" he whispered. "Laura? You haven't harbored such thoughts?"

"Ha! Not for a moment, so don't raise your hopes!" She flopped down on the edge of the bed again when she realized she had been stamping about just as Sean had done.

He approached her carefully, as though he expected her to lash out. And she did think about it. Seriously. It must have shown on her face, she thought, for he stopped out of arm's reach. His voice remained low, just above his former whisper. "I will leave if that is what you want. We will talk about all this when you are calmer. I regret that I upset you."

"Ha!" She huffed again and looked away, crossing her arms over her chest. The click of the door closing softly behind him signaled Laura that it was safe to collapse. She did so, pounding her fists into the same pillow where she buried her face.

No more tears. She would get up and pack, Laura decided. Even if she must stay married to the beast, no woman in her right mind would stay and listen to this harangue day after day. Lambdin would take her in until she could think of a better destination.

Chapter Thirteen

~~~~~~⤜⤛~~~~~~

"This definitely reinforces my belief in bachelorhood," Campion quipped to Sean as he welcomed the waiter with a smile.

They sat at a corner table in the Truncheon, a public house they had often frequented on London frolics during their university days. "If you cease riding the roads searching for your habitual runaway wife, you can still approximate that blessed state. Just let her go, why don't you?"

"Shut up, Camp," Sean said, sitting back to allow delivery of his pint. He avidly wished he had never confided in the fool about Laura's absence. Far worse than the embarrassment of her desertion, however, was the desperation he felt. Desperation to have Laura back. She did not deserve it and he hated feeling it.

And he didn't think he was hiding it well at all. Camp always had read him like broadsheet. "I don't want to discuss it."

The rogue laughed. "Should think not! At least this time, you know no one took her. That is something, anyway."

Sean said nothing. As long as he and Campion had known each other, the man's audacity never ceased to amaze him.

Usually, Sean found it easy enough to laugh at or overlook, but today Camp had latched onto the wrong subject.

Panic had undone Sean yesterday when he discovered Laura missing from their rooms. If, indeed, he could call the rooms *theirs*. He had not slept there at all since he had returned to London with her four days ago. Fortunately no one had observed his half-mad state when he found her absent. Then he'd seen that her clothes and travel bags were also gone. No one had taken her. Laura had left under her own steam.

Further investigation revealed her passage on the mail coach, headed in the direction of Bedfordshire. Gone home to her little brother and the horses. Gone to ground, secure in the knowledge that her husband would not follow. After all, hadn't he had made it quite clear he wanted none of her unless she groveled for his forgiveness? Sean could kick himself.

Right from the beginning, he had realized that Laura held the power to hurt him. More power than he had ever allowed anyone else in his life since reaching adulthood. Well, he hadn't exactly allowed it, had he? He had tried to limit his feelings to friendship, fought his desire as well as hers. Then all she'd had to do was smile and twitch her skirts once too often. His resolve caved in like a sinkhole. What the hell had happened to his self-control? To any kind of control? He felt scattered, undone, not to mention anxious that he might have lost her forever this time.

Pride. There was the culprit. Both possessed an abundance of that, and each had torn away at the other's until neither of them dared sacrifice what little they had left. Right now, however, Sean admitted he felt damn near ready to let go of his entirely. He wanted Laura above anything in the world. He needed her. Wasn't certain why he did so, but there it was.

Camp rattled on. "You needn't worry she's in trouble if she took the post coach. Safe as the mail. Cheap transportation, too. Didn't you provide her any money?"

"Drink your drink." Sean drank of his, wiping his mouth with the back of his hand.

"Gone off to rusticate," Camp continued with a mocking grin. "Why do you suppose she would do that when she schemed so hard to get you shackled? Did you disillusion her, wild man? Did you show her all the pitfalls of the married state?"

"I do wonder that you've never had that nose broken."

Camp's long, slender fingers examined the object in question. "That might lend me a bit of character, what?"

"You could damn well use some of that," Sean observed.

He sighed and polished off the ale, turning the mug round and round on the table surface, wondering whether he should order another or simply get up and go after Laura. Why did he sit here ruminating, as though there were a decision to be made? As if he had a choice in the matter?

"I shall have to go and get her, but you need not come," he told Campion.

"Hell, I wouldn't dream of it! Not for me to ride off again after the deceitful little b—"

Sean backhanded him out of his chair.

Half-prone on the floor, swiping with one hand at the blood running from his nostrils, Camp grabbed Sean's ankle with the other. "*Dieu!* Sean, wait a moment, will you? I but played devil's advocate here. A stupid thing to do."

For a time, they simply stared at each other, a wealth of unspoken words in the prolonged exchange. Sean understood then that Camp only meant to help, to goad him into doing the right thing. His methods might be crude, but they were effective.

Sean had always valued Camp for his virtues, and also accepted his faults. Friends just did that. Why couldn't lovers? Why expect perfection? He knew he was far from perfect. Why should he expect it of Laura?

He finally reached for Camp's hand and helped him rise. "How's your character now, Doc?"

"Much improved," Camp said wryly. He settled back in his chair and fished for his handkerchief. "Why did she run, Sean?" The seriousness of his concern prompted Sean to explain.

"I drove her to it. Ordered her to repent like I was some Calvinist preacher on crusade. *Atone and ye shall be saved.* I deserve a lightning bolt."

Camp winced. "You can act a bit above us all now and again. Had a big scene, did you?"

"She asked me to divorce her," Sean admitted.

"You refused."

Sean couldn't help rolling his eyes at the unnecessary question. "Of course I refused! Divorce was never an option. Laura would be ruined. And I would be destroyed, as well. Irrevocably. And I don't mean my reputation."

"Quite," Camp agreed. He fell silent for a few moments, lost in thought, drumming his fingers on the table. Then he sat back in his chair and crossed his arms; the doctor, observing his patient.

Sean thought he was about to field questions concerning his mental well-being. He could use some help there at this point, come to think of it. The good Dr. Campion could not make any decisions for him, he knew, but Camp always had been a good sounding board.

"You still believe she is lying about the pregnancy? That the child is not yours?"

Sean nodded, then grasped at the nearest straw. "Don't you? Do you suppose it's possible that it could be mine?"

Camp's typically French shrug annoyed Sean. His words compounded it. "The bit about that fatal illness was a proper scam. She must have had a reason for that other than your pretty face. However, in answer to your question, if she had sex with you, then there is the possibility. You would certainly know more about that than I."

When Sean said nothing, Camp fanned out his fingers in a dismissive little gesture. "Who planted the seed is anyone's guess. Perhaps she doesn't even know herself. She came to you a woman of experience, no?"

A heat suffused Sean's face and he couldn't meet Camp's gaze of inquiry. "Perhaps."

Camp expelled a harsh grunt of disbelief and sat forward, hands clenched on the table, peering at him intently. "Sean? What do you mean *perhaps?*"

"Virginity can be faked!" Sean declared defensively. "A matter of pretended pain, a bit of blood, a few tears! You're a doctor, surely you know the scheme! It was an old gambit used by Madam to up the price on her new girls. There are advantages, growing up in a brothel. One learns these things early on."

"Imbecile! That is mere physical evidence, and sometimes missing even when it truly *is* a woman's first encounter." He took a calming breath and lowered his voice. "Have you never had an innocent?"

"Not bloody likely!" Sean grumbled. "Where the hell would I get one? Unless I procured some schoolroom miss, I doubt I could find one in all of London! And even that would offer only the odd chance."

"Hmm." Camp at his most noncommittal, playing doctor again. "You must judge by the woman's attitude," he advised Sean. "By her expertise under fire, so to speak. Did she seem uneasy? Frightened? Did she wait for your lead?"

Sean laughed without mirth. "She practically dragged me back to my flat immediately after the ceremony and initiated the whole episode herself. We had known each other for a total of about two hours."

"Not good," Camp muttered, staring into his ale.

Not good might be the shortest understatement in history, Sean thought.

"But you do love her. Do not bother to deny that," Camp warned, "or you shall insult my intelligence."

"No denial. It's true enough." Sean rested his head in his hands. "Camp, I don't even care anymore. What's that say about my wits, eh? I just don't care what she's done. She must come back to me. Any way that I can have her. If she lies, then she lies."

"What of the baby? You will resent it. Any man would. If she were widowed and left in such a state, things would be different, but she used this child to try and hold you. Thought to pass it off as your heir."

Sean's temper flared again, not at his friend, but at the situation Camp defined. "My estate's not so paltry that I need hoard it for those of my own blood. This one may have a share if it comes to that. No bastard ever *asks* to be born, and well I know that! The child is not at fault here."

"It will bear your name," Camp reminded him.

"Oh, my name, is it? Whores gave me the damned name, for God's sake. I kept it and made it legal just to spite my grandfather, who would undoubtably have been glad of it had he even known. No sacred lineage there."

Camp grasped Sean's wrist and squeezed it. "Then go after her, Sean. Assure her that you love her despite everything, and that you will accept the child no matter how she got it. Once you convince her of that, she will beg your pardon. Laura is only afraid. I think she must love you."

Sean wondered. She had certainly made him believe she did during their last night together. But then, Laura had also convinced him she was slowly dying of a damned insect bite. Some man of the world he was. God, he felt mortified just thinking about his former gullibility and his present lack of dignity.

"Well, will you do it?" Campion asked, leaning forward expectantly.

"Right after our next pint," Sean promised, and rewarded Camp with a wide smile of thanks for the advice. "And I'm buying."

When the rascal looked at that swollen nose of his in the next mirror he passed, Sean hoped to be well on the way to Bedfordshire.

Frost sparkled the landscape visible from Laura's second-floor window. She glanced down at the ground and, for a moment, considered jumping. Broken legs and dragging herself through the chill November morning to parts unknown held little appeal, however. She allowed the curtain to drop back in place. Never had she imagined being held prisoner in her own home.

But since yesterday, Laura really did not consider Midbrook her home. The realization occurred just after she had stepped out of the coach. Lambdin had greeted her with apprehension instead of the expected open arms. And her stepfather was in residence. She wondered at her mother's absence, but received no answer when she asked.

"I wish you had not come back," Lamb had whispered. Now she knew why.

Fury at her stepfather, despair over the state of her marriage, and ordinary hunger tied Laura's stomach in knots. She had not slept at all last night, wondering when the next family confrontation would come. The one immediately after her arrival had ended in a shouting match that precipitated her imprisonment without dinner. Apparently, the punishment extended to breakfast, luncheon, and tea as well, for now it was late afternoon the next day. Was he trying to starve her into submission?

The key turning in the lock interrupted her dark thoughts.

"Laura? Are you all right?" Lamb asked, hurrying toward her. "Father sent me to bring you downstairs. I promise I had no idea he intended to lock you in your room."

"You allowed it, however." Laura couldn't help the accusatory tone. Lambdin's fortitude when it came to his father wouldn't half fill a demitasse. "Are you in agreement with all of this, Lamb?"

"Certainly not!" he vowed, looking hurt. "You'd best come along now. He's waiting."

"Let him wait!" Laura cried. Contrary to her words, however, she swept past him and out of the room. She couldn't stand the dread and isolation for another moment.

Her stepfather waited in the study, poised at the window with his back to the door. When she and Lambdin entered, he turned slowly and moved to the desk. "I have the document ready for you to sign."

"Well, good day to you, too, Father," Laura said, braving his wrath with her sarcasm. "Am I too late for breakfast?" Her stomach rumbled.

She ignored the pen he held out to her. "It's definitely too late for that." Laura pointed to the sheaf of papers in front of him. "My inheritance belongs to my husband."

He smiled and shook his head. "This is already witnessed, and dated before your marriage. You give over everything to your brother. It should have been his to begin with. This will make it official."

"Tell that to Sean Wilder, if you dare," Laura said with a smirk. "I should really like to witness the occasion."

With the suddenness of a snake striking, he moved around the desk and raised his hand to strike her. Lambdin blocked the blow. "Stop this, Father!" Lamb ordered.

Laura had jumped back out of the way. She could not

believe it! Never in her life had either of her parents attempted to strike her for any reason. Of course, they had never been around long enough for her to misbehave in front of them.

Her stepfather knocked Lambdin aside. "Shut up if you know what's good for you. I'm trying to secure your future, you ingrate!"

"But, Father, I don't need Laura's money!" Lamb insisted.

"The hell you don't! What my shipping managers haven't stolen from me, I have tied up in investments. Your pockets will soon be as empty as mine. Then how will you support that simpering little fiancée of yours when you wed her, eh?"

He dismissed Lambdin with a snarl and directed his attention back to Laura. "And you! Your brother will have to take care of you as well now, won't he? And your whelp, too, unless you were lying to me in Paris. Now that you've left that bastard, Wilder, who but Lambdin here will give you shelter?"

"That document is fraudulent," Laura declared. She knew the door behind her stood open. Maybe she could run for it. "Starve me, beat me, or throw me out, but I will not sign!" She inched backward, intending to turn and flee.

"You will!" With a grunt, he lunged, grabbed her arm and twisted it behind her back, forcing her back to the desk. Lambdin raised his voice, objecting.

"Sign now or I will break this arm," Middlebrook threatened.

After a sudden wrench upward, he abruptly released her.

A harsh snap and a scream occurred before Laura could turn around to see why.

"Goddamn! You broke—" her stepfather sank to his knees, cradling one of his arms with the other and gasping "—my arm!"

"Your neck is next if you've injured my wife," Sean growled.

"Sean?" Laura cried. She threw herself at him, uncaring whether he welcomed her.

"Are you hurt?" he demanded.

"Not physically," she assured him. Murder seemed imminent if she admitted otherwise.

"Send someone for her things," Sean ordered Lambdin. "Do it *now!*" he shouted when Lamb just stood there gaping.

"But what about Father? You've broken his arm!" Lamb said, hovering over the man.

"He's not going anywhere," Sean said brusquely. "If he moves from that spot, I promise to break his legs."

Lambdin hurried out and Laura heard him shout for Clary, the maid, to run and fetch help.

Moments later, Lambdin, himself, came back carrying her bags. She had never unpacked, thank goodness, for she'd had no intention of staying after her shoddy welcome.

Lamb halted at the study door. "I'll just, uh, put these in your carriage then," he said, looking from Sean to his father and back again.

"Do that," Sean said. Then he glared down at her stepfather, who moaned and rocked back and forth. "And as for you, Middlebrook. If I ever see you again—anywhere, at any time—or if you try to contact my wife in any way, I shall kill you without warning. Do you understand?"

Sean seemed content with the answering nod, for he turned Laura about and lifted her in his arms.

"May—may I write to her?" Lambdin ventured as he held open the coach's door.

"No, you spineless wonder, you may not!" Sean declared heatedly.

He deposited Laura inside and climbed in behind her. Once he settled himself on the seat opposite her, Sean slammed the door and faced Lambdin through the coach window. "I will consider it," he said, only a bit less brusquely than before. With a pull on the signal strap, they were off.

After countless miles of tense silence, Laura decided enough was enough. "Lamb did prevent his striking me," she said, feeling obliged to defend her brother.

Sean huffed and shot her an angry look. "Then Lamb saved his miserable life, didn't he!"

He leaned his head back against the wall of the coach and took a deep breath, letting it out slowly. "Why, Laura? Why in the world did you come back here?"

"I had to go somewhere, didn't I? I couldn't very well stay with you!"

"And why not, may I ask? I am your husband!"

Laura sighed and smoothed her gown over her stomach, offering Sean a reminder as she spoke. "You know why. You believe me to be a conniving liar and a woman of low morals. There is nothing I can ever say or do to prove to you that I am not. At first, I thought that the timely arrival of the child would prove to you that you fathered it, but Dr. Campion neatly killed that notion."

She bit her bottom lip to still its trembling. Weeping would not do. It was true that tears affected Sean deeply, but now he would only believe them a ploy to elicit sympathy. And sympathy definitely was not what she wanted from Sean.

He cleared his throat and stared out the window for a moment. "Laura, I promise to claim your child and forgive you completely. We will never mention it again."

She jerked to attention, all thought of tears forgotten. "Imbecile! There is nothing to forgive, I tell you! And fie on your grudging acceptance! That's worse than outright rejection!"

He reached for her hands, but she snatched them away. "Leave me alone, Sean. I do not wish to live with you! I want a divorce!"

"I do not wish to live *without* you," he countered, speaking through gritted teeth. "And you may not have one."

Laura flopped back against the seat and threw up her hands in defeat. "Then what am I supposed to do here? We are at an impasse."

"Just so," he agreed. "But you are my wife and you shall stay my wife. Regardless."

Silence descended again as they trundled on toward London. Laura could not imagine why he would still want her as a wife, believing as he did. Though she understood the suspicion he harbored, considering the circumstances, she sorely resented his not giving her the benefit of the doubt.

If she relented and stayed with him, she would suffer his constant distrust and, unspoken or not, Laura knew she could not stand seeing that look in his eyes each day.

"Sean," she said earnestly, "if you have no faith in me, then we will have no marriage. I do not see how I can bear to live with you that way."

The spring green of his eyes clouded nearly to gray as he held her gaze. Was it disappointment, or disgust she saw there? No, it looked more like resignation. And surprisingly, anguish.

"I'm afraid you must," Sean said at last. "You have nowhere else to go even were I willing to let you."

Laura searched his features more closely than ever, wondering at the profound sadness he now allowed her to see quite clearly. No wall of pride or anger stood between them now. That he did not even try to hide his feelings confused her.

Could he love her still? She realized then that he must. Probably as much as she loved him. But it was no use. More than love was needed to make a marriage work. But, oh, how desperately she wished there were a way to save what they had found together so briefly.

Suggesting that he provide a place for her to live separately in London occurred to Laura, but she simply couldn't form the words. If she truly insisted, he might agree. And despite the heated words she had thrown at him, she felt much as he did about a divorce. Deep inside her, a vestige of hope remained that Sean would eventually see the truth.

"Very well," she agreed softly, smoothing down the fabric of her skirts and then clasping her hands together. "We shall make the best of it. I shall try to be a good wife. And mother," she couldn't resist adding.

He turned to regard her with a curious look. "You are consistent, if nothing else, aren't you?" Though the wrath was missing, Laura detected exasperation. He went on, obviously struggling to sound reasonable. "All I ask of you is that you acknowledge an error in judgment, Laura. Is that so much?"

"The only error in judgment that I made was in not confirming with my brother what I overheard that day. For that, I am truly sorry, believe me."

"Oh, for God's sake, I give up!" He almost shouted with exasperation.

"It's about damned time!" Laura said, more than a little exasperated herself.

Chapter Fourteen

Sean sat at his desk, fingers steepled under his chin. He stared past MacLinden's head to the reversed letters showing through the glass on his door. *Wilder Investigations.* They should read *Ostrich with Head Buried in the Sand,* he decided. Laura had him so befuddled, he had simply submerged a fact he did not want to recall. MacLinden's new information had just triggered the memory of Simms signing his confession with an *X*. How could he have forgotten that? Simms could not even read, let alone write, and could not possibly have written the threatening notes.

Lindy took out his pipe and tamped its nonexistent tobacco with his thumb. "Coroner's report reveals no bullet wound other than the one that killed him. Dr. Killeen says Simms had never been shot before. If your wife wounded the assailant at your Paris hotel," he said, putting the pipe to his lips and making a little sucking noise, before continuing, "Simms is not your man."

"At least we know that the man we are after looks like him," Sean said.

"Yes, she and Dr. Campion here said Simms matched the

description of the man she shot." MacLinden turned to Camp, who had not intruded on the conversation.

"The right size and a dark beard," Camp affirmed, offering Sean a look of apology. "I fear that fits many men, my friend."

MacLinden nodded. "Simms was merely a highwayman, just as the smithy suggested. Oh, I don't doubt Simms would have killed your Laura once he'd finished his business with her, but he definitely is not the man she shot in Paris. That wound would hardly be healed if it existed, Sean. It simply wasn't there." He stuck his empty pipe back in his pocket and leaned forward, both hands on Sean's desk. "Seems we still have a problem."

"Why the devil did you wait so long to tell me this?" Sean demanded. "You have had the body more than a week now."

"Just read the report. You know as well as I how busy they are at the morgue. And my office is in bloody chaos at the moment what with the recent murder in George Alley. Damned fellow's struck again and every man jack in London is hounding us for an arrest."

"I know, I know." Sean settled again in his swivel armchair, resting his chin on one palm, thinking. "There have been no further notes," he said, still angry with himself. He had allowed Laura to dull his wits to the point where his investigative talents were practically useless. Objectivity seemed impossible where she was concerned, but the danger remained and he had to deal with it. "Whoever wrote them must not have located us yet."

"That lets out your father-in-law, I suppose," MacLinden suggested.

"Not necessarily. He *is* here in England now. Traveling without his wife, which is unusual and suspicious. And he did lock Laura in her room with the intention of forcing her to sign over her inheritance to her half brother."

"Could he have written the earlier threats, do you think?" Lindy asked.

Sean sighed. "Laura says they're not in his handwriting, but he could have altered that easily enough. Trouble is, now that we know the culprit isn't Simms, I want so much for it to be Middlebrook, I may not be the best judge in this."

"Where is Laura today?" Camp asked, rising from his chair.

Sean got up abruptly and skirted the desk. "She's out shopping! I have to go and find her. What if—"

"Calm down," Camp advised, restraining him gently with a hand to his shoulder. "There are not that many places she could be. Now think, what is she shopping for? Did she tell you?"

"She said she needed…larger clothes," Sean said, feeling his face heat with the thought of Laura swelling soon with child. Someone else's child. "I don't know where women get those sort of—"

"Expandable gowns?" Camp offered, smiling.

MacLinden laughed merrily and slapped Sean on the shoulder. "Why didn't you tell me, son? We'll have to celebrate! This is wonderful news!"

Sean met Camp's eyes and read the dare. But he could not bring himself to sully Laura's name, not even to Lindy, who would hold the secret safe to his grave. "Yes. Thank you," Sean said simply. Camp's tongue-in-cheek expression did nothing to help matters. The only important thing right now, however, was Laura's safety. Sean dismissed all other thoughts.

"Let's go," he ordered, grabbing his hat and giving Camp a rough shove out the door.

Laura wandered out of Madame Renee's, her attention on one of her gloves, which had lost a button. The air felt cold and damp, but thank goodness the rain had stopped. How foolish she was to venture out in such unpredictable weather. She had no enthusiasm to continue what she had started—the purchase of a serviceable wardrobe to accommodate her soon to change waistline—but at least it gave her something to do.

Sean had greeted her plan with a dark look of accusation and a hefty stack of pound notes. Why did she persist in prodding his anger with reminders of her pregnancy, she wondered.

He had acted pleasantly enough once they had arrived at his rooms last evening. If by *pleasant,* one meant strictly polite. The landlady sent up a cold collation for supper at his request, but Sean departed before it arrived. She had no idea where he had slept, but he had returned for breakfast.

Did he have a club to go to? Other than a plethora of wild rumors and the bare facts her solicitor had gleaned before her marriage, she realized how little she really knew about Sean's life in London. She should have asked much sooner if she wanted to know, for he certainly didn't seem disposed to share anything about it now.

Perhaps the shopping excursion had occurred to her as a way of shaking up that very correct stranger he had become. Or maybe it was sheer perversity on her part, an attempt to force him to accept their coming child as a reality. One he had helped create.

She stepped off the curb, headed for the Silken Thread shop across the street to buy her unmentionables.

The sudden clatter of a speeding carriage alerted her just in time to step back, too late to avoid a collision altogether. The hooves missed her, but some portion of equine anatomy sent her tumbling out of the way of the wheels.

Laura landed in a puddle of mud at the edge of the street. She glared at the dirty carriage disappearing round the corner. Several gentlemen rushed to her side, offering assistance, and she allowed a portly gentleman to give her a hand regaining her feet.

"The bounder didn't even slow his team!" the older man declared, shaking his fist at the now-absent culprit.

"Are you hurt, miss?" another asked. Their murmurs grew louder and angrier as they hashed over the recent accident.

Laura shook her head and tried wiping a splatter of muck off her cheek, smearing it even worse with her filthy glove. "I am fine, I think. I do appreciate your assistance, sir," she said a little breathlessly. She spent a few moments brushing at her wet skirts and righting her hat, which had tilted to an odd angle over one ear.

She heard the clatter and splash of running feet and someone shouting her name. Before she could register the familiar sound of it, a figure plowed through the meager crowd and huge arms enveloped her.

"Oh, Laura!" Sean snapped. "Must I follow your every step to keep you out of trouble? What am I to do with you?"

She pushed away from him, using all her force. "Well, thank you for your tender concern," she replied with a huff. "Hail me a ride home and I shall see to myself!"

"Over there." He pointed to a conveyance waiting just down the street.

"I shouldn't like to inconvenience you," she said, striving for dignity, which proved difficult to muster with mud dripping off her chin.

"Camp's here," he stated, stepping back so that she could see the doctor. "He should check you over, see if you were injured. Are you?"

"Kind of you to ask, however belatedly, but no." She flounced through the bystanders and stalked to the waiting carriage. The dirty carriage. One uncomfortably similar to the one which had just tried to run her down. It had been no accident, of that she was certain. And afterward, there had been plenty of time for the carriage to circle round. No, Sean

would never do such a thing. And Campion wouldn't coun-
tenance it, even if Sean would.

What was she thinking? It was the shock of falling, surely.
She was not herself yet. Even now, bones ached and bruised
muscles began screaming for a hot soak.

Sean opened the door and lifted her inside the vehicle. She
cried out in spite of herself when he grasped her waist.

Campion climbed in quickly and had her damp cloak off
in a trice. She felt his long fingers probing her ribs. He
grunted and continued his ministrations, even when Sean
protested.

"Get over on this side, Sean. She should lie down. No,
you cannot hold her in your lap. She must lie flat," Camp
insisted. *"Move!"*

Sean slid to the opposite seat while Campion arranged Laura
in a reclining position. "Nothing seems broken. Do you have
any discomfort here?" he asked, gently touching her abdomen.
"Any sensation that might mean bleeding? I can't examine
you fully here, but we shall have you home in a few moments."

Then she realized what he meant. The baby. She concentrated, but didn't feel anything to indicate there might be
trouble in that regard. Had that been the purpose of the fright
she had endured? Could the incident have been meant to induce
serious injury or such terror so that she would miscarry?

She turned her eyes to Sean, who had his averted. He
looked terribly agitated at the moment. Disappointed his
scheme had not worked?

"Answer me, Laura," Campion demanded.

"I am well enough," she said vehemently, still watching Sean.
"And you won't have another chance. I promise you that!"

"Chance?" Sean looked confused. "What do you mean?"

Laura quailed under the fierceness of his glare. Suppose
she was wrong? Even if she was right, it would be incredibly

stupid to let on that she knew. "Nothing," she murmured softly. "Never mind."

She watched the men exchange an unfathomable look. *Guilt?* Nothing else was said until they arrived at Sean's rooms. Sean lifted her out of the carriage and carried her up. Campion followed.

Laura hurried into the necessary the moment Sean set her on her feet. She slid the latch inside and quickly checked to make certain there was no evidence of a possible miscarriage. Then she huddled in a corner of the room, aching all over. They would be out there waiting, and she doubted they would exhibit much patience.

"Are you all right?" Sean called out. "Laura?"

"Go away," she pleaded. "Just go away, both of you."

"Open this door, Laura!" he ordered.

"No."

"If you don't, I'll break it down!" he warned.

Laura regarded the stout oak and wondered whether he really could. Probably. Still, she had no choice but to trust it would hold. If she gave Campion the opportunity, he might rid her of the child without her knowing what he was about until it was too late. He was a physician. And Sean's best friend. Neither of them believed the baby legitimately conceived. Even if Sean did want her, she knew he did not want what he thought to be her bastard.

A heavy thump rattled the hinges.

The murmur of voices followed, Sean's argumentative, Camp's placating. She could not understand the words.

Then Campion raised his voice enough for her to hear clearly. "We will leave if that is what you wish, Laura, but you must come out and go to bed."

A trick, she thought, and not a very good one.

"Later," she answered. She turned on the water in the huge

claw-foot tub. If she had to spend hours in here until they gave up and left, she figured she might as well use the time to advantage. The mud had already dried on her face and her body felt like one huge contusion.

After a long, leisurely bath, Laura dried herself. She bundled up her wet clothing, and then dressed in the night rail that hung on the hook by the door. No sounds were audible from the bedroom.

Quietly she disengaged the latch and cracked open the door. The draperies were closed and the lamp beside the bed threw shadows around the darkened room.

One of them had laid a fire, which silhouetted the two armchairs facing it. Laura tiptoed out and rushed to the door that opened onto the upstairs landing. She shot the bolt and leaned against it for a moment, eyes tightly shut in relief.

"It's about time," Sean muttered, rising from one of the wing chairs she had thought to be empty. "We feared you had drowned."

The scream stuck in her throat. She whirled around and fumbled with the bolt, but Sean caught her before she managed to open the door.

"What the hell—?"

She fought with all the strength she possessed, kicking, clawing, biting, until her energy deserted her completely. Hanging limply against him as he carried her to the bed, Laura wanted to weep with defeat. No use. He would do what he would. Nothing stopped the wild man.

She lay quietly under Campion's gentle probing of her ribs and belly. He never touched her intimately as she had feared he would. When he had finished, he covered her to the neck with the heavy comforter. Only when he poured a mixture of something into a water glass and offered it to her, did she refuse to cooperate.

"This is not laudanum, Laura," he assured her gently. "I know you wouldn't take that. But you do want to feel better, do you not?"

"Drink it!" Sean ordered in a brusque voice. He stood right behind Campion, looking like a man bent on mayhem.

"No," she whispered, horribly certain the glass contained something meant to vacate her womb. She had heard there were herbs that did just that. Would a doctor carry them around in his bag? She wasn't about to take the chance. "Just leave me alone. Please."

Camp set the glass on the table beside the lamp. "Come away, Sean. I think it is best if Laura rests now." When Sean obstinately remained where he was, Camp grasped his elbow and repeated softly but insistently, "Come with me."

They left the room and Laura, despite her exhaustion, leapt up to lock the door behind them. Only then did she crawl back into bed and give way to the pain and weariness.

"Good Lord, what is wrong with her?" Sean bellowed once they reached the street. "She acts as though I am responsible for what happened!"

Camp sighed and shifted his bag to his other hand. "I believe that is exactly what she thinks."

Sean stopped walking. "You're not serious!"

"She is terrified, Sean. Of both of us. She believes we want her to abort the child."

"Good God in heaven! That's absurd!"

"Is it?" Camp asked. "Think, if you will. We show up immediately after she has been run down in the street. You are not overly solicitous to her. And then I immediately ask if she is about to miscarry? Add all that to the fact that she suffered a tremendous shock only moments before. It seems a reasonable assumption on her part, don't you think?"

Sean felt absolutely deflated. "But I would never harm her, Camp. Surely she knows that. Once she's rested, she will realize how ridiculous—"

"Do you wish her to lose the child, Sean?"

"No! Of course not!"

"Then you must somehow rein in all this anger you exhibit every time you approach her. Exactly who are you angry with, anyway?" Camp glanced heavenward and shook his head. "As if I did not already know."

Sean threw out his hands in a gesture of surrender. "Myself, of course. Why do I do this, Camp? I love her, damn it! Why can't I simply tell her? Make her believe it?"

Campion sighed. "Pride, my man. You've said as much. And fear of the uncertain future." He walked on down the street, hands locked behind him, thinking. Then he turned to speak. "Sean, why not send Laura away for a while?" He held up a hand when Sean started to protest. "Not long. Just until you can come to terms with what all of this means to you. And," he continued, "to give Laura time to collect her thoughts. After all, during these past two months, she has been under constant pressure of one sort or another, even if some of it was of her own making."

Sean considered it. "The danger remains. What happened today could very well have been an attempt on her life. It seems rather too convenient to have been accidental."

"Yes," Camp agreed. "Your note writer, no doubt."

"That being the case, I've no place really safe to send her, Camp. If we separated, how could I draw an easy breath, knowing someone might be arranging yet another attack? No, I have to keep her with me and find some way to convince her I mean her no harm. And that I want nothing more than to make the best of our marriage."

They walked on. Sean led, taking them in the direction of

the In and Out, a club off Piccadilly where both he and Camp would be welcomed.

"I should think you would be going back home to settle things then," Camp remarked.

Sean shrugged. "Tomorrow's soon enough. My outer door's sturdier than the one to the necessary and my shoulder's already killing me from my attack on that one. We'll have a few brandies, scare up a game, and then you shall have an overnight guest."

Camp snorted. "Nothing like inviting yourself."

"You'll be glad to know I've overcome my shyness," Sean quipped.

With that sally, Sean got the laugh he sought from Campion, but it did not lighten his own mood in the least. Here he was, trudging toward a last refuge away from home, and dreading the hours he would spend apart from Laura. Hours she would no doubt spend dreading their next meeting. He wanted nothing more than to retrace his steps, force entrance to his rooms and shake her until she came to her senses. But that would only frighten her more.

She would be safe where she was for the moment, however, and he could certainly use the time to get his wits together. And to get rid of the anger, as Camp had suggested.

Tomorrow he must use all the persuasion he could summon to allay Laura's fear and suspicion of him. If he had to lie to her, he would do that, too, Sean decided. He would tell her he believed everything she had ever said, if that was what she wanted to hear.

Yes, he would play the fool with bells jingling. Turn cartwheels and dance attendance on her like the lack-wit she thought him to be. If that's what it took to wipe that terror off her precious face, he'd do it. Such an existence would be a sham, of course. But life without Laura in it, regardless of what she had done, would be a travesty of the worst imaginable magnitude.

Chapter Fifteen

⁓

Laura snuggled into the covers, groaning as she drew her knees up to her chest. She ached abominably but felt too lethargic to get up and draw a bath. Hunger triggered nausea, for she had not eaten since yesterday's breakfast. And Sean's stiff politeness had wrecked her appetite even then, she thought with a sigh.

Dawn had come and gone. She had to get up and dress herself. A delivery person would be bringing her purchases from Madame Renee's this morning. Mrs. High would send someone with food if she did not appear soon in the dining room where the regular boarders ate. And, of course, Sean would be back to pound on the door, demanding yet another confrontation.

What should she do when he came? Face him, of course. She had no other choice really. Anywhere she ran, he would probably find her just as he had always done. Courage did not rank very high on her list of attributes this morning, but somehow, she would stand up to him. If she decided he did have something to do with yesterday's incident with the carriage, she must think of some way to escape and locate a place to hide permanently. The authorities would never believe her. Since her shock had abated and she could think more clearly, she did not really believe it herself. Only a small doubt remained. He had rather conveniently been there at the scene within moments.

Just as she had predicted, a gentle knock rent the morning silence. Mrs. High with the food. She could smell sausage. "Just a moment," she called, rolling from the bed with a wince.

She donned her blue velvet robe and limped to unlock and open the door.

"Good morning, Laura," Sean said softly.

"For whom?" she snapped, retreating, wrapping her arms about herself.

"For you, I hope," he answered, setting down the tray he held and drawing up two chairs to the small table. "I've brought your favorites. See, those little pork links you love. And brioche fresh from the bakery. Mrs. High did not take kindly to my replacing her scones, but—"

"Oh, leave off it, Sean! You didn't come here for that. Not unless you've poisoned the coffee!" Heavens, but it smelled so good, she was tempted to drink it anyway.

He puffed out his cheeks and released an exasperated breath. "You aren't going to make this easy, are you?"

For a moment she thought he referred to making her drink the stuff. But he abandoned the food tray altogether and drew her to one of the chairs, kneeling in front of her. Laura knew then that he meant the talk they were about to have. She did not delude herself that he intended to confess, apologize or declare undying love. But he must be about to tell her just what he expected her to do. Would he demand that she give up the child? Would he want her to go away to have it? If he so much as mentioned a word about the baby, she would—

"I want to talk about the baby," he said.

"No! There is no point in that. Just leave me alone."

He took her hand, holding it tightly to prevent her withdrawing. "Laura, I came to tell you that I want the child. I promise you that I am sincere."

"Liar," she accused, leveling on him her most cynical glare. Behind it, she prayed. *Oh, please let it be true!* After all his ranting about the importance of honesty, surely he meant it. He had said this before, however, and attached a price to it— her confession and apology. Sean only meant to humble her, that was all. "I do not believe you," she said.

"But I do want it," he vowed, his voice more tender and conciliatory than she had ever heard it.

"And just what occasioned this radical change of heart?" she asked sarcastically. "Do you suddenly yearn for the scent of used nappies, or do you finally concede the baby might possibly be yours?"

"It might be…it *is* mine. Yes. I'm certain of it," he said, looking wary. And so totally dishonest she wanted to slap his face.

Instead, she laughed. Bitterly, but she laughed. "Oh Sean, you should never lie. You do it so wretchedly."

He sighed heavily and frowned, the faint lines between his dark brows deepening. His huge shoulders drooped. "You once told me that my ears turned red when I did so. I forgot to cover them this time, didn't I? But, Laura, I—" He swallowed hard, visibly, and looked away. "I want *you*."

Laura shook her head and leaned back in the chair, remembering the time they had laughed about his fabricating an adventure for her. How she wished they could erase all that had happened between then and now. She would almost rather have faced a real death sentence than to have endured all that had gone on since then.

"I'm too weary for this, Sean. You don't believe me. You never will. Why not just let me go?"

"I cannot," he whispered. "I promise I will love the child as best I can. And neither of you will want for a thing, ever. Can that not be enough?"

"I suppose it will have to be. What do you expect of me in return?"

He took her other hand and pressed them together. "I want you to be my wife."

Red flags went up. Laura knew very well what he wanted and it was not someone to send his suits out for cleaning. "You want me in your bed."

"Yes," Sean admitted freely. "I do want that. But I also want us the way we were before, laughing, happy, living for the moment. Why can't we be that way again, Laura? Why? I know you never pretended all that. That much had to be real."

He seemed earnest now, she thought. And so troubled. "Could we, Sean? Could you put aside all your accusations, all your doubts?"

"Could you?" he countered. "After accusing me of causing what happened to you yesterday? Laura, I swear by all that's holy, I had nothing to do with it. MacLinden found that Simms is not the man you shot in Paris. We think whoever wrote the notes has found us again. I suspect he was the one in the carriage."

"That's why you were there so soon after?" Hope returned, if it had ever really gone away. Somewhere, deep inside her, Laura knew she had never convinced herself that he and Campion had arranged the mishap. She had suffered shock, perhaps. Or had been trying to focus her overwhelming terror on something—someone—known to her rather than face a phantom.

"I feared you might be in danger once Lindy told us about

Simms. Camp and I were looking for you when we heard the commotion." He released one of her hands to brush his over his face. "God, when I think what might have happened! I might have lost you. Times like this make me feel exactly the way Wade Halloran looked when Ondine died. I'm likely to end in the cell next to his if we don't resolve this madness soon!"

Laura watched him closely. If Sean lied now, he had certainly improved his delivery in the past five minutes.

"All right," she agreed, her voice barely audible.

"What?" Sean asked, looking confused by her words. "All right, what?"

"All right, we will try to mend things as best we can," she clarified. "But I will brook no further bitterness or reproach from you, Sean. I have had enough of that."

"I promise," he said with all sincerity. "No more. The past is over and done."

Laura nodded, considering all that had been said between them. Sean seemed willing to begin afresh, but he did not yet believe a word she had said about the reason for their marriage or that the child was his. Still, she supposed this was the best offer she was likely to get from him at this point. If he thought to have her groveling at his feet in appreciation, however, he had best think again.

"It's agreed, then. We will say no more about it," he said with a decisive nod. "From here on, we live for the moment."

"Fine," Laura said. "Then move out of my way, please. At this particular moment, I wish to live for food. Are you not having anything?"

He smiled and gestured toward the tray. "You see that I brought enough for two."

"Precisely!" Laura allowed. "Perhaps you could get something else for yourself downstairs."

She gave Sean credit for not grumbling aloud as he left.

He had even struggled to hide his disgruntled look. She lifted a sausage and bit into it, her lips turning up in a smile she couldn't suppress. *We will win him over to you, little dear,* she thought to the child within her. *Just you wait and see.*

Things had progressed better than she could ever have hoped when she first awoke this morning. At least Sean did want her. Of that she had no doubt at all. It was a start.

The envelope rested on the table in the foyer, right where Mrs. High had said it was. How benign it looked, so nondescript and harmless. Sean knew, however, by the handwriting that it was another of the threatening notes. It had been delivered less than half an hour before by a small street urchin.

No point seeking the lad who brought it. Sean had spent several years doing the same sort of messenger work and knew the boy could have grabbed onto the back of a carriage and reached anywhere in London by now.

He pocketed the note without reading it, determined not to allow it to ruin his morning. Instead, he opened the other missive that had lain beneath it.

Expensive, hand lettered, and rather too formal to the occasion, Mrs. MacLinden's invitation brought satisfaction. If Sean needed to court his wife to gain her good graces again, he could not have asked for a nicer opportunity. Or a safer environment in which to parade her about. They would hardly be accosted in the chief inspector's own home.

Mrs. High had Sean's tray ready when he returned to the kitchen. He thanked her profusely, garnered a motherly cluck from the usually taciturn woman and took his breakfast back up the stairs.

No work today. In fact, Sean had almost decided to close down his enquiry business altogether. His investments were sound and the bank account very healthy, even without

Laura's inheritance. That would be saved for her child. *Their* child, he corrected, frowning at the lapse. At any rate, he did not want to leave Laura alone any more than necessary. He couldn't count on her staying safely locked in his rooms every day while he worked.

He entered without knocking. Laura glanced up, her mouth full, her eyes smiling. At her expression, Sean's heart swelled with something akin to the joy she had brought him weeks before, only without the apprehension of her death to spoil it. He smiled back, noting the plates on the table were nearly empty. "Need refills?" he asked, raising his brows, mocking her healthy appetite.

She touched the serviette to her lips and gave a small, self-deprecating laugh. "No thank you," she said when she had swallowed. "I've quite finished. Please, sit down and eat. Shall I serve you?"

"Not necessary," he returned, taking his seat and arranging his plate. "I'm fair starved." But not for the food, he thought, looking at her hungrily. Did he dare approach her so soon? No, then she might believe that getting under her skirts was the only reason he had forgiven her. Best do the pretty for a while yet, much as it fueled his frustration.

"We have an invitation to dinner tonight," he said, changing the subject and tucking into his breakfast immediately. "I believe you would enjoy it."

Laura rose and began tidying around the room, fluffing a pillow here, straightening an antimacassar there. Her nervous energy alerted Sean that something worried her. Small wonder, he thought. She knew none of his London friends. After their experiences in Montmartre, she probably thought his usual social life here consisted of the bohemians who made up the art circles, or worse yet, those who peopled the streets where he made his beginnings. This was partly, but not altogether, true.

"Inspector MacLinden and his wife have asked us," he said casually. "You will like them, I know. Helen MacLinden is a very talented woman, as well as a beautiful person."

"You know her well, then?" Laura asked, buffing a brass cricket box with the tie of her robe.

Sean grinned. That was the same tone she had used when he first told her of Lou Lou. Jealous? A devil tempted him to provoke her further and find out, but he resisted. "Not well, really. We met a few times at award ceremonies when I was with the Yard. You met Lindy the night we found you at Barnswallow. Remember?"

She brightened and turned to beam at him again. "The older gentleman from Scotland Yard? Yes, of course I remember him. Wasn't he your superior at one time?"

"My superior, always," Sean admitted with affection. "Not a finer man alive that I know of. Shall we go?"

"Oh, yes! I should love it," she said with enthusiasm, then glanced toward the dressing room. "What shall I wear? I've not gone about much to...well, to anywhere except where you took me in Paris."

At once, Sean felt glad that Laura had not been provided with the chance to meet many men, and incensed with her stepfather for stifling her socially. Though she *had* managed to meet one man, hadn't she? He thrust the dangerous notion away. He had given her his promise.

Sean pushed his plate aside and stood up, crossing the room to take her hands in his again. The need to touch her overcame him at the strangest moments, as though touching could banish the darker thoughts intruding on his mind. This time it did.

"Dress to the nines, my dear. And if you haven't anything appropriate, then we shall go out and buy you a gown that shines. Something in silver, I think, to match those lovely eyes of yours."

She sighed with what appeared to be overwhelming relief, or perhaps pleasure. Her blush undid him so completely he leaned down and kissed her. A mere brush of lips, but it enkindled the fire inside him that he had so carefully banked. The effort required to prevent a regular conflagration proved almost too much to handle.

"Sean," she whispered, looking up at him, tear-glazed eyes shining like the silver he had just compared them to. "Oh, Sean, I have missed you so."

He slid his arms around her and drew her as close as he possibly could, his face buried in the thick tumble of satin coils loosely pinned atop her head. No words would come. His chest felt too full of love to issue the breath required to speak. He simply held her, swaying infinitesimally side to side, a slow dance of comfort and caring.

Eventually he became aware of her moving against him. How warm, her breasts pressing into his chest. How slender, her hips, unable to attain the height to reach his, though she must be raised to tiptoe. He lifted her, relishing the slide of her shapely body.

She was hardly dressed at all. An open robe, a silken night rail. So easily removed. The thought stirred his hardening loins to near bursting. Now? Would she have him now and think none the worse of him?

"Will you love me, Sean?" she asked so softly he barely heard. Had he wished the words or had she really spoken them?

"Laura?" he rasped, his voice husky and low. "I want you above everything. Not just this way, I promise." He kissed her soundly, invasively, and as thoroughly as he knew how. The welcome pliancy of her sweet mouth spurred him on. And on, until she began to draw away. Reluctantly he broke the kiss, feathering her lips with coaxing touches of his, moving to her cheek, her ear.

"But this way, too?" she asked, all but pleading.

"Oh God, yes!" He freed one hand to drag open her robe and find the full, soft weight of her breast. "You are willing?" he mumbled, settling his mouth on her neck, then nuzzling her ear again. "Tell me you want this *now.*"

"Oh no, I thought we should wait till dark."

Her breathless words made him pause, uncertain whether she meant it.

"Idiot." She laughed softly and slid a trembling hand up the front of his shirt, tugging ineffectually at one of the studs. "Shall I revoke that rake's license of yours? Must I do everything?" Her lips, rosier than ever from his kisses, turned up enticingly while her lashes lowered and then lifted with unmistakable invitation.

"Flirt," Sean said, pulsing with the pleasurable pain of hot anticipation.

"Tease," she countered with a throaty whisper.

He scooped her up and crossed to the bed. Gently he placed her on it, and followed her lips with his. She made an impatient sound, which he drank in like nectar. Laura wanted him. She wanted *him.*

Her warm, womanly scent invaded his senses, melded with the softness of her skin, the sound of her sighs, the sweet heaven of her mouth. He welcomed the heady invasion and demanded more.

Without thinking, Sean pulled at their clothing, ridding himself and her of any and all that lay between them. He could not taste enough, feel enough to assuage the fiery longing that burned so hot within him. Words tumbled out along with his branding kisses, ardent words of love and need, compelling suggestions and erotic promises.

But underneath the keenest of pleasures lay a pervasive fear of feeling his soul laid bare, bare as her body beneath him. Both vulnerable, exposed to the risk of selfishness or betrayal. Each trusting the other to go fairly and gently about the matter of loving.

Trust. The word echoed in his brain, even as he accepted hers and denied her his own. "I love you, Laura. Love you," he repeated again and again, as though the offering could replace the trust he could not give.

Love and lust came together like thunder and lightning, storming through him so violently he thought he might not last.

Her breasts, ripe and fuller than ever before, greeted his fervent touch, his kisses. The surprising strength of her slender arms held him fast, urged him close, offered him a security he had never known he sought. Soft thighs cradled him as naturally as though born to do so, which he knew they had been. Laura, ordained for him at her very birth. The only one. The love he had searched for all his life.

"I love you," he rasped again as he drove deeply into her, desperate in his claiming of her heart and urgent in his need of her body. The rush of sensation robbed him of control. "No," he groaned, willing her to lie still. But she met his every move, rose against him, taking, giving, throwing him into such wild abandon, he erupted with a shout. She clenched around him, arched and trembled with her own release even as he thrust his last.

With a shudder of relief, Sean enfolded her completely and rolled to his side. "Laura," he breathed into her hair. "My Laura."

No matter what, he thought, he would never let her go. For all their lives, they would remain just so. As they were this moment, joined at the soul. Just the two of them.

Then, in spite of his best intentions, he remembered. There would be soon be three.

Sean fought the thoughts that assailed him in the wake of their lovemaking. Why couldn't he simply dwell on the remarkable intensity of their pleasure, Laura's willingness, his own embarrassing urgency? Better to feel even a bit of chagrin over that than to consider Laura lying with another man. Somehow, he couldn't quite form the picture of that in his mind, thank God.

He did recall the aura of innocence she retained even though they had been intimate three times now. Just how long could a woman project that quality after maidenhood, he wondered.

Sean remembered Campion's recent advice on determining a woman's experience. Her eagerness did not necessarily equal frequent practice at the art, he told himself. Laura was a sensual woman right enough, but certainly no accomplished wanton who had indulged herself often.

A worse thought occurred. Suppose she had been taken against her will. No, he quickly dismissed that possibility. If that were the case, Laura would never have hurried to repeat the act. She would have insisted on a platonic arrangement, at least after the one occurrence required to make him believe the child was his.

Her angry and continued insistence that he was the father could be righteous indignation, couldn't it? He hoped with all his soul it was so, but his old, pragmatic self resisted the idea. She had felt obliged to trick him into marriage with that cock-and-bull story about the fatal illness. Why do that if she had not already been with child and in dire need of a husband?

He turned his head on the pillow and stared at her, wishing he could see into that mind of hers and determine the truth. How childlike she looked now, tousled in exhausted sleep, cheeks and lips reddened, her hands tucked beneath her chin.

Hadn't he said the lies did not matter? They did, of course, but she had his promise not to mention any of that again and he would not. To seal the silent reaffirmation, Sean leaned forward and kissed her lips, the barest touch so as not to wake her.

His eyes traveled down to the curve of her waist and the all but indiscernible swell of her abdomen. Soon she would have no waist to speak of, would blossom with fecund roundness, her shape taunting him unmercifully. Would he go mad with the questions he could never ask?

No, he vowed to himself, he could not allow that. Nothing must mar the perfection they had found together. He would begin to think of this child as his, theirs. Tentatively he pressed his palm to her middle and held it there.

After a moment, he withdrew his hand and turned away from her, unable to feel what he needed to feel inside himself. Acceptance. Trust. Absolute forgiveness. The incapacity disturbed him even more than the reasons for it.

Chapter Sixteen

When they were shown into the drawing room of the MacLindens' elegant town house, the chief inspector greeted Sean like a son, slapping his back as he shook his hand.

He grinned at Laura and wriggled his reddish brows as Sean made the unnecessary introduction. "You will remember Laura, sir? Though I daresay she looks somewhat changed from the last time you saw her."

"Bonny then and bonny now," the older man avowed. "Come, come, here's my Helen. Dearie, meet Sean's bride."

The woman confirmed the theory that opposites attract. Tall and willowy, elegant and beautiful, Helen MacLinden proved to be all that her short, sturdy, energetic husband was not. And yet, they seemed somehow the perfect match for each other.

Laura envied the casual aura of love that surrounded them. No touches passed, no impassioned looks, just a comfortable and steady knowing that communicated itself to all around them. How sweet it must be, that knowing, she thought wistfully.

Their hostess took Laura by the hand after their greeting and drew her away from the menfolk. Eventually their conversation centered on a grouping of pictures distributed along the mantelpiece. Judging by sheer numbers alone, the MacLindens must be extremely prolific, as well as lucky in love. None of their progeny were in evidence tonight, however. Laura wondered at that. Were she and Sean to be the only guests?

Apparently so, for after a half hour of polite conversation, Inspector MacLinden ushered them downstairs to the dining room.

Dinner proved a marvelous affair. Laura could not recall having had such a delicious meal. The girth of their host's waistline indicated that sumptuous fare was not all that unusual. She sighed with pleasure as the maidservant removed her dessert plate.

Mrs. MacLinden suggested they leave the gentlemen to their port and retire to the drawing room. Once they were alone, she politely offered directions to the necessary, just off the hall. Laura took advantage and rejoined her hostess.

Helen MacLinden smiled sweetly at Laura as she settled on the brocade settee. "I recall how it was every time I found myself increasing. I must have availed myself of every convenience in London at one time or another."

Laura laughed at the impertinence. Women usually did not mention their interesting states, even to each other. She liked Mrs. MacLinden and her unassuming ways. "I am going to have a child," Laura admitted, excited over the opportunity to tell someone who might possibly act as though they were happy for her. Thus far, no one had.

"Oh, I know," Mrs. MacLinden said. "Isn't it wonderful?"

"How did you know?" Laura immediately looked down at her own stomach as though its size had given her away. No one could tell yet, surely.

"Sean told Trent. I do hope you don't mind that my husband shared the news with me. He has known Sean since he was a boy, and was very excited about his becoming a father."

The thrill Laura felt made her giddy. Sean had told someone! He had bragged that he was to be a father. He did believe her after all.

Perhaps resuming their intimacy had caused him to reconsider. But when had he told the inspector? Not tonight, she thought. The inspector and his wife had not even spoken with each other alone.

No matter when Sean decided she had told the truth, Laura treasured the fact that he no longer thought she had come to him a fallen woman. Suddenly she could not wait to go home, to have Sean all to herself. He would love her again as he had done today, and then they would speak openly about all the misunderstandings.

Her eagerness embarrassed her, but she could not deny what she felt. The very sight of Sean stirred her senses to fever pitch. The gravelly sound of his voice alone sent a thrill racing through her.

After she had awoken from her nap, Sean had taken her shopping. All afternoon he had teased her and made all those wicked promises with his eyes. Within his smiles, Laura had detected a wistful sadness and attributed it to his continued lack of faith in her. A mistake on her part, surely. He must have been reflecting on all the time they had wasted when he didn't trust her. Everything would be fine now. Better than fine.

She heard the men coming up the stairs from the dining room and so said nothing further to Mrs. MacLinden. At the moment, her happiness seemed too great for words anyway.

MacLinden greeted the ladies and offered Sean a seat. "Might as well get comfortable. We've a bit of business to discuss." He cleared his throat for the attention he already had. "Regarding the notes. Helen offered to assist me in the investigation and she has found something very interesting."

Sean sucked in a quick breath as though to protest Mrs. MacLinden's involvement.

"Wait, wait!" MacLinden said, holding up a palm to forestall it. "You see, she's well acquainted with all the stationers in town, having seen to the printing of numerous wedding invitations for our brood, sheet music for our son's compositions, and so forth. Compared 'em all for just the right paper. Knows what they have available. I've had her check with them concerning the type of paper your notes were written upon."

"Ordinary stock?" Sean said, questioning the lady with raised brows. "Readily available anywhere, I should think."

"Not really," she argued. "It is a rather expensive linen weave, if you look closely, though the color is certainly unremarkable. Only three of the businesses carry it. I've a list of twenty-odd customers who order regularly by the ream. Small individual packets are not available for sale."

"Remarkable!" Sean exclaimed. "I'm impressed by your expertise, ma'am."

"Take a look at the list, Sean," the inspector ordered. "See if you recognize any names." He handed it over.

Laura read, as well. Suddenly she saw it. "Sean! Mr Batts is the stationer in our village! I order through him for Midbrook." She felt ill. "Let me see one of the notes," she demanded.

MacLinden reached into his pocket and withdrew a packet of envelopes, handing one over to her. Laura opened it and drew out the page. For a long moment, she stared at it, felt the texture, ignoring the threatening words it contained. Then in a small voice, she confessed. "I have a standing order with Batts for this very kind. We have used it for as long as I can remember."

She handed the note and envelope back to the inspector. Sean took her hand and squeezed it, offering reassurance, his eyes still locked on the page of names.

MacLinden fiddled in his pocket, leaned forward in his

chair and clasped his hands together over the pipe he never lit. "Any more names that you recognize?"

"Two," Sean said. "Garret Hufflinger, a solicitor I've known for years. Not a friend, exactly, but not an enemy, either." He paused, darting a glance at Laura and then up at MacLinden. "And there's Magnus Norton."

"Mmm-hmm," the inspector hummed, tapping the pipe stem against his knee. "I noticed. And what do you make of that?"

He and the others exchanged pointed and wary looks. Sean stared at the ceiling as though expecting help from above.

"Well, who is Magnus Norton?" Laura asked, since everyone else seemed to know the man.

Sean blew out a breath, curled his lips inward for a moment and then turned to her. "My former fiancée's father."

"Fiancée?" Laura gasped.

"Former. I was betrothed to Camilla Norton. She cried off only a few days before I met you."

"Why?" Laura asked.

"That's not important," he muttered.

"It very well might be!" she retorted. "If someone is trying to kill you, Sean, then we certainly need all the facts about these people." She thumped the list he held. Not a little of her vehemency had to do with jealousy of the unknown woman who had almost married her husband. "Now tell me why she ended your engagement!"

Sean smirked. "She thought she was getting a *royal* bastard apparently. A bastard I am, but royal, I ain't. She felt a bit cheated. No princely blood for her offspring, you see."

"You're certainly better off without her!"

"And much better off with *you*," he said, smiling. "No arguments there, Laura."

Helen spoke up. "You can cross Camilla off your list, I believe. She may have delusions of grandeur, but she can't be capable of murder. Forgive me, Sean, but you must know she isn't overly endowed with brain power."

"Just what *is* she endowed with?" Laura demanded, curious about Sean's reasons for choosing the woman.

"A truly estimable chest!" the inspector declared and then slapped a hand over his mouth. "I never meant to say such a thing!"

Sean threw his head back and roared with laughter. The inspector covered his embarrassed grin with one hand.

"That was unseemly, Trent!" Helen MacLinden scolded. "Now, get back to what we were about!"

The men sobered instantly, but remaining crinkles around their eyes betrayed them. How could Sean join in jest about the woman's physical attributes? Laura shot him a quelling look and ignored Mrs. MacLinden's desire to change the subject. "Sean, for heaven's sake, you almost married the woman!"

"Well, she seemed eminently suitable when she proposed," he explained, all feigned innocence.

Laura huffed. "Oh, *truly estimable,* I suppose. Just like her—"

"Ahem!" MacLinden cleared his throat again, and resumed his assessment of the previous topic. "Well then, chests aside," he said, pausing to smooth down the corners of his mustache, "I do think we may discount the Nortons. Camilla, we agree, hasn't the mental equipment to arrange things, and Magnus has one foot in the grave. He simply isn't able."

"Could he have hired someone?" Laura asked, anxious to erase everyone's memory of her petty display of jealousy.

"I doubt that he could," Sean said. "Old Magnus doesn't even know his own daughter a good part of the time. Some debilitating illness has rendered him nearly incoherent for over a year now."

"Then that leaves my stepfather," Laura said softly,

dropping her head and staring at her lap, horribly ashamed of her connection to the Middlebrook name.

"You know no one else on the list?" MacLinden asked again.

"No," Sean said. "No one."

"Camilla may have been seeing someone else," Helen MacLinden offered. "I saw her entering a closed carriage with a man in Pall Mall not long after you were with her at the Havingtons' ball. Trent tells me that was the night she cried off your engagement. I assumed the fellow was a relative since I believed you still engaged at the time."

"If she has another suitor, she would have even less reason to hold any grudge against Sean," MacLinden pointed out. "Why should she anyway when she was the one who ended the engagement? Surely she wouldn't shoot him because of who his father was—or rather, was not."

Sean rose and paced back and forth, abandoning the list where he had sat. He paused behind Laura's chair and laid a hand on her shoulder. "Another note came today," he announced in a low voice.

When Laura started at his words, he soothed her with his hand. "Please, don't be frightened. I would have told you earlier, but I didn't want to spoil your day. Now, however, I believe we should have everything out in the open."

He reached into the inner pocket of his jacket and withdrew the envelope. Then he unfolded the note and read. *"You have not yet suffered enough, but I weary of the game."*

"Let me see that," Laura said, grabbing it from him before he could refuse. She examined the letters closely. "This isn't my stepfather's handwriting. Nor is it Lambdin's or my mother's."

Sean reached for the note, but Laura held it away. "Wait a moment. Don't you notice something peculiar about this? The shape, I mean."

He looked at it. "It seems smaller than the others. Square."

"Yes!" she exclaimed. "And see these three small specks of blue here at the top edge? Something has been scissored off, but he didn't quite get all of it."

Helen hurried over to kneel before Laura while MacLinden moved the floor lamp closer. "Not the same color as the writing ink. Something was printed on the cutaway portion, a business trademark, do you suppose? The blue spots are like downward points," Helen said. "The writer must have used up all the unmarked second pages and had to resort to trimming off a first page of its identifying symbol. Let me take it to the stationers and try to match it. I shall get to the bottom of this."

"You need not do that," Sean said, heaving a sigh and taking his seat again. "I think I know what it was."

"Well, man, don't keep us in suspense!" MacLinden exclaimed. "What the devil was it?"

"A design, or a device, if you will. A sort of faux heraldry. The spacing of the blue bits is just about right for the lower points on the medallion I have in mind. It would have had a gaudy gothic *N* in the middle. For Norton." Sean grimaced.

He addressed Helen. "What did this man look like, the one you saw with Camilla?"

"Tall, well built, with a dark beard. Expensively dressed, but rather rumpled for all that. I remarked it as odd. Feather-witted, she may be, but Camilla Norton is dreadfully particular about personal appearances."

"Sounds like our fellow, doesn't it?" Sean asked Laura.

"Good Heavens! Then it *is* Camilla!" Helen MacLinden whispered. "She planned to have you murdered!"

"Mmm-hmm," her husband agreed. "I guess she has more brains behind those vacant blue eyes than we credited her with."

"She has brown eyes, Trent!" Helen admonished. "Some chief inspector *you* are. You probably never made it up past her neck!"

MacLinden grinned and winked at his wife.

Sean took the letter and handed it over. "Put this with the others, Lindy. I suppose you will handle things from here on?"

"Of course. Think no more about it. I shall question Camilla first thing in the morning and make an end to all this. Not to worry a moment longer. I shall have the name of her accomplice and take him into custody before you can say what's what!"

"Thank you. Both of you," Sean said, assisting Laura from her chair. "I do believe we should be going now. It has been an interesting evening. Most rewarding," he added with a smile.

Laura and Sean took their leave with promises to meet the MacLindens again under happier circumstances. She had made two new friends. As her first social evening in London, Laura believed it had gone exceptionally well.

As an added bonus, they had discovered that her stepfather was not responsible for the attacks on them, and ascertained the source of the threat that had hung over them ever since they had met. Now, with that worry removed, they could really begin anew.

Best of all that had happened tonight, Laura found that Sean looked forward to the child they would have. He had told his old mentor, Inspector MacLinden, that he would soon be a father himself.

Laura could scarcely contain her joy.

Chapter Seventeen

Sean took her in his arms the moment the door to the carriage closed. Laura laughed merrily when he immediately began planting urgent kisses on her neck and nuzzling her ear. "Sean! Not here! We'll be home in ten minutes."

His mouth ravaged hers as though he fully meant to possess her right there on the carriage seat. She pushed at his chest while she still had sense to do it, and reluctantly he let her go.

Laura laughed nervously, a bit undone by her own ready response and devilish inclinations. "Perhaps you are used to unusual places and positions for this, Sean, but I've not yet graduated to total impropriety."

He grinned wickedly and framed her face with his hands. "You will graduate tonight," he promised. Then he sat back and stretched, closing his eyes and looking supremely satisfied. "Ah, Laura, life's going to be good for us."

"I know," she said. "What do you think we will do for excitement now that we needn't dodge bullets?"

He relaxed and took her hand in his, playing with her gloved fingers. "Any number of things we could do, but you know what's first on my mind."

"And mine," she whispered, turning her hand palm up to grasp his. "Sean, I had a wonderful time tonight. I liked the MacLindens very much. She is a very warm person, isn't she?"

"Good of her to help Lindy trace the notepaper."

"Yes, but I didn't mean just that. She told me that you spoke to him about our child." Laura said happily. "I'm so very glad you look forward to it enough to confide it to your old friend."

Sean stiffened and withdrew his hand, then seemed to think better of the move and clutched it again, squeezing her fingers too tightly for comfort. "Yes. Well." He paused and drew in a deep breath. "I really had hoped Helen would sing for us tonight. Or play, at the very least. She has an extraordinary voice. Their son is a singer, too. Now there's a talent, that one! Brilliant future, I predict. He'll go far, that Scot—"

"Sean!" Laura said, interrupting his prattle. "Whatever is the matter? You obviously told Mr. MacLinden about the baby. Why won't you talk of it to me?"

He remained quiet for a long moment and then sighed. "Of course. What shall I say, then? I hope it is healthy."

"That's all?" Laura asked. "Do you want a boy or a girl?"

Again he sighed and shifted on the seat. "A girl."

Laura smiled. "Well, I hope for a boy. One who is just like his father. Exactly like you."

"We're here," he announced curtly, not even waiting for the driver to open the door. He turned and grasped her waist to help her down. "Best get upstairs and get some rest."

"Indeed," Laura said, disappointed by the chill in his voice. The November air seemed warm by comparison. "I suppose we should. If that's what you want."

Sean opened the downstairs door for her and handed her his key to the door upstairs. "I'll be along directly. I just thought, I really should go and tell Camp about our findings tonight. He'll want to know."

"Tonight? But you said…shall I wait up for you?" she asked, in no way hopeful.

"No. If I see I'm going to be very late, I will stay at Camp's place." He turned away and was back in the hired carriage before she could stop him. As though she would want to do so. If he couldn't bear to stay here with her tonight, he could bloody well live at *Camp's place.*

Disheartened, dejected and absolutely furious, Laura let herself into their rooms, changed into her nightgown and went straight to bed. She did not weep for all that might have been, or dwell in much detail on what lay ahead. But she did promise herself that she would never mention the child again in Sean's presence. Not one word. Let him pretend it did not exist if that's what he intended. She just wondered how in blazes he thought he would ignore it once it got here.

Maybe he felt she was pushing him too hard, dwelling more on the baby than on him. Could Sean be that jealous of her attention? What if she used a little reverse persuasion? If he thought she did not want him to have anything to say about the child, would he begin to insist on it? He was contrary that way.

It was a far reach, perhaps, but Laura was all out of reasonable plans. She couldn't leave him again, for she had nowhere to go. What would that solve anyway? She and the child would be even more alone than if she stayed with Sean. He would never divorce her, but she didn't want that, either. In spite of his mistrust and pigheaded ways, she loved him.

All she did want was for them to be a normal, loving family. Laura suspected Sean simply didn't know how to be a part of that. She wasn't absolutely certain she knew, either, but more than anything in the world, she wanted to try. First, she had to make Sean want the same thing.

* * *

Sean bypassed the building where Camp rented a room and ordered the carriage take him to the In and Out club. He had no desire to talk to anyone he knew well. Camp would be full of questions about the situation with Laura, and Sean had no answers.

There, for a while tonight, Sean had thought things were splendid. The mystery of the notes and attacks was all but solved. Laura liked the MacLindens and had charmed them both. He had her half seduced on the way home with the prospect of a wonderful night ahead. How could he have been so bloody brainless? Freezing up like that at the mere mention of the child she carried. He pounded his fist in his palm and knocked his head back against the wall of the carriage. *Stupid!*

Maybe the night air would clear his head. He signaled for the driver to stop, paid the man and began to walk.

It was hours later, returning home half-frozen, when he almost knocked the woman down. She exited the alley at too brisk a pace and they collided. With a cry of surprise, she clutched the bundle in her arms and tumbled back against the brick wall of Talloway's tobacconist shop.

"I beg your pardon!" Sean said, reaching out to keep her from falling. She swayed and moaned, obviously terrified.

"Don't hurt me!" she cried, pushing at him with her free hand.

Sean schooled his voice to gentleness. "I would never hurt you, madam. Why are you out here on the streets so late and in such weather?"

The weak wail of her infant cut into the night.

Sean wasted no time on further questions. He took the woman by the arm and guided her to a small inn he had passed only moments before.

Once inside, he led her to a table and pushed her down into

a chair. The place was nearly deserted. Only two of the tables were occupied in the public room, both by men nursing a late-night pint. Still it looked a fairly respectable place.

He returned his attention to the woman. "You look done in. What were you doing out there with a little one? Why aren't you home?"

She sniffed and brushed back the kinked strand of red hair hanging in her face. "I have no home," she explained in a flat voice. Then she looked up at him, her wide blue eyes red rimmed from weeping. They reminded him of Laura's eyes as he had seen them once, not lacking spirit, however desperate. "I will not go upstairs with you," she declared.

"I didn't ask you," Sean retorted. "Look, ma'am, I knocked against you accidentally when you came flying out of that alley. All I am trying to do is make amends. Now then, you will have something hot to drink, and then I'll hire you a cab to take you wherever you need to go. Fair enough?"

She nodded, softly rubbing the now silent child she held. Her cracked lips pressed together. She sniffed and then raised her gaze to him again. "Could...could I please have milk? Warm milk?"

"Of course," Sean said, waving the publican over. "Warm milk for the lady. And a brandy for myself." The man nodded and disappeared toward the back.

"My husband is dead," she said suddenly. "There's no money. I have nothing to pay for the drink. I have nothing."

"No family?" Sean asked gently.

"None. Frederick was a soldier. He died last year. I told no one. It took every cent I made sewing, but I managed to hold on to the house until I lost my employment. They made me leave yesterday."

Sean nodded. He knew where this woman eventually would go if he did not intervene. The poor house, a whorehouse, or to another alley to freeze to death. Probably the latter. "I am Sean Wilder, ma'am. Would you accept my help?"

Her laugh sounded more like a strangled cough. "I would take help from the devil himself at this point. I cannot cling to pride and let my Freddie starve."

"You sound well educated."

"My father was a minister. He taught me well enough."

The drinks arrived. Sean slapped down coins and pushed the milk toward the woman. "What is your name?"

"Sylvia Moresfield." She dipped a finger in the milk and touched it to the barely visible lips enclosed in the blanket. A sharp sob escaped her and frantically she tried again. Her hands trembled so violently she couldn't manage.

"Here, allow me," Sean offered. He left his chair and went to kneel beside hers. He withdrew his clean handkerchief and dipped a corner into the milk. With his thumb and fore-finger, he gently opened the little lips and inserted the milky cloth. The baby issued a kittenish mewl and widened his mouth for more. Carefully Sean repeated the process, heedless of the attention he had drawn from the publican and the other customers.

"Best get some of that in the mama, too," one fellow advised. She 'pears right faint."

Sean looked up. He had an audience as rapt as if he con-ducted a bearbaiting. Sylvia Moresfield did look fit to collapse.

"I need a room," he said to the innkeeper, "and food. Anything nourishing. You there—" he motioned one of the customers toward him and fished a gold coin from his pocket "—fetch Dr. Campion at 112 Adkins. He's only a few blocks over, just off Long Acre. Tell him Sean Wilder needs him."

"Cor, th' wild man? You're 'im?" The man's eyes grew wide. At Sean's growl of frustration, the fellow grabbed the coin and raced out the door.

By the time Sean had the Moresfield woman upstairs and settled on the bed, Camp had arrived.

"We've got a problem here," Sean said, not bothering with a greeting.

"You've got a *woman* here!" Camp observed wryly.

"Spare me your wit. She's ill and so is the little one. See what you make of it."

Camp checked the infant first, muttering to himself. Sean looked on, fascinated by the tiny limbs Camp uncovered. "Five or six months old. Low fever. Dry skin. Lethargic. Lax muscle tone." Then came the diagnosis. "Dehydration. Malnutrition. Addiction to laudanum would be my guess."

"So young!" Sean exclaimed. "And her?"

He staggered backwards when Camp thrust the baby at him. "What do you expect me to do with it?"

"Feed it. Here." He handed Sean a spoon from the untouched tray of food and pointed at the food itself. "Mash the peas to pulp and coax in whatever you can. Alternate with spoons of milk. Watch for gagging." Then he turned to the woman, leaving Sean to tend the baby.

Sylvia Moresfield lay unconscious while Campion examined her. By the time he had finished, Sean had arranged a workable solution to the feeding problem. He sat in the chair, one ankle resting across the other knee with the child cradled in the triangle formed by his legs. He worked his own mouth in unison with the baby's as he plied the spoon. "Little devil's got teeth," he announced to Camp. "They clink on the spoon."

Camp laughed. "Unusual technique you have there. Did he eat much?"

"How much is much?" Sean asked. "A few bites. He's had a fair amount of milk, maybe half a cup."

"That is fine. Now pick him up and pat out the wind."

"Beg your pardon?" Sean said, frowning at Campion.

"Put him onto your shoulder and pat his back."

Sean lifted the limp child against his chest. The weightless body felt incredibly warm. Warm and trusting. He heard a soft whimper and felt a feathery sigh. When he looked down, Sean's nose and lips brushed the downy head. He pressed his large hand to the infant's back. So fragile and weak. "He's not going to die, is he, Camp?"

The baby belched louder than Camp in his cups. Sean laughed. Frightened by the unexpected sound, little Freddie began to cry.

"Bounce him," Camp advised, and Sean did so until the howling dwindled to hiccups.

After a while, holding it felt rather natural, so that even after the baby fell asleep, Sean kept it in the crook of his arm. Absently he stroked and patted to keep it content. "The mother?" he asked.

"Exposure. Exhaustion. Mild grippe. I see no signs that she is drugged. It is fairly common to give babies laudanum to keep them docile. Contributes to the high death rate, however. Tend to starve."

"That's abominable!" Sean said, holding little Freddie even closer. He'd had no truck with infants before tonight, but this little fellow began to seem rather special somehow.

"What will you do with them?" Campion asked as he re-arranged his bag to make room for his stethoscope.

Sean considered. "She says she sews. I'll ask Mandy Peebles over on Fairhope to hire her for alterations. That way she can keep little Freddie with her. I suspect she's had to leave him with someone to work. She can let a room from Mandy as well."

"I will stay with them for now," Campion offered. "It is almost morning. Your wife may be wondering where you are."

Sean looked down at the baby resting so comfortably in his

arm. He didn't want to leave it. Neither did he want to be away from Laura a moment longer.

Horrible pictures of Laura and her child chased through dark alleys by shadows, poverty and hunger ran through his mind. Had he really threatened her with that only weeks ago? Never mind that he hadn't meant it. Laura wouldn't know that.

She probably thought he didn't care at all. He had to tell her how untrue that was. More than anything, Sean wanted to love her and keep her safe. And the child, as well. Never again should Laura have to worry what would become of her and the baby, especially not now when she was so vulnerable.

That reminded him, she must have greater worries than just his attitude. "Camp, you will still be here, won't you? When Laura's time comes? You'll ensure that everything goes well?"

"You want me to deliver the child?" Campion asked.

Sean shrugged. "Well, you seemed…capable enough at handling these two." He glanced down at baby Freddie and then over to the mother. "And you are the only doctor I know well."

Camp laughed and rolled his eyes. "Drown me with praise!" Then he sobered and rested a hand on Sean's shoulder. "I will be here, Sean. I have decided to stay in London indefinitely."

Sean puffed out a breath of relief. That was settled.

"And I shall arrange for Mrs. Moresfield's employment first thing tomorrow," Camp said. "You have enough to dwell on. Let me have that little fellow now."

Campion lifted the child from Sean's arms and laid it beside the sleeping mother. "Go home, my friend. See to your own."

Sean felt like running all the way.

Laura awakened to Sean's distinctive knock. He must have misplaced his key. Then she remembered he had given it to her the night before. One glance at the window told her dawn was arriving already. She ought to make him sit on the landing until breakfast, but he would probably wake the entire neighborhood. She slid out of bed, donned her robe and went to let him in.

The moment he entered, he grabbed her close to him, running his hands over her back and shoulders. His face felt frozen when pressed to her cheek, but his voice against her ear was warm and fervent. "Oh, Laura, I can never tell you how much I regret what I said to you. I never meant it, please believe me."

"Are you drunk?" she asked. She hoped he was. If not, he must have taken leave of his senses.

"When I said I would turn you out. You and the child. I would never have done such a thing. I swear it."

"I believe you," she assured him. What in the world had come over him? Where had he been? On pain of death, she would not ask him.

He answered anyway. "I found this woman—"

"Now why does that not surprise me?" she asked, pushing out of his arms and turning away.

"No! No, you don't understand at all," he said, sounding eager to reveal every detail. He crossed his arms over his chest and shook his head as though hopelessly searching for words. "You see, she had this baby and—"

"You *are* drunk!" she declared. "I have no desire to hear this, Sean. Go to bed."

"Come with me," he implored, catching one of her hands. "If you won't let me tell you, then let me show you how sorry I am for all I said."

For a moment, Laura felt tempted. Then she remembered the sudden coldness that had come over him last evening in the carriage. The moment she had mentioned the baby, he had withdrawn as though she had plague. "No, thank you," she murmured. "You obviously need rest. Excuse me." With that, she swept away to the necessary and closed the door between them.

"Laura, please don't do this. We need to talk," Sean said, his voice muffled by the thick oaken door.

Remaining silent, Laura leaned against the door and wondered if she was making a mistake. No, she decided, she did not want to hear about this woman he had found. Or the baby he mentioned. If he couldn't bring himself to speak of their own baby, be damned if she would converse with him about someone else's.

Curiosity nearly overwhelmed her, however. Sean had been gone for hours on end. Who were this woman and child he spoke of? And what was it about them that had stirred Sean to such a state? He had seemed almost frantic. Well, she supposed if he felt so strongly about whatever it was, she would hear all about it soon enough without asking. Sean Wilder certainly was not the most reticent person in the world.

After her bath, Laura slowly opened the door enough to see the bed. His clothes lay on the floor where he had shucked them off. Sean stretched out, half-covered, one arm thrown back over his head, sound asleep.

She tiptoed into the bedroom and lay down carefully, so as not to wake him. It was a long time until breakfast and she had nowhere else to wait. Angry as she was, Laura refused to bed down on the floor or in the bathtub. Her thoughts kept her awake for what seemed hours.

She had just begun to drift into sleep when she heard his lazy whisper. "He didn't appear that appealing at first glance, you know? A rather ugly little imp, come to think of it. The mother was no prize, either, dirty and nearly frozen to death, but how fiercely she loved that baby! The attachment to him just grew in me, Laura. So quickly I didn't even realize it was there at first. I held him and dribbled that milk into his mouth and just sort of started caring. I saved him. *Me.* Well, Camp helped, I suppose, but I felt…responsible for him. More than that."

For a while, Sean remained silent. Laura breathed in and out, keeping the slow rhythm of it so he would not realize she was awake. She needed to think about this. Who were these people he spoke of? Someone he had met with last night, obviously. Some woman he had known before? One who had borne his child and searched him out to tell him so?

"Where he came from didn't matter, you see?" he continued. "Given a bit more time, I could have loved that little boy. I think I must have a strong affinity for children, after all. And I'm so *damned* glad of it, Laura. I wish I could tell you." His sigh was prolonged and contented.

As soon as she felt certain he slept, Laura rose, collected her clothing and dressed. She knew there was no point in trying to sleep after hearing all of that. What should she make of it, his strange revelation? It made her vaguely jealous of this unknown woman and homely child he felt such an *affinity* for. And thanks to her pretense of sleep, she couldn't very well question him about something he thought she had not heard. Better to dismiss it from her mind altogether. If she could.

She went downstairs and was having her third cup of tea, waiting for the other boarders to arrive for breakfast when MacLinden arrived, shown in by Mrs. High. "Laura," he said urgently, his unusual agitation frightening her. "I hope to God Sean is here."

"He is upstairs asleep," she said. "What has happened?"

"A murder," MacLinden declared, mangling the brim of his curly-brimmed bowler. "Camilla Norton is dead."

Chapter Eighteen

Sean struggled out of the fog of exhaustion, certain he could have slept only for moments. Lindy's voice prodded him, "Come on, man! We have a situation here!"

"What?" Sean asked sleepily. He slid his legs over the side of the bed and sat up holding on to the sheet with one hand. Then he yawned and briskly rubbed his face with his hands.

"Camilla Norton's been murdered," Lindy announced. "We found her in the Norton town house. Stabbed. Dead at least a month."

That woke him up. "Camilla? But who—"

"I've sent to their house in Kent to see whether the servants know anything. Apparently everyone else accompanied the old man when he left town. We simply don't know any more than that. One of the staff spoke with a friend next door before the household packed up. Said they were retiring to the country for Norton's health. Why Camilla stayed behind, we haven't a clue. Surely we can surmise what happened to her as a result of it."

"Damn!" Sean rasped. The implication was that the bearded man Helen had seen Camilla with had killed her. Had her deal with the man hired to kill Sean gone awry somehow? Or could it be because Camilla had been betrothed to Sean and someone thought to punish him with her death? The latter seemed more likely. Even though the writing paper for the threats had probably come from her, Sean could not believe that Camilla had such a vindictive nature. Would she have sought his death over a broken betrothal? Even though she had broken it herself? Sean didn't think so. And how would she have established the contacts to hire an assassin?

"Suppose someone befriended her," he suggested. "Someone bent on revenge toward me. He could have used her to find out what he could about me, then killed her. That would explain the stationery. He could have stolen that from her father's study easily enough while visiting. Helen saw Camilla with the man, so we know they were not strangers."

Sean paid no attention to Lindy's answer. His mind was busily engaged in sorting out facts and applying them to possible theories about how his former fiancée might have courted death.

"Might this have anything to do with the murders of the other women you are investigating?" Laura asked, taking a seat beside Sean on the bed. She felt an insurmountable need to be near him, no matter how much he had disappointed her last night. All that seemed so insignificant in light of what had happened. MacLinden's news made it quite clear that they were not out of danger yet. She did not even think to protest when Sean's arm drew her close.

MacLinden heaved a sigh and clasped his hands behind him. "Oh no, I don't believe this is connected at all. All the others have happened in the streets and alleys where women should not venture in the first place. This took place in her own home. Also, there's the fact Miss Norton was stabbed repeatedly with a knife, but not slashed or mutilated in any way. Whoever did this made no attempt to hide or move the body. That's why we found her."

He continued, all business now, his earlier excitement banked. "We went there early this morning, intent on questioning Camilla about all we spoke of last night. Maybe to arrest her if what we thought proved true. I stationed men all around the house in the event someone might try to evade us. One of the men passed the library and glanced in. She was on the floor right by the floor-length window."

"Stabbed," Sean repeated. "Poor Camilla." He looked at Laura with regret in his eyes. "I don't believe she tried to have me killed. And it really seems unlikely after what's just happened. She was not all that bad, you know?"

"I should hope you didn't think so when you meant to marry her," Laura said.

"She only wanted acceptance by the elite," he explained. "I found it amusing that she would try to accomplish that by marriage to me. She was a wealthy merchant's daughter, her station not unlike your own, Laura. And beautiful. But even those attributes didn't bring her the invitations she wanted so much. At the time, I thought a wife might be just the thing. Someone to accompany me to social functions I had to attend, the very ones Camilla sought.

"Living as a bachelor can be, well, inconvenient at times. But I had no urge to commit myself to a woman I might develop a tendresse for. I'd had my lesson in that with Ondine. No danger of that with Camilla, though I liked her well enough. We might have gone on fairly well together, had she not kept harping on my *royal* connections. Once I confessed that was merely a foolish rumor, she cut me dead. I thought that rather sad."

"Rather shallow, if you ask me," Laura said, moving a little away from him and chafing her arms when she shivered. "But I certainly wouldn't wish anyone dead for that."

Sean scoffed. "Were that a cause for death, London would be damned near full of corpses."

"Be that as it may," MacLinden interrupted, dismissing the subject, "we must get you both to safety. There is no way we can find this bloke who killed her with such a limited description. Why, he could turn up anywhere you go."

"Then how do we catch him if we don't set a trap for him?" Sean asked. "I think I should send Laura to my mother and then wait until he strikes again. He won't kill me if I stay on guard."

"No! I refuse to go unless you come, too. You cannot protect yourself against the unknown, Sean! How would you know when or where he might find you?" Laura gripped his forearm and shook it. "Please come with me!"

MacLinden looked from one to the other, waiting for their decision. Laura pleaded with the man, "Tell him I'm right, Inspector! Tell him!"

"Sean, I can't promise you adequate protection here. I can assign a man or two to hang about, but that may not be enough. Why don't you accompany Laura to Cornwall, stay there at least until we discover what we can from all of Camilla's acquaintances? Perhaps one of them will know who our culprit is, or at least give us more to go on. I promise to wire you the moment we have any more news."

Sean reluctantly agreed. "The man has already killed once, perhaps three times, if he was responsible for the deaths of Mr. Beaumont and his nephew in Paris. I suppose if nothing turns up about him on further investigation, we can always arrange to lure him in later. We won't wait until dark to leave. At least in daylight, I will know if we are followed."

MacLinden nodded. "I'll say goodbye to you then, and get about my business. You two have a care. Watch your back, son." He took his leave and saw himself out, closing the door behind him.

Laura closed her eyes and sighed with relief. Sean would not send her away alone.

After MacLinden had gone, Sean took her in his arms and pressed her face against his chest. He sat very still, as though lost in thought. The sleepy male scent of him surrounded her, stirring feelings she did not welcome, yet clung to. But he was so warm, his embrace so protective, she couldn't move away.

Then she opened her eyes and found herself gazing straight down his body. He was completely naked. Only a corner of the sheet draped across his lap provided any cover at all. And that did not begin to hide what his thoughts concerned.

"I want you," he said in a low, determined voice. "I want you *now.*"

"I want you, too," she replied, her own words a mere whisper.

No matter what the differences between them, only the physical difference counted at the moment. Laura needed to banish the frightening imaginings MacLinden's news had wrought. Of a dead woman lying in a pool of blood. Of Sean suffering a like fate.

She had faced her own death, even resigned herself to it once. But she knew that facing Sean's would destroy her completely. At the very thought of it, dignity deserted her. Laura slid her arms around his neck, drew his head down to hers and kissed him for all she was worth.

Sean's mouth ground on hers, devouring it, stealing her breath, filling her senses so completely the outside world might not have existed. His groan of urgency mirrored her own as he lay back on the bed and rolled her beneath him. She felt his hand drag up her skirts, tear at her lace pantalets, and at last find the part of her so desperate to have him.

"Mercy!" she gasped, digging her fingers into the muscles of his shoulders.

Sean devoured her mouth again, and braced his lower body

away from her only long enough to position himself. He thrust into her with such fervor, she cried out, the keening sound muffled by their kiss.

He tore his lips away, uttered a rough murmur, an apology or perhaps a curse, she didn't care. She grasped his hips with both hands and arched to meet him, matching that fervency, reveling in each wild and mindless lunge. Her fingers scraped up his back, scratching, kneading his body. They slid up the column of his neck to twist in the soft waves of his hair.

Sean's grip on her shoulders, holding her steady for his un-relenting invasion, slackened as he opened his hands and sought her breasts. He squeezed roughly as though angered by the interfering fabric of her dress, and then abandoned the effort. Again he clasped her, long fingers pressing into the softness above her collarbone. Tortured sounds issued from his throat as he pounded into her furiously.

The deep, pulsing ache inside her demanded more and he gave it, driven, hastening his momentum, hurtling her over the edge of madness with a mighty roar that matched her cry of completion. Again he thrust, and once more. She felt the heat of him suffuse her, the sweet, liquid fire that burned away her tension, her fears, and offered the sweetest peace.

For a long while, he lay there, his face nestled in the curve of her neck, his long supple hands still clutching her shoul-ders. The heaviness of his body precluded all but the shallow-est of breaths. She thanked heaven she no longer wore a corset.

Suddenly he lifted away from her, propped on his elbows, his face only inches from hers. Laura sucked in a deep draft of air and smiled up at him. How uncertain he looked. Or shocked.

"That was unforgivable," he murmured. "Unforgivable."

"I'm sorry. Did I hurt you?" Laura asked with a grin.

He rolled away from her and sat up, cursing.

"Sean, what is it? What is wrong?"

"I hurt *you*," he said, staring down at his hands as though they had betrayed him.

"You did no such thing," she assured him softly. "If I ever felt more fit, I cannot recall it." She pushed herself up and spread her dress down. "All right then, a bit breathless and weak in the knees, but certainly not hurt."

If he heard her at all, he gave no indication. "Never. Never have I taken a woman that way. I...I lost control. That's no excuse. I know it's no excuse."

Laura draped her arms around his shoulders. "It's all right, Sean. Really."

"No!" he declared, turning swiftly to face her, glaring. "It is not all right! I could have damaged you seriously, or injured the child!" He dragged a hand over his face, his whisper distraught. "You begged mercy."

"And you gave it! So thank you," she replied, exasperated with his self-reprimands. "Fishing for compliments?"

"God, no! What is wrong with you?"

She groaned with frustration. "Nothing! Absolutely nothing." Lud! It wasn't as though he had been brutal! Just carried away. She had quite enjoyed every second of the encounter, had loved the fact that she could drive the wild man even wilder. The thought made her smile even now. She had felt quite feral herself. Never had she felt the child in danger or she would certainly have let him know it.

But she must not talk about the baby with him, she reminded herself. She had promised herself she would never mention it again to him. Not until she was absolutely certain he accepted the fact that it was his. He looked so distressed right now, however, she felt she ought to do something to convince him she was not about to expire or miscarry.

"Laura, I am sorry," he said simply, sincerely.

"Well, I would take a fire poker to you and make you feel

better, but I expect we had best get up and pack our things. You did say you wanted to leave today." Summoning some hidden reserve of energy, Laura hopped out of bed and proceeded to the necessary room to set herself to rights. At the doorway, she turned and flashed him a bright smile for good measure. "Get the traveling cases out, would you? We don't have all day."

Two days later, Sean still felt the dismay. She totally confounded him. Laura had turned him inside out in the brief time they had known each other. She had changed him from a streetwise business man with a firm handle on his world, into a love-struck fool who hardly knew what to do next. He should hate her for it.

He watched her every move. He had done so ever since she had adopted that attitude of false gaiety after their lovemaking. *Lovemaking.* Ha! It qualified as a debauch, plain and simple. He had never even treated a paid lover as roughly as he had Laura, his own wife.

News of Camilla's murder, following so closely the near death of Sylvia Moresfield and her child from exposure, had unnerved Sean. Envisioning Laura in both situations, he had reacted too desperately, too harshly, to the fear he might lose her. Despite the brief engagement, he had not known Camilla very well, and the Moresfield woman, not at all. But they both represented what fate might have held, and might yet hold, for Laura. Still he would have behaved with more finesse had Laura not responded with such exceptional vigor. No, he would not blame her. Not for any of it. He had done the inexcusable.

And she would hear no apology for it, would allow him no way to make amends. Every time he broached the matter, she changed the subject.

She did the same thing whenever he mentioned the child.

He had wanted her to listen to his experience with Sylvia Moresfield and little Freddie. He needed to reassure her that he had discovered he quite liked babies. Even monkey-faced little fellows with jug ears and eyes too close together.

Unable to discuss his latest transgression on her person, or Laura's pregnancy, it seemed all they had left to talk about was their impending arrival in Cornwall and the reason for it. That was no pleasant topic, raising as it did visions of murder and stalking villains. And that thought brought him right back where he'd begun, to two days past. The time when he had tried to assuage his terror for Laura on her body.

It was worse than a single thought, however. His wayward mind constantly repeated the episode in vivid detail. He closed his eyes against the picture of Laura's exquisite breasts, heaving and hidden beneath the fine lawn and moire of her clothes. His hands clenched into fists trying to prevent the tactile memory of her softest skin. He even breathed through his mouth to avoid her scent. All of that—all of her—kept him randy as a half-grown lad in the first throes of lust. Maddening. And damned uncomfortable.

The whole trip to Cornwall was proving a nightmare, one that could only grow worse once they reached their destination. Then he would have his mother to deal with, as well. More guilt. Lord, it was enough to make him swear off women altogether.

They were two days out of London now, traveling by train and nearing the coast of Cornwall. Though he would have preferred a ship, he couldn't bear to have Laura endure seasickness again, especially in her condition.

Their private compartment on the railcar was comfortable enough, but Sean wondered if he shouldn't have bought regular seats just for the company of other passengers. As it was, Laura spent almost every waking moment in the dining car, chatting with perfect strangers. While he brooded. Bad form, he knew, but the whole situation gave him far too much time to think. Thinking led to examining all the motives for his recent actions, not a pleasant pastime, to be sure.

Now, for once, he had her alone and awake. They sat in their private car, on opposite seats, anticipating their arrival at the station nearest his mother's home. Laura stared out the window at the passing countryside. Sean stared at her.

"We're almost there. Are you feeling well?" he asked.

"Of course! Never better," she said brightly, pointing out the window. "Look there, so many cows! Do you have cows on your estate?"

"Some, I think," he replied carefully. "Laura, we really should talk about things. Settle a few matters."

She adjusted her velveteen hat, fiddling with the pin. "Matters are quite settled, I should think. We weren't followed to the train station. The trip has been lovely. No one but MacLinden knows where we will be."

"Not that," Sean said with a frown, "I think we should talk about the child, Laura. I've wanted to tell you—"

"Will I have any specific duties about the house once I'm settled in? I do hope I might help your mother in any way I can," she said, smoothing her skirts and buttoning on her gloves.

"Laura, look at me. I want to tell you something," he said. "I have realized that—"

"La! Will you look at the time?" She glared at her lavaliere watch and started to rise. "I did promise Mrs. Williams I would say goodbye before we arrived at our destination. She's to go on to Havers to disembark. I do believe we shall be neighbors, however. At least within riding distance. Might I have her over for a visit one day? Yes, of course I will. She will be good company for your mother, too, don't you think?"

"I think you're babbling, Laura," Sean interrupted, speaking through his teeth, struggling with his impatience.

"Well, you are absolutely right, I'm sure," she said, sounding distracted as she hurried out of their car. "I shall meet you at the exit."

The closed carriage Sean had hired to drive them from the train station clattered up the paving stones to the front entrance of Willow Weep. "Charming!" Laura exclaimed. "Absolutely charming."

She had expected the place to look cold, forbidding and battered by sea winds, rather like the setting for some gothic novel. In fact, the house sat almost a mile distant from the cliffs and was surrounded by lovely, well-kept grounds. The gray stone structure with its white-painted wooden trim looked warm and inviting.

"You'll find it modest compared to Midbrook Manor," Sean commented as he leapt down and held up his arms to assist her. For a long moment, he held her, molded her to his body. She shifted closer in spite of herself. Then he shook his head as though to clear it, set her down and turned away. Laura took perverse pleasure in cracking that polite reserve of his, however inadvertently it had happened.

"Willow's smaller, at any rate," he said, as though nothing untoward had taken place. "Only twelve bedrooms and that's counting the servant's quarters."

In spite of the deprecation, Laura could tell he loved the place. So did she. The facade, at least, possessed an aura of welcome Midbrook did not. She watched as he and the driver unloaded their luggage, wondering what life at Willow Weep would hold for them.

"Master Sean!" a gravelly voice greeted them from the front doors. "You've come home!"

"Sonnet, you old reprobate!" Sean strode forward and embraced the tall, portly older man. "Still spouting that twisted verse you call poetry?"

"Rhyme a day, or the devil to pay," the man admitted with a throaty laugh. "Welcome home, son." His large, capable hands slapped Sean's back. "Your mother has missed you dreadfully."

Sean released the fellow and reached for Laura's arm to draw her near. "My wife, Laura," he said with a distinct note of pride. Proud of whom, Laura wasn't exactly certain. "This is Byron Sonnet, butler, steward, friend and poet extraordinaire!"

"How do you do," Laura said, extending her hand.

"Wife!" the man whispered the word. "Heavens above! What wondrous deeds have you performed lately to merit this sort of luck? She's prime, lad, simply prime!" He pumped Laura's hand, grinning all the while. "Married, imagine! Her Ladyship's going to faint with glee!"

Ladyship? Pet name or reality, Laura wondered. Sean had said his mother was wellborn. She shot Sean a questioning look which he ignored. Instead, he grabbed one of her smaller travel bags and ushered her up the steps and through the open doors.

Sonnet virtually danced around them all the way to a small salon and preceded them inside. "Anne! You'll never guess! Look who's here! And a wife, darling! He has a wife!"

Darling? The butler called Her Ladyship *darling?* Laura suppressed her shock and dropped a curtsy to the smiling woman in a bath chair with wheels. Highborn or not, Laura knew the value of first impressions. This was her mother-in-law.

Sean bowed stiffly. "My mother, Lady Anne Cavendish," he said formally, and presented Laura, "Mrs. Laura Wilder, my wife."

The woman bit her lips together for a moment. Tears hovered on the edge of her lower lids and finally trickled

down her cheeks. When she spoke at last, she addressed
Laura. "My dear child. How delighted I am to meet you."
Then the sea green eyes turned to Sean. "Thank you for
coming, Sean. You will stay?"

"For a while," Sean replied. "Unless you prefer we find
other accommodations."

"This is your home, Sean. Nothing makes me happier than
to have you here."

"Ah," Sean said, looking away from her as though examining every object in the room, "I suppose that is why you
weep whenever I appear." He backed toward the doorway.
"Excuse me while I collect our things."

Before anyone could object, he disappeared.

"I ought to cane the scamp," Sonnet said under his breath.

Sean's mother chuckled. "I should dearly love to watch you
try that. He seems to have grown even larger in the past year,
don't you think?"

They laughed together, an abbreviated sharing fraught with
meaningful looks and remembered conversations. Like
longtime friends. Or lovers. Laura noted for the first time that
Byron Sonnet wore clothing every bit as finely made as Sean's
own things. This Mr. Sonnet cut a fine figure, almost as tall
as Sean, and rather handsome, in a rugged sort of way. He
looked nothing like a butler or a steward, however. And not
at all like a poet. His bearing seemed that of a noble—at the
very least, gentry—and totally lacked subservience. And, if
he really was a servant, why was Sean seeing to the baggage?

The small Lady Anne looked nothing like her son, except
for her bright green eyes. Dark curls wisped around a creamy
oval face remarkably free of age or worry lines, though she
must be nearing the half-century mark. Beautiful, almost clas-
sical features relaxed into a comfortable, genuine smile that
settled on Laura like a benediction. The woman held out both

hands to her. "So you're to be my daughter, child! Will you call me Mother?"

Laura felt her own eyes fill. Sean's mother accepted her? Just like that, she accepted an unknown woman who could very well be an adventuress or an unlikable creature of the very worst sort? No artifice. No suspicion. No wait-and-let-us-see. Laura felt herself drawn to the older woman. She recalled a similar reaction to Sean, but had attributed that to pure physical attraction. Perhaps there had been need involved in that instance, as well.

Laura knelt just to the side of the bath chair's wheel and looked up at Lady Anne. "Most gratefully, Mother," she whispered, her voice thick with emotion.

Lady Anne leaned over and kissed her cheek. "I am honored. Now why don't you run along with Byron. He will show you to your room so that you may rest and freshen yourself after your journey. Later, we shall have a long talk and become acquainted."

"Thank you, ma'am," Laura said, rising. She followed Sonnet from the room and up the stairs, unable to think of anything but the fact that she had just acquired a mother, one who had kissed her and made her welcome. She didn't know why she should feel so heart-warmed and flattered to tears by all that. The woman even loved the butler, for heaven's sake.

"On the left," Sonnet proclaimed. "Your room is just here." He threw open the door to a chamber tastefully dressed in pale yellow. Perpetual sunshine, she thought, smiling.

"And through there is the master's chamber. Aha, I hear the rascal rattling about. Excuse me, please." Sonnet whisked through the dressing room. Laura peeked into the other bedroom before the door closed and saw Sean placing her portrait on the mantel. A warm, hopeful feeling suffused her. Laura heard the two men exchanging their good-natured insults. Strange how close they seemed. Like brothers. Or father and son.

Why did Sean hold this man in such friendly regard and yet puff up with all that formality when he faced his mother? It must have to do with the accident Sean said had crippled her. He had told her he felt responsible for that. Laura recalled mocking him for it at the time. Now she must figure a way to reconcile mother and son. A worthy goal for her stay here, she thought.

As she opened her case and laid out a change of clothing, a timid little voice intruded on her thoughts. "Ma'am? I be Emmy, at yer service. 'Er Ladyship says ye might be liking a bath?"

"That would be heaven, Emmy. I am Mrs. Wilder."

"Oh, I know," the maid said with a wide gap-toothed grin. "Master's got hisself marrit. We are that proud, all of us belowstairs. I'll just go and see to th' water, ma'am."

"Thank you, Emmy," Laura said, unbuttoning the jacket of her traveling costume.

She wondered why Sean had not written to his mother of their marriage. Almost three months wed, and the bride exactly that far gone with child. Heaven grant the baby would go full term and more. She did not want Sean's mother to think the worst of her. But beyond that, and even more important, Laura knew it was the one thing that might help convince Sean he was the father. Even then he would have room for doubt, but it was the best she could hope for.

Laura wondered if not discussing the child with Sean had produced the desired effect on him, and made him want to talk about it. She could not count the times he had tried to introduce the topic. Cutting him off midsentence with a change in subject had worked thus far. She had limited the opportunities by avoiding him as much as possible on the train. His frustration was mounting and she expected an explosion anytime now. She hoped that this time it would clear the air.

Laura felt that something other than her mistake about her dying prevented his accepting her word that he was the father. She had accused him of not wanting the commitment of a permanent marriage and fatherhood. But he had been perfectly willing to marry Camilla Norton at one time. Besides that, if he were so dead set against marriage now, wouldn't he have jumped at the idea of divorce? It must be the responsibility of rearing a child, any child, that troubled him. He had promised to accept this one, even while insisting that he had not sired it. But that offer had been grudgingly made.

She looked forward to her get-acquainted talk with Lady Anne. Surely the woman could give her a better understanding of Sean. He had been open about some events during his childhood, but Laura thought there might be a number of devils not yet exorcized.

Laura wished to heaven she knew him better. The man she had married and the Sean Wilder most of London knew hardly bore any resemblance to each other. His reputation—which she now knew he had encouraged if not fostered himself—declared him a rogue, a man given to violence, one who could be hired for the darkest and most dangerous deeds. Laura knew Sean as a compassionate, tender husband, a man who gathered friends and inspired their trust and respect. Yet she also understood that a part of the public's perception of Sean must be true. Though never violent with her, he certainly had been volatile at times. And she had witnessed his justified brutality with others, such as her stepfather. He had broken the man's arm without exhibiting a shred of remorse.

Doubtless he had done other, even worse things for which he could not forgive himself. One of those had to do with Lady Anne's confinement to a bath chair. How many other acts preyed on Sean's soul? And were they what caused him to fear the responsibility of loving a wife and child as he should? Did he use her supposed lies as a protective measure?

And a better question, could she help him past that barrier and reinforce the bond they had begun to form soon after their marriage?

Now that they were safely ensconced here in Cornwall, Laura felt her chances of that happening improved. At least they need not be on guard against a threat to their lives while settling the problems confronting their shaky marriage.

Chapter Nineteen

"You and my mother seem to be getting on well," Sean observed as he seated Laura for breakfast.

They had been here nearly a week and all her fine hopes for enlightenment and reparation remained unfulfilled. Sean spent most of his time out-of-doors despite the chill of late November. "Seeing to things," he explained when she questioned him about it.

She and Lady Anne had engaged in several long and interesting talks, none of which addressed Laura's concerns about Sean. Mr. Sonnet remained present most of the time, adding his wry comments and ready wit. Enjoyable, those conversations, but not the least informative.

She still had no idea exactly what Sonnet's relationship really was to the family. He answered the door and directed the other servants as though he really were the butler. He pored over the account books with Sean and complained about matters of the estate just like any steward might. But he also teased Sean unmercifully, calling him "master" in one breath and "scamp" with the next. And he looked on Lady Anne as a devoted husband might do.

Since she had Sean alone this morning, her curiosity finally overcame good manners. "Just who *is* Mr. Sonnet?"

His laughter burst forth unexpectedly, thankfully banishing the serious demeanor that had grown rather tiresome. "Ah, our Mr. Sonnet. Just what is he?" He folded his arms across his chest and seemed to ponder it, still wearing a smile. "I suppose I shall have to tell you a story in order to explain."

"I'm all ears," Laura invited, encouraged by Sean's apparent good humor. "He is a most charming fellow, but he doesn't seem to fit in any particular role. Or rather, he fits too many roles. And as yet, I haven't heard a single line of poetry, good or bad."

Sean assumed a thoughtful look and leaned forward in his chair, his elbows on the table. He toyed with his coffee cup. "Byron was an actor who frequented Ruffles House when Mother and I lived there. He befriended me when I was around five or six. Used to give me coins to run errands for him. And no, he wasn't a private customer of my mother's, if that's what you are thinking."

"Never entered my mind."

"It entered his, I'm sure. And possibly hers, after knowing him a while," Sean said wryly. "Byron patronized the other women occasionally. That's how we met him. He was always kind and friendly to the both of us whenever he came round. I knew from the first he loved her, and used to pretend to myself that he was my father, before Mother told me who really had done the wicked deed."

He sighed and swept a hand over his mouth before continuing, "When I was…taken away that time," he said, glancing up briefly at Laura, and then back down at his coffee, "and when Mother was injured, Byron looked after her for me. He simply refused to leave her side. Madam threatened to throw him out of Ruffles, of course. He paid the going rate, just to stay."

Laura smiled at the sweetness of that. "Is he a paid companion of sorts now?"

"Heavens, no, never that! Byron has money. He had offered to take Mother away from Madam's employ long before we actually left, but she refused him. At the beginning, I suppose she believed he had ulterior motives. Later, I think she didn't want him embarrassed by her past. Then when Grandmother rescued us, Byron immediately followed. He applied for a position as footman here, and progressed to butler within the year. Once Grandmother died, he assumed full responsibility for Mother and everything else around the place. I was away at school and then with the army. Went directly to the Yard after I mustered out. Byron assumed all the duties I should have. He still does."

"I see. They are lovers now, aren't they," Laura said, more a statement than question.

"Undoubtedly."

"Then why don't they marry?"

"Why should they?" Sean countered defensively. "Propriety's sake?" He huffed. "They seem incredibly happy as they are, don't you think?"

"You don't believe in marriage much, do you, Sean?"

"Now why would you say that?" he asked with a dry half smile. "I wed Ondine, didn't I? And considered it a second time with Camilla, if you recall. And then I married you. It is the only way to get heirs. And speaking of that—"

Laura rose quickly, abandoning her breakfast uneaten and heading for the door. "I have something I must—"

"I shall say goodbye now, then," Sean said, effectively halting her in her tracks. He got up and came to stand before her.

"Goodbye?" She felt at a loss for words. He was leaving. Because she wouldn't speak of the child?

"I've decided to return to London and assist Lindy with the investigation."

"No!" she exclaimed. "No, you can't!" She grasped the front of his coat as though she could physically prevent his going.

His hand closed around hers. "I think I must. You will be safe here and I will send Campion to you when your time is near. Mother and Byron love you already, and they will look after you in my absence."

Rage overwhelmed her. "Leave, then! Get out! Go and get yourself killed as you've tried to do since you got out of knee pants! First Africa, then the Yard, and God only knows what hazards you've taken on since then. I don't know what propels you to throw yourself at death the way you do, Sean. I suppose I never shall. But someone will shoulder your responsibilities for you, won't they? Someone will pick up what you toss away because it got too close. Because *I* got too close. And you'll no longer have to worry, will you? All you must do is seek one danger after another, until one of them kills you. You did say there are worse things than death, Sean! Is staying with me worse than death to you? Do you want to die?"

With a jerk, he dislodged her hand from his lapel and shoved past her without another word. She stood motionless, listening, jumping when a heavy door slammed. Soon after that she heard the sharp clop and scrape of hooves on the paving stones, changing to thundering thuds once he reached the road.

He must be desperate to get away to travel horseback, came the ridiculously superficial thought. Laura sank to the floor, wrapped in her own arms.

An hour later, she wished she had simply kept her mouth shut and waved goodbye.

"Laura is probably right," Byron Sonnet said softly as he rested his hands on Lady Anne's shoulders. "I have wondered as much myself."

Laura wished now she had not poured forth the story of her altercation with Sean to these two. They had caught her at the worst possible moment, in the dining room, before she had recovered herself. The pain on Lady Anne's face shamed Laura for indulging in the confidence. They could not possibly alter the situation, and it only added to their obvious worry over Sean's comings and goings during the past few years.

"It was that time he spent with Aversby," his mother stated with a meaningful look at Byron. She pounded her palm with her fist. "My God, I wish I had killed the man myself."

"Well, he's quite dead, I assure you," Byron said. "I saw to it."

Laura gaped. This jaunty old fellow had murdered a lord? Because the man had bought Sean away from his mother? "Perhaps Sean believes *he* killed Lord Aversby," Laura suggested. "He was very young at the time. Maybe guilt over that troubles him. He did hit Aversby over the head."

"He discussed this with you?" Byron asked, disbelieving.

"Yes, of course. He said he escaped that first night, before anything untoward happened, by knocking the man out."

Lady Anne squeezed her eyes shut and shook her head.

"No, my dear," Byron said to Laura, "though it was quite obvious Sean had tried to get away time and again. You see, he was there for three weeks. Until I discovered where he was and shot Lord Aversby through the heart."

"Oh, dear God!" Laura pressed her hands to her mouth and thought she might be sick.

Byron went on, "I carried Sean back to Anne. The poor lad had been beaten within an inch of his life and looked a proper corpse. When I entered Ruffles with him in my arms, Anne collapsed at the sight of him. Fell down the stairs." He brushed a hand over Anne's hair. "Too frightening, wasn't it, darling?"

Laura went to her, knelt and took her hand, as much to

comfort herself as Anne. "Sean feels responsible for your accident," she explained. "That is why he seldom visits here. Though he says the memories he brings with him are too much for you, he must find them even worse than you do. What are we to do for him? How can we help him?"

Anne sighed, a forlorn sound, sad as her eyes. "I have to speak of it with Sean when he comes back again. We should have straightened this out long ago, but I thought he had put it all behind him. Somehow, I always believed his avoidance of me was due to shame over my mistakes. Heaven knows I made enough of those to turn the best of sons bitter."

"Now, now," Byron comforted. "What's past is past. Sean loves you dearly." He turned his gaze on Laura. "And you as well, my dear girl. I see it in his eyes whenever he looks at you. He will return soon. I cannot imagine his doing without you for very long. Not to worry. Sean will finish that nasty business in London and be back straight away, I'll warrant. Our lad can take care of himself."

"Yes, of course," Laura said without conviction. Sean had not told either his mother or Byron Sonnet why they had come to Cornwall. He hadn't wanted them to worry them about the threats. Thanks to her, they now had that cross to bear, as well. "If you will excuse me, I need to think about all of this."

Byron nodded. "So do I." Then he leaned over Lady Anne's chair and patted her hands. "I'm going to take you up to your room and leave you by your window to sew. You put on that thinking cap of yours while you're about it, sweetheart. I am due over at Briarhaven this morning to select one of their bulls to buy. When I return, we shall all put our heads together and decide what must be done about the boy when he gets back. He'll come for Christmas, no doubt, and we shall have him put to rights by Boxing Day, you'll see!"

Laura watched Byron lift Lady Anne from her chair and

carry her to the stairs as though she were weightless. There was a mighty strength in Byron Sonnet that had little to do with his size.

For a long time Laura sat alone before the fire in the small salon, contemplating what must be done about her husband. Byron had ridden off to Briarhaven, while Lady Anne must be upstairs mulling over the same thoughts Laura struggled with. She really ought to go and keep her new mother company.

Just as she rose to do so, someone knocked loudly on the front door. They were on short staff today, with only her, Emmy and Mary Lou, Lady Anne's maid and sometime cook, about the house. The rest were on days off she recalled, it being Sunday. Laura hurried across the foyer and swung open the door.

A stranger waited, a clean-shaven, dark-haired, handsome man of around thirty years. Before she could greet him, he grabbed her, twisted her around and covered her mouth with one hand. He hauled her, kicking and struggling, down the steps and across the side lawn toward the trees.

She clawed at his wrists, lashed backward with her feet, tried to open her mouth wide enough to bite his hands. Even as she fought tooth and nail to escape him, Laura prayed to God he was not who she thought he was.

Only when they reached the copse of evergreens that lay between the house and the sea, did he release her mouth and set her firmly on the ground.

Laura tried again to break away, but the bruising grip on her wrist prevented it. "Who are you? What do you want?" she demanded.

"Wade Halloran, at your service," he said with a mock bow. "And I want to kill you." His deranged trill of laughter made her skin creep.

"You are mad!" she gasped without thinking, frantically twisting, fighting his hold on her wrist.

"Mad?" he shouted, then went immediately calm. "All right. Mad, then. Your sainted husband thought so, anyway."

He dragged her, stumbling and pulling against him, through the trees. Branches slapped at her face and roots tripped her. The cold permeating her very bones had more to do with their obvious destination than the temperature of the air. She could hear the breakers from here.

Salt tanged her nostrils as Laura heaved in breath enough to fill her aching lungs. They had covered nearly a mile as they approached the cliffs overlooking the sea. For the first time, Laura viewed the Cornish coast, a wild and frightening sight. Her imminent fate made it even more so.

Had anyone seen them? Byron would not return for at least two hours. The maids had probably been in the kitchens preparing the light luncheon they were to serve in Cook's absence. They would not have heard. Lady Anne's room faced the side lawn. But even if she had seen what happened from her window, what could she do about it?

Wade Halloran meant to kill her. He had said so in no uncertain terms. The best Laura could do at this point was stall the inevitable and hope for a miracle. "At least tell me why you are doing this," she pleaded, digging in the heels of her house slippers.

He laughed again and shrugged as he dragged her on toward death. And he didn't seem at all inclined to explain why.

Chapter Twenty

Sean saw no reason to hurry the rebellious excuse for transportation he had chosen. He was no more enthusiastic about leaving the warmth of Willow Weep than the gelding seemed to be.

Foolishly he had stormed out of the house without a coat, and unarmed except for the ever present derringer in his boot. The old cloak someone had left hanging in the stable held in most of his body heat, but it smelled strongly of horse sweat and made him slightly nauseous.

The gelding automatically turned toward the local pub, the Keg o' Silks. Sean imagined that the animal's main function must be hauling Byron here and home again. He had been here a few times himself on his infrequent visits to Willow Weep.

He dismounted, now almost over his wrath at Laura's accusations. Why not nurse a pint and warm his blood awhile? Plenty of time to catch the train for London. He could arrange for someone to return Byron's gelding while he was here.

After dismounting and flipping a coin to the stable lad, Sean entered the alehouse and settled at a corner table. His thighs and backside ached and his hands were nearly frozen.

He spent the first pint thawing out and damning the rough-gaited creature that had brought him here. During the second tankard, he decided that if he had any sense at all, he would hire a closed carriage and go directly back to Willow Weep.

Laura had overstepped herself, no question about that. Even a wife had no right to presume on a man's thoughts. But they *were* his thoughts, he admitted reluctantly. Until she had voiced it all, he had never considered why he courted death so avidly. What she said did make sense in a convoluted way.

From the moment Lord Aversby had taken him away from Ruffles House, Sean had fought like a wild thing for escape. Byron had blessedly granted that in the physical sense with the rescue, but the memories of what happened between his purchase and his deliverance had assaulted Sean daily for at least a decade. He had battled those in every way he could, seeking any kind of release. By the time the horror had faded to a tolerant level, the habit of risking his neck had become an ingrained way of life. He had become addicted to hazard as surely as if it were an opiate.

He did not want to die now, of course, and had not for so many years he had forgotten that he ever really wanted to. But Laura had guessed the original motive behind his risk-taking right enough.

Once he had taken full control of his life, he had righted himself somehow. Gone was Madam, who had made a virtual slave of his mother, despite Sean's attempts to get them out of the place. Gone was Aversby, who thought to make him into something he could never be. Gone were the officers, who ordered his every move for two years. Ondine, with all her demands, had died. Then he had quit the Yard, because even good old MacLinden's directives rankled. Finally Sean had felt himself free to choose his own course, make every decision that affected his life. Until Laura.

Suddenly everything came clear. The anger that he couldn't seem to subdue had actually begun the day Laura told him she was to die. But at the time, it had been directed at fate for dealing him a hand he could not change. Then, when he found she would live and he was to spend the rest of his life with her, he resented that the marriage had not been his idea, but hers.

Control. It had all been about control. He had become obsessed by it and did not even know until now.

He had always believed that lack of it had caused his mother's crippling accident. If he had not appeared half-dead that night, she would not have fallen. Stupid to blame himself for it, when he looked at it that way. Might as well blame Byron for presenting a child to its mother in such a bloody state. Aversby's fault, all of it. And that man was dead as a bullet could make him.

His mother didn't blame him. But Sean wished his presence at Willow Weep did not upset her so. He could hardly bear to see the misery in her eyes. She still loved him, he knew. How he had missed their early closeness all these years.

And he would miss Laura even more, if he left her. How could he have treated her the way he had done? Especially that last day in London.

He took a long swig of ale and shifted uncomfortably. Talk about an embarrassing lack of control.

That one night in Paris had been wild enough, but this last time, he had tumbled her as though she were some back-alley tart and he, a sailor just come ashore. For all that, perhaps she had found a bit of pleasure in it. He could only hope Laura knew that desperate coupling was not really his way.

He hadn't even the excuse of long abstinence, since they had made love only the day before. Perhaps she would remember that time with fondness. And the first time. Ah, there had been heaven incarnate, for the both of them.

While sipping his ale, Sean relived their first experience in clinical detail, initially to erase the more recent occasion. And then, as he progressed, for verity in the act itself. In doing so, he could not envision how Laura could possibly have tricked him about her virginity. She had no way to acquire the knowledge to do that. And for all her zeal during the act, she had exhibited no expertise other than that which might be instinctive in a woman of her passion.

Her sickness on their way to France had surely been due to the rough crossing. Hadn't his own stomach gurgled once or twice? And he certainly wasn't pregnant. Was, in fact, a seasoned sailor.

The only thing Sean could not get past or explain away was the ridiculous story about her dying. An insect bite? That was almost too silly to be a fabrication, considering all the causes for death she might have chosen for the lie.

He just hated to be thought so gullible. Sean Wilder, man of the world, duped like a green youth right off the farm. But had Laura been duped, as well? Had she really overheard something and misconstrued it? Sean remembered the very real tears and her preoccupation that day he first met her. All right, he admitted her tale was possible. Not very probable, but possible.

Forget whether she'd lied about that. Whatever her reason for getting him to marry her, Laura had been a virgin on their wedding day. And that certainly meant the child she carried really *was* his. The ripple of fear and dread that rose inside him during that revelation told Sean more about himself and his motives than he really wanted to know.

Control aside, Sean had another reason for resisting the idea so vehemently. His baby would need a father, and Sean had no idea how to be one. Laura had been right after all about his not wanting the commitment. If she bore another man's child, then Sean would not feel quite so responsible for the person it turned out to be. He could blame all its faults and misdoings on the bad blood of its sire.

Fatherhood? What did he know of babies? Nothing, other than how to feed one mushy peas and milk with a spoon, and only that just recently learned. Damn! He would probably ruin a child for life, teach it all the wrong things, offer the worst kind of example.

But after all this hard reflection, Sean finally concluded that he had done Laura a major disservice. And that he had to have fathered the child she carried, like the truth of that or not. And with the realization came the pride, as well as the fear. Natural things, he figured. All expectant fathers probably felt them. His feelings were only exacerbated by the kind of life he had led.

Being a bastard himself, Sean gloried in the fact he could offer his surname, fabricated though it was, to a son or daughter of his own blood. But he feared a child of his might suffer the same sort of things he had endured if his protection—and his control— should prove inadequate. Laura would be there, however. She would help. For that, he'd gladly surrender a little power.

Well, now that he had more or less accepted his fate as a parent, he really should tell Laura he believed her after all. He couldn't prevent the smile that formed while thinking of doing that. They could plan the baby's future, choose names, talk of nurses, nannies and tutors. He could hardly wait.

But how should he approach the topic? Laura had not mentioned the child once since leaving London. No accident there, either, he was certain.

One thing he did know, he would not be catching the train today. Sean slapped another coin on the table and stood.

"See you, Bodman," he said to the publican as he passed by the bar.

"Anytime, Wilder," the man replied. "Saw your friend Halloran today." He blew on the glass he was polishing with a towel.

"Who?" Sean snapped to attention, his every nerve on alert.

"Wade Halloran. Guess he's recovered, eh?" The sly look encouraged a bit of gossip.

Sean's heart almost stopped. Suddenly everything fell into place. *Wade*. The notes made perfect sense now. Yes, Wade might very well want to kill him. Sean had been the one to bind Wade and deliver him to the authorities after Ondine died. The man had lost his mind and tried to kill himself, but a madman would not understand that Sean's actions had no malice attached to them.

Befriending Camilla certainly would have been easy enough for a man with Wade's looks, accomplishments and titled father. That would explain their being together in London, assuming that Wade was the man Helen MacLinden had seen with her. Also Wade would have had access to Norton's stationery and probably attached some twisted significance to using it for the death threats.

Upon receiving the first, Sean had decided the notes must be from someone he had apprehended and sent up. He had checked all the lists of reported escapees from both the prisons and institutions for familiar names and found none. Wade must have been released. That would have been quite possible since no criminal charges were involved. Sean cursed the oversight.

"Where did you see him?" Sean demanded, grasping the bar with both hands.

"Right here," Bodman said, his grin laconic. "Seemed right sane, he did. Unlike the last time we saw him, eh?"

Sean didn't wait to hear more. He pushed away from the bar and hurried outside to the stables, leapt onto the gelding and thundered away toward home.

Please, God, he was wrong. Or please, God, he was not too late.

He reached the house in record time, slid down off his mount and dashed inside.

The moment he opened the door, his mother's voice reached him from two floors above. "Sean, thank God it's you! A man took Laura away by force! I couldn't see who he was, but he meant her harm. I sent Emmy to Briarhaven for Byron, but she had to go afoot. You have to help Laura, Sean. Please hurry!"

"Which way did they go?" he called up, his voice echoing in the stairwell.

"Through the wood, toward the cliffs!" she called down. "Oh, Sean—"

He didn't wait to hear the rest. Tearing outside, he scooped up the reins of the gelding and mounted with a leap. Sweat froze on his face as he kicked to a gallop and sped toward the trees.

When he had reached the far edge of the wood that opened onto the terrace of the cliffs, Sean realized that he still had only his derringer. No use for it, he decided once he saw them standing face-to-face near the precipice where Ondine had fallen to her death. Given the boot gun's lack of accuracy at a distance, the risk of hitting Laura with a bullet would be too great. He'd improvise. A distraction, maybe, so Laura could run.

Sean drew in a deep breath, willing himself to calm down. Panic solved nothing. Then he strode halfway across the clearing, determined to draw all the attention to himself. "Wade!" he called. "I am here!"

With relief, he noted Halloran brandished no weapon, either. He had grabbed Laura by both her wrists as he turned halfway round.

"Eye for an eye! Woman for a woman!" Wade said in a singsong voice as he grinned at Sean. Then he released Laura with a shove.

Sean froze with absolute shock. The breath left him as suddenly as Laura's scream rent the air. For seconds, he could do nothing but stare at the edge of the cliff where she had disappeared and deny what he'd seen.

Gone, just...gone.

Rage did not grow inside him. It sprung fully formed and bursting through the skin of his body. The overwhelming urge to kill, minus any thought of self-preservation, poured out of every pore. He advanced on Halloran, set on tearing him limb from limb, snatching the still-pumping heart out of his chest and making him eat the bloody thing.

Even as he stalked, Sean glanced one last time at the cliff's edge, mouthing a silent promise to Laura to avenge her death and that of their unborn child.

Then he saw them. *Fingers.* Grasping at the rock ledge not three feet behind Halloran.

Sean halted. He jerked his horrified gaze back to the man just above her. Halloran's evil grin had settled on his next victim, thank God.

"Come and get me, Wade," Sean taunted. "Come and do your worst." He motioned with his hands. "I'm waiting. Are you afraid to tackle a man, or are women all you can handle?"

Halloran sauntered closer, reaching under his jacket to withdraw a gun. A repeater, Sean noticed with dismay. Somehow, he had to draw him away and hold his attention so that Laura could make her way back up.

Already, in his peripheral vision, Sean could see her arms up to the elbows, and the top of her dark head just above the ledge. The surf crashing against the boulders below covered the sound of her scrabbling climb.

Come on, Laura, you can do it.

Sean backed up slowly, one step at a time until he was almost at the edge of the woods that grew in a semicircular pattern around the large clearing. Halloran followed, putting a good thirty feet between himself and Laura. Now to keep the lunatic busy while Laura got up and away.

"Ah, Wade, you are a wonder. How did you manage to get free? Bedlam getting lax these days?"

"Walked right out," Halloran said amiably. "Aren't you happy I'm well now, Sean? Everyone else seemed delighted. Father even provided me another tour of the Continent, bless his heart."

"Including Paris, no doubt."

"Oh, especially Paris! Such a rat's maze, that place!"

"Did you shoot Beaumont and his nephew?" Sean asked.

Wade shook his head and thumbed the cocked hammer of his pistol. "An unfortunate error. I thought you were there that evening." He rubbed his shoulder with his free hand. "Had to hurry the plans along. The day your woman nicked me with that bullet in your hotel room, I thought you might have recognized me."

"No," Sean admitted with a shrug, "I couldn't see."

"I didn't intend to kill you in the street, Sean," Halloran said, almost apologetically. "I only wanted to frighten you. When you were hit, I realized our little confrontation had to happen immediately. Before you died, you see. So I followed you inside."

Sean nodded, snatching a glance at the cliff. *Come on, sweetheart, pull up!* Quickly he retrained his gaze on Halloran. "But you didn't figure on Laura shooting you, of course."

Wade tittered. "More woman than you deserved, wasn't she! Ha! And more resourceful than I expected, certainly. She helped you dodge me again. You thought you hid so well that time, Sean, and in the gutters where you felt so at home!"

"Right you are!" Sean admitted, forcing a laugh to try to cover the sound of Laura's scuffling against the rocks.

Wade's attention seemed fixed on him for a moment. Sean dared not look directly at her, but shared her struggle. *Hang on,* he prayed.

"You must have read my mind," he said to Halloran. "A stroke of genius that you found us."

"It was, wasn't it? I knew you hadn't left Paris, so I simply played tourist while looking for you," Wade bragged. "Where would you go to ground? I asked myself. Then I recalled your penchant for sketching in school. You were quite good. And you still are! I even purchased two of your pictures from that little gallery. For old times' sake." He threw back his head and regarded Sean through narrowed eyes. "Really stupid to sign them as *Sauvage,* Sean. Campion always called you that. *Wild man.*"

Sean sighed loudly, projecting defeat. "You outwitted me, what can I say?" Then desperate to keep Halloran talking—though he already knew the answer—Sean demanded, "Why involve my wife, Wade? To what purpose?"

Halloran waved the pistol back toward the cliff without turning. He grew visibly agitated, his movements rather jerky. "After my hasty mistake with the Beaumonts, I decided to kill your woman first. Allow you a little time to grieve. I made that clear enough? Didn't I? Well?"

Sean's stomach clenched painfully when he heard the clatter of rocks tumble against the cliff.

"To make me suffer. Yes, I recall you did mention that."

Halloran sighed. "I had hoped this would upset you a bit more than it has, Sean. Don't you care for her after all? Must I hunt down another one that you haven't tired of yet?"

"You stabbed Camilla," Sean stated. "Why? That was over."

Wade giggled, causing the pistol to waver. "I thought you still loved her. She said you did, silly chit. You've never loved any woman, have you?" Then his face changed dramatically.

His mouth pulled down into a grimace and his eyes went wide. "That's why you killed her. Why you killed my Ondine!"

"No, Wade! Not I. Remember? You were there first. You saw her fall."

"I pushed her," he said in a horribly flat voice. "But you killed her. You made her believe you loved her. She carried my child, Sean. Mine! I loved Ondine before you, but then you married her. Made her love you. You *made* me push her!"

Sean risked a brief look at the cliff. Laura had half her body up and was almost safe. *Hang on. Rest a moment. Easy now.*

Wade had come nearer to him, but not close enough yet to make a grab for the weapon. He looked as though he might fire at any moment. Sean bent his knees slightly, ready to lunge when the time was right.

"Wade, you were out of the country on your tour, remember? Ondine had to do something, for God's sake. She was with child and afraid. I didn't know she was pregnant when we married. I didn't know the two of you loved each other."

"Of course, you knew!" Halloran shouted, gesturing angrily with his free hand. "You seduced her just like you did all those girls when we were in school! Barmaids, village girls, even that sluttish vicar's daughter! Ondine meant nothing but another conquest to you, did she?"

His voice lowered, almost inaudible over the sound of the sea below them. At that moment, when he met Sean's eyes directly, he looked perfectly lucid. And horribly grief stricken. "But I loved her, Sean! I loved her more than anything in my life!"

Wade's gaze dropped to the pistol and he raised it higher to aim.

Sean glanced behind Halloran for one final look. Laura was up and running, but not away from danger as he had hoped. In her hands, above her head, she held a large stone. But not large enough.

Sean threw himself forward just as she struck.

Halloran staggered forward under the impact but did not go down. Sean grabbed his wrist with both hands. The gun discharged harmlessly into the air as they grappled for it. Sean wrestled it free and jumped back, leveling the weapon on Halloran with the same motion. "Get behind me, Laura!" he ordered, fearing Wade would grab her as hostage.

Shaking his head erratically, Halloran began walking backward. His voice grew louder as he went. "You have not won, Sean. I shall have her. She will be mine. Mine!"

Sean followed, powerless to stop what was happening.

When Wade reached the edge of the spot marking Laura's desperate climb, he turned and dived, arms stretched like wings.

For a long moment, Sean stood there, gun at his side, and stared at the empty space before him. He supposed he should look over and see where the body had landed. No question Wade was dead. He had leapt out too far to grab at the craggy face of the cliff as Laura had done. And not far enough to miss the boulders below and land in the sea.

It was over. He turned in time to see Laura approach with fire in her eye. She hefted the rock she had crowned Halloran with a second time and dropped it directly on his foot.

"Fool!" she screamed.

The pain set in. "Damn it, Laura! You've broken my toes!"

"I ought to break your ruddy neck, you idiot! What do you mean waltzing out of the woods like that? 'Wa-ade, I'm heeere!' You're as crazed as he was! And with no weapon! Oh, no! Bullets bounce right off the wild man, don't they? Standing there like a witless *tree,* conversing as though you hadn't a care in the world!" She kicked his shin. His good one. "While I'm losing all my fingernails trying to stay out of the bloody *ocean!*" She drew her foot back again, but Sean hopped out of reach.

"Now, Laura—"

"I'm going home!" she stated, whirling around, her sodden skirts tangling against her legs.

"There's a horse just inside the trees," he called out.

"Good!" she shouted. "I'll take it, too, don't think I won't! Stupid, maggot-brained, imbecilic *man*..." Her muttering drifted off with the freshening wind.

Sean sat down on the frozen ground and blew out a breath of profound relief. It was over and they were alive.

The gelding wouldn't carry them both and Laura would reach the house faster than if he walked beside her while she rode. What was a mile's walk on broken toes? Laura was safe. Safe and unharmed.

He smiled wryly at her reaction. It brought to mind his mother's anger when he had gotten into dangerous scrapes as a boy. Partly shock and relief, he was sure. Mostly fury, which was good. Most women would have collapsed in a heap. But Laura was not most women. No, indeed.

She would recover from fury once she had a hot bath and a bit of coddling. He would see to that coddling himself once he had made arrangements for Wade's body to be recovered. A couple of hours' time to settle down wouldn't come amiss for either of them.

Slowly Sean got to his feet and limped toward home. Willow Weep *would* seem like home now, even if they decided not to live there. Wherever Laura was would always be his home. All he had to do now was convince her that he believed her every word. That would take no pretending at all. Besides, Laura could always tell if he was lying.

The next order of business would be to make things right with his mother. He should have done it years ago. Perhaps if he gently insisted, she would finally accept Byron's proposal.

Love. It felt so damned good, he wished it on everybody. And to think he had almost thrown it away.

He felt sympathy for Wade Halloran and almost understood the madness that drove the man. Hadn't he felt an uncontrollable urge for vengeance when he'd thought Wade had killed Laura?

Love could make or break a man, Sean decided, proud of the profound thought. Byron could probably construct a very serious work around that concept. If the real Byron hadn't already done that. He shrugged. At any rate, he felt remade, reborn because of Laura and the way she loved him. Soon things would be perfect. He just knew it.

Four hours later, Sean hopped into the small salon on one foot, balancing against the walls and door frame. Laura wasn't there. Byron greeted him with a brandy. "Son, I don't know about you, but today has just taken ten years off my life. How's the foot?"

"Sore," Sean replied with a wince. "Not broken, though. I had Dr. Folson take a look at it after you left the scene. We had plenty of time while the crew climbed down to retrieve the body. He drove me home in his trap."

"Figured he would. Just glad we met up in the woods so you didn't have to walk far." He gestured toward Sean's bootless foot and frowned. "Can't imagine why Laura would just leave you out there like that."

"Mmm, I sent her on home. Say, Byron, did you realize there's an equine disease that is caused by a fly bite? Dr. Folson just explained it to me in great detail. Not too well known. Affects Arabians."

"Why no, I don't believe I've heard of such. I didn't think you were interested in horses, son."

Sean grinned from ear to ear. "Only one in particular. It died."

"I see," Byron said, when obviously he did not.

"Where's Laura?" Sean asked, feeling on top of the world. Everything she had said was true. She had never lied. There was the proof, though he hadn't needed it really. He could not wait to see her, hold her, treasure her for a lifetime.

"Upstairs with Anne, I believe."

Sean pulled off his other boot and tossed it aside. "Byron, do me a favor?"

"Certainly, my boy. Just name it."

"Have Emmy bring up food now and then and leave it outside the door. I don't want us interrupted for a solid week. Can you arrange it?"

Byron clucked his tongue. "Can't imagine why you'd want to spend seven whole days secluded with your wife *and* your mother, but whatever you wish."

Sean threw his head back and laughed. "You're a rotten clown, you know that?"

"Part of my charm, boy. Just part of my charm." He winked and downed his brandy. "Let me find one of the girls to bring the chair down, and I'll meet your mum at the top of the stairs."

"Thank you, Byron. A bit late in the saying, perhaps, but I do thank you for everything."

"Oh, it's never too late, son. Trust me on that."

Sean found walking much easier with both boots off. He stopped near the open door to Laura's room, wondering if his mother would scold him for the impropriety of appearing in his stockinged feet.

Their voices drifted out and Sean remained where he was, thinking to gauge Laura's mood before going in. He hoped she had calmed down.

"Oh, I'm certain! I don't ever want to see him again!" Laura stated emphatically.

"How difficult to face such a thing. Surely you must have grown to love him?" his mother sympathized.

"No, I don't believe I ever did really. He's simply not the man I once hoped he was. All he has ever done is disappoint me."

"I daresay that's true enough after all you've told me. I am so sorry, child."

"I'm well over the shock of it now, and ready to get on with my life. So you mustn't worry," Laura said brightly. "I truly am fine."

His mother hummed a little sound of resignation. "Well, what's done is done, I suppose, and no mending will fix it. I'd better go below and see if we are to have any supper at all. Would you pull the bell rope for Byron, please? He's in the salon, I believe."

Sean stood stock-still, listening to the jingle in the distance below. Then he began easing down the hallway to the stairs, hoping to escape unseen. He couldn't bear Laura telling him to his face what he had just overheard. Not today. Not after all that had happened. Not after embracing such hope for them.

He covered his face with one hand, unwilling to believe the words that had dashed all his dreams of home and family. Laura would leave him. Never wanted to see him again. Had never really loved him at all. He had disappointed her, made her unhappy.

"Sean?" his mother said softly. "Are you unwell?"

He slowly uncovered his eyes and looked down at the woman in the bath chair. Suddenly he felt five years old again with her as his only salvation. "I am sick to death, Mum," he whispered. "And you can never make this better, even with a kiss."

"Would you let me try?" she asked with a smile.

Sean leaned down and met her soft lips with his own.

"There, you see?" she said. "Almost well. Go in to Laura now and take your medicine like a man. She was frightfully piqued with you for risking yourself the way you did." She noticed something behind him. "Ah, here's Byron to fetch me already. Run along now, darling."

Sean felt as though he faced the gallows. But there was no escape in sight. He might as well get it over with. He sucked in his breath and marched into Laura's room.

"Sean!" she cried. She leapt up and rushed at him, flung herself against his chest and hugged him hard. "I've been so worried. I'd never have left you but I was so upset. You nearly got yourself killed because of me and—"

"Just what is this all about?" he growled, enraged that she would feign all this caring after what he had just heard her say.

"I feared you would have to walk all the way home and just as I started turning around to go back, Byron appeared and sent me on home. Then it took so long for you to get here—"

"Never mind all that, Laura! Do you want to explain what I just heard you tell my mother? Or did you plan to let me guess what happened after you—"

"Oh, that. Nothing important. Just a letter from my stepfather begging me to come home. I haven't the vaguest idea where he got the address, but I suspect Lamb—"

"You—you were discussing Middlebrook?" Sean stilled, drawing a little away from Laura's embrace.

"Yes, we were. You don't mind that I told Mother everything, do you? She saw how agitated I was when I opened the letter."

Sean began to laugh. He laughed so hard, he couldn't hear what she was saying. When he finally got his mirth under control, he kissed her. Nothing ever tasted so good as Laura. Nothing smelled so heavenly, felt so soft or looked so beautiful. But he had no urge at all to hear anything she had to say.

It would only take another moment for her to figure out what he had thought he overheard. He was in for a lot of I-told-you-so's about eavesdropping and knew he deserved every one. To prevent that, Sean took her mouth as hungrily as he would soon take the rest of her.

When she eventually broke the kiss, he managed to catch his breath before she did. "Laura, I love you," he said quickly. "And our baby. I know it's mine, and I never should have doubted you. I believe every single word you ever said to me. Everything. Even about the horse. Especially about the horse." He rushed on before she could get a word in. "Thank God, you're going to live! Every day I'll thank Him." Sean squeezed her so hard, he felt the breath she'd just drawn rush out of her. "I am so very glad we have a future. We do, don't we? Have a future? Together?"

"And a present," she gasped, her fingers busily working buttons through buttonholes on his waistcoat. "Let's not put off till tomorrow what we can do today!"

"So practical," he murmured against her mouth, tracing her lower lip, feeling her hands tug his belt.

"And greedy as Goulue," she assured him breathlessly. "Will you stop talking now or must I find another stone?"

"Mercy!" he whispered, laughing, trailing kisses down her throat.

"In a second," she said on a shuddering breath, "just this one last button…"

* * * * *

On sale 1st August 2008

HERS TO COMMAND
by Margaret Moore

Finding Lady Mathilde waiting in his chamber,
Sir Henry is irresistibly drawn to her intelligence.
Steadfast and determined, Mathilde is a proud woman
and as complex as her secrets…

Henry agrees to help save her lands, but as invaders
close in, Mathilde must dare to trust not only her deepest
desires, but the man willing to fight for all he is worth
to prove his honour…

"Ms Moore is a master of the medieval time period."
—*Romantic Times*

2 FREE

BOOKS AND A SURPRISE GIFT!

We would like to take this opportunity to thank you for reading this Mills & Boon® book by offering you the chance to take TWO more specially selected titles from the Historical series absolutely FREE! We're also making this offer to introduce you to the benefits of the Mills & Boon® Reader Service™—

- ★ **FREE home delivery**
- ★ **FREE gifts and competitions**
- ★ **FREE monthly Newsletter**
- ★ **Exclusive Reader Service offers**
- ★ **Books available before they're in the shops**

Accepting these FREE books and gift places you under no obligation to buy, you may cancel at any time, even after receiving your free shipment. Simply complete your details below and return the entire page to the address below. You don't even need a stamp!

YES! Please send me 2 free Historical books and a surprise gift. I understand that unless you hear from me, I will receive 4 superb new titles every month for just £3.69 each, postage and packing free. I am under no obligation to purchase any books and may cancel my subscription at any time. The free books and gift will be mine to keep in any case.

H8ZED

Ms/Mrs/Miss/Mr ....Initials ....
BLOCK CAPITALS PLEASE

Surname ....

Address ....

....

....Postcode...............................

Send this whole page to:
UK: FREEPOST CN81, Croydon, CR9 3WZ